The Lauras

Sara Taylor was b   ginia.
She has a BFA from   College and an MA in
Prose Fiction from the University of East Anglia. She
is currently chipping away at a double-focus PhD in
censorship and fiction at UEA, and splits her time
between Norwich and Reading. *The Shore*, her debut
novel, was shortlisted for the *Guardian* First Book Award
and longlisted for the Baileys Women's Prize for Fiction.
In 2015, Sara was shortlisted for the *Sunday Times*/PFD
Young Writer of the Year Award.

Praise for *The Lauras*

'Taylor's sense of place is one of her greatest strengths ... An
extraordinary journey ... *The Lauras* is a fine achievement,
engrossing, original and eloquent, and Taylor has more than
fulfilled the promise of *The Shore*.'

Helen Dunmore, *Guardian*

'Elegiac and beautifully observed ... Taylor has a great ear
for language, with the kind of sentences that make you pause
and read a second time ... It is such acute observations of
her imaginary world that saw Taylor's debut novel, *The Shore*
longlisted for the Bailey's prize, and it should be no great
surprise to find her second novel following in its footsteps.'

Observer

'[*The Lauras* is] a work that looks to combine the epic sweep
of America with an intimate study of a mother and her
child   scape,
so cle   urney
Taylor   oise.'

                                                    Times

'Taylor's writing is poetic and emotionally sensitive.'

Kate Saunders, *The Times*

'It is exceptionally moving, and the novel it reminded me of most is James Baldwin's *Giovanni's Room* ... in beguiling the reader into identifying with someone they thought they couldn't ... Some of these scenes are gut-wrenching; some of them are quietly beautiful. Taylor's prose is remarkable; both intense and expansive, both precise and wonderfully sfumato ... The writing about Alex exploring different wildernesses is astonishing ... A joy.'

Stuart Kelly, *The Scotsman*

'*The Lauras* is the (still) rarely told story of a girl's romance about the life of her mother ... What marks Taylor's novel out from many of its contemporaries is how little psychic damage Alex and her mother sustain – or pass on – from their experiences ... There's an important lesson here, important for storytellers and for women, about not giving yourself away too easily, about possessing your own life.'

Times Literary Supplement

'Gorgeously written and the characters of Alex and Ma are so brilliantly drawn they'll haunt you long after you've turned the final page. Quirky, original and moving.'

Sunday Mirror

'Taylor is a phenomenally talented novelist as this riveting depiction of a mother and daughter relationship amply demonstrates.'

Fanny Blake, *Woman & Home*

The Lauras

SARA TAYLOR

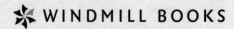 WINDMILL BOOKS

1 3 5 7 9 10 8 6 4 2

Windmill Books
20 Vauxhall Bridge Road
London SW1V 2SA

Windmill Books is part of the Penguin Random House group of companies
whose addresses can be found at global.penguinrandomhouse.com.

Copyright © Sara Taylor 2016

Sara Taylor has asserted her right to be identified as the author of this
Work in accordance with the Copyright, Designs and Patents Act 1988.

The line 'myself three selves at least' is reprinted from 'I am Myself Three Selves at
Least' copyright © 2009 by Jennifer K. Sweeney from *How to Live on Bread and Music*,
with the permission of Perugia Press, Florence, MA (www.perugiapress.com).

First published in Great Britain by William Heinemann in 2016
First published in paperback by Windmill Books in 2017

www.penguin.co.uk

A CIP catalogue record for this book is available from the British Library.

ISBN 9780099510642

Typeset in 13.44/16.10 pt Fournier MT Std by Jouve (UK), Milton Keynes
Printed and bound in Great Britain by Clays Ltd, St Ives Plc

Penguin Random House is committed to a
sustainable future for our business, our readers
and our planet. This book is made from Forest
Stewardship Council® certified paper.

To Laura, who left a hole in me.

'Every day is a journey, and the journey itself is home.'
Matsuo Basho

'Don't make me turn this car around.'
Mom

CHAPTER I

I could hear them arguing, the way they argued nearly every night now, their voices pitched low and rasping in that way that meant they thought they were being too quiet to wake me up. They were right in that their fights never did wake me up—but that was because I always stayed awake until they started. I could feel one coming like the promise of a storm thickening the air. When rain's on the way I can't sleep either. Even though I always heard them, when morning rolled around I pretended that I'd slept through it all, because I didn't know what else to do.

I listened to the rise and fall of their voices for hours some nights, for as long as it took for them to gradually calm. So on that last night, when they went from full pitch to silent in a moment, my stomach fizzed with swift fear: they never broke off in full flow. Then the sound of my mother's boots on tile as she came down the hall. When my bedroom door squeaked open I went stiff and limp at once, hoping that she'd think I was asleep and go back to the fight.

"Get up, Alex. Now."

1

Ma's hand on my back made me jump; her voice was urgent, hard-edged, and I guessed in that moment that something was really wrong. I sprang up, comforter bundled around and over me, and she pushed me towards my bedroom door. The mix of dark and light and the gumminess of my eyes made everything smeary so that I almost walked into the door frame. As she hurried me out with one hand gripping too tightly to my upper arm I dove for the mottle of shoes in the entryway, scrabbled, then clutched my muddy-soled hiking boots to my chest. Across the front porch, the splintered edges of the boards catching on but not quite sticking in the tough soles of my bare feet, then down the steps. The gravel of the driveway chewed them, and I jumped into the back seat when she opened the car door for me. I twisted up to look through the rear windshield, blinking to clear my eyes enough to see, searching for smoke, fire, anything that would explain the urgency, but she lifted a fold of my comforter over my head and pushed me down, so that the bump in the middle of the seat pressed against my hip.

I couldn't tell if Dad was still inside the house or if some of the footsteps were his, or if he'd gone out the back door while we went out the front. Then nylon rustled and something heavy landed in the footwell below my head: the backpack that Ma had kept by the shoes in the front hallway for so long that I'd stopped noticing it was there. Then the thunk of the car doors shutting and the grind and catch of the engine, the world dipping as we drove away.

It was a few moments before I realized that Dad wasn't in the car with us. I wanted to sit up, to ask why we'd left him behind, what had happened to make them stop fighting so suddenly, but I stayed where my mother had put me.

When she turned on the radio I pawed the cloth from my eyes, felt the chilly night air gusting through the fine opening of her window, watched the stars rotate over us as we turned under them, a right and a right, and a right, getting farther and farther away. I knew better than to ask questions, or to say anything—give her the slightest reason and all that cracking anger I'd heard her unleashing at Dad would be turned to me.

At some point my eyes closed on their own and the seat became comfortable beneath me, and I stopped pretending to be asleep.

"Hey there, chickie pie," she said, and I felt her hand shaking my leg.

I realized that we were no longer moving.

"You awake?"

The clouds were pink. We were caught on the thin, hungry edge of the morning, before the sun sliced itself open on the horizon and bled out across the sky. In front of us, on the far side of a sorry strip of dirt and weeds, was a freeway, cars zipping by now and then with their windshields dewed and misted, some with their head-lights on. We were parked up at a truck stop, the few people moving slow, the eighteen-wheelers looking like they were asleep. The air was greased with the smell of Southern-fried breakfast, stronger even than the smell of Ma's cigarettes.

"You hungry?"

Walking into the truck-stop diner I felt naked—I'd gone to bed in thin flannel pajama bottoms, one of my dad's old shirts—chilly with the breeze that made my clothes feel like tissue paper and made my skin go tight and prickly. It felt obscene being in public in my pajamas, but Ma said that thirteen is just young enough to still get away with it; I look younger. She hadn't thought to grab my jeans on the way out.

Elsewhere, my classmates were getting ready for school, and I wondered if Ma would call in to say I wouldn't be there. My school backpack had been left in the car the day before, so at least I'd be able to get my homework done.

The smell of old fryer oil turned my stomach, which was still tight with sleep, but I dutifully flipped through the menu full of laminated pictures of pancakes and waffles and ugly pucks of sausage doused in lumpy brown gravy. Breakfast was a normal thing to do, even a truck-stop breakfast, even if I was wearing pajamas and boots without socks; it was like being on a road trip. Ma sat across from me and scanned the menu, and I imagined for a moment that we were on our way somewhere fun, taking a day off from life, and when evening rolled around we'd go back home and Dad and dinner would be waiting for us. Then she set down the menu and pulled out her wallet, slid the credit and debit cards out of their slots, then got up, went to the ATM near the door, and started withdrawing great wodges of bills.

While I chewed a biscuit and washed the pasty slurry down with chocolate milk she sat across from me, ignoring her plate of eggs but sipping at her coffee, and I listened while trying to make it seem like I wasn't paying attention as she pulled out her cellphone, called the number on the back of each card in turn and reported it lost, then carefully cut them all into pieces with scissors she'd borrowed from the waitress. The little phone had sat in the cup holder of her car, except when it was charging on the kitchen counter, for as long as I could remember, in case of flat tires or accidents that never happened; I had never seen her use it before.

Usually when a person looks back they have to reconstruct, invent, guess at what was said or felt or smelled. That twenty-four hours, starting with the moment we left home, was burned into my memory. Even now, years after, I can't forget the grease and smoke, the flannel on skin, the fear of realizing that my life was taking a ninety-degree turn. Some part of me knew, as I listened to my mother's footsteps coming toward my bedroom door, that everything was about to change, wouldn't admit it to the rest of myself in the diner as I watched her turn her credit cards into confetti. The tipping feeling, of everything I knew and thought and trusted being pulled out from under me, has stayed with me for thirty-odd years, as if she branded it into my skin with her fingertips when she dragged me out of the house.

She dropped the card bits into three different garbage cans on our way across the parking lot, put the backpack in the trunk, tossed the cell into the passenger footwell as if it had outlived its usefulness, put the car in gear while I was still buckling my seat belt.

The phone began buzzing as we got onto the freeway. She'd let me sit in the front seat, to keep me from throwing up or to make things easier when I did throw up, and after a few seconds I reached for it.

"Leave it, kid."

"It's probably Dad."

"I know."

The phone continued to buzz every little while, skittering on the floor like a giant insect. I wondered what she'd do if I picked it up and answered it myself, decided that, given the circumstance, that was a bad risk to take.

While we were stuck in rush-hour traffic halfway across a bridge Ma decided she'd had enough. She flicked her cigarette butt out the open window, ducked abruptly to the side, her hand flailing between my knees but eyes still on the road, and pitched the trembling phone off the side of the bridge and into the river.

I was too stunned to say anything.

"It was more than six years old," she said after a little. It sounded almost like an apology. "I should've thrown it away with the cards—cops can use them to track you down if they want to. I'll get a new one once we sort life out."

"Couldn't you have just talked to him?" I asked.

"Peanut, sometimes things go way beyond what talking can fix."

I didn't say anything, but she must have read my silence as expectant because, after a few minutes, she continued: "Maybe I'll give it a shot, in a while."

*

My mother had never been much of a storyteller. I knew the vagaries of her life—the foster homes and that she had a green card, the fact that she hadn't spoken to her parents since she was a teenager—but it wasn't until we left home that she began writing in the details. Maybe she began telling me then because she felt guilt, or whatever her version of guilt was, over leaving and taking me with her and not explaining anything. Maybe the stories had finally backed up in her and she had to let them out.

Around sundown on the day that she threw her phone out the window we pulled off the highway into one of those graveled roads that cross the tree-covered median where cops sometimes sit to watch for speeding drivers, and that's when she started telling me about her childhood. I wanted us to be stretched opposite each other on the cold, solid ground, with a wood fire between us casting shadows across her browned, unlined face, because that's how stories were supposed to be told. Instead, we were in the front seat of the Civic, my feet barely reaching the dash but propped up anyway, passing deli bags of salami and provolone and a can of Tab back and forth, the windshield dark with evening, the headlights rushing by on the highway on either side of us blocked out with spare clothes and the blanket from my bed, their edges caught between the windows and frames to make curtains. I sucked the flavor out of each slice of salami before swallowing it whole, kept my eyes wide and intent on her and nodded at intervals, trying to show how close I was listening.

When we'd stopped in the late afternoon for the salami and Tab and more cigarettes we also went to the Goodwill next door, found a few pairs of jeans that fit me, several men's flannel shirts that were too big for both of us so we could share them back and forth, plus odds and ends like socks that we couldn't do without. It was cold for May but the flannel would keep us warm enough, and I hoped that the fact that she'd not gotten jackets or coats or even sweatshirts meant that Ma wasn't planning on us being away from home long enough to need them, even though she'd pitched her phone rather than talk to my dad.

She ate six or seven pieces of salami and cheese rolled up together like a cigar, cracked open the soda, took a swig, handed it to me, then said, "When I was fourteen, just a few months older than you are now, I ran away from home to be a ranger," like she was talking to the steering wheel or the night on the other side of the windshield.

She wanted to be a caretaker of the wilderness, wandering the national parks counting birds and paring back mistletoe, carrying all that she needed with her and going days and weeks without seeing another person. She checked all of the survival books out of the library, read them under her bed because it felt more secret there, and took notes in a marble composition book that she'd shoplifted from the five and dime. When she had filled three of these with lists of things you could eat and things not to, instructions for making fires and building shelters and choosing drinking water, she set off, in her younger brother's boots—her parents said that girls didn't need boots—with as little as she couldn't spare crammed into a backpack fished from a dumpster. She made her first mistake then: the boots didn't fit properly and her socks were too thin. Her feet blistered, and they found her a day later.

"The first thing you do is take care of your feet," she told me. "Keep them dry and comfortable, stop when they tell you to stop. Good shoes aren't cheap, but you only ever have one pair of feet."

After that, she began to save her lunch money and the pennies she found in the sidewalk seams and the crumpled one- and five-dollar bills that her mother forgot crammed deep in the pockets of her jacket, and on the day that she had enough she dumped it into a one-gallon freezer bag, skipped school to go into town, bought a pair of size five-and-a-half putty-green walking boots with yellow laces and space in the toes, and three pairs of cotton boot socks, because she's always had a weakness for good socks. They felt like sinking her feet into cake batter. She hid the boots under her bed until the days lengthened and warmed, then photocopied maps from library reference books and bought lightweight food. When they found her the second time she'd hiked nearly one hundred miles of the Appalachian Trail.

I was scared to ask where we were going, but even so I wasn't relieved when the cop knocked on our window at five the next morning and asked the question for me.

"To my parents' house in Lexington," Ma said, not

bothering to specify whether it was Lexington in Pennsylvania, Kentucky, Virginia, or somewhere else.

"You realize your husband's called out a search for this car?"

"Domestic tiff. We didn't get violent, and the car is in my name. I can take my kid to visit my parents for a few days, can't I?"

I shuffled in the glove box for the registration, which was in fact in her name, and after some hemming and hawing and muttering into his radio he had to let us go.

"I can't tell you how to run your marriage, lady, but I recommend you make up quick. Your kid or not, your husband can charge you with kidnapping."

"We aren't actually married," she said levelly as she took the registration back, but I could tell she was getting annoyed. "So there isn't, in fact, much he can do. As you undoubtedly know. Good day, officer."

"Are we really going to Lexington?" I asked as we pulled back onto the highway, and then when she didn't answer for a few minutes added, "Where *do* your parents live?"

"We are going to find somewhere to get breakfast. Then we're going to get ourselves to the other side of the West Virginia border, just in case the state brass are still looking for us. And then we're seeing what we can do about this car."

We pulled off a while later in a one-horse, one-stoplight town, where the morning sun didn't touch yet because it had gotten caught on a spur of the mountains. It was nothing more than a strip of buildings along the highway—a diner with a *Waitress needed* sign in the window, a post office barely worthy of the name, and a gas station/convenience store/mechanic's garage with out-of-date sodas and stickers on half the pumps that said they'd failed inspection by a representative of the Bureau of Standards—with the barest promise of more buildings farther into the trees. Ma said she'd be right back, and as her boots crunched across the gravel and scattered the auto glass that littered the parking lot I crawled into the footwell and peeled up the carpet. Linty coins were ground into the floor and stuck to the inside of the cup holders and fallen under the seats. I left the little caddy of quarters alone; that was for tolls. Ma didn't carry a purse, instead crammed a billfold into the back pocket of her jeans until it wore permanent lines into the denim, so my scope for plunder was limited. She'd disappeared into the mechanic's garage; I cracked the door open wide enough to slip out, and padded down the grassy shoulder of the road to the post office.

The counter was manned by a single perm-haired postal worker, who watched me through eyeglasses with plastic frames the same clear red as jolly ranchers as if she suspected that I was going to take off with her entire stock the moment she looked away. Her glare made my spine crawl as I picked out a postcard, not one of the *Welcome To!* or *Greetings From!* ones, but a placeless one with dogs playing around a water pump on the front—I wasn't worried about being tracked down by the postmark, since we were on the move, but I didn't want to make it too easy, if Ma really didn't want to be found.

11

Daddy— I started it because Ma said he sometimes worried that I was getting too old to want him around, to not be embarrassed of him. Too old for him to be my daddy. Which I was, but hey. The cheap blue pen chained to the counter spluttered, and I went over the word again and again, until it stood out in ridges on the glossy side of the card.

Mom is all right and I am all right. Though I think she's still upset. If she doesn't want to come home, I will when I can, so don't rent my room to anyone.

I'd meant that to sound funny, but it just sounded juvenile. But you can't erase pen.

I love you. And miss you. —Me

I counted coins into the woman's hand to pay for the card and a stamp, then held it for a moment before dropping it into the dark slot of the blue U.S. Post box, not quite a wish and not quite a prayer, but something between the two.

Ma was leaning against the car when I walked back, watching a man with pierced ears and a goat beard inspect the workings of her engine.

"Where'd you get off to?" she asked when I got within hearing distance.

"Looking for something to read," I said. "Nothing."

"Your school books are in the back seat—you should take a crack at them."

The bearded man finished his inspection, nodded at her, and ambled back to the garage.

"What's he doing?" I asked.

"Mr. Freeborn over there is willing to trade out this car for a hatchback he owns," she answered, "and to throw in a set of plates registered to a woman too blind to drive anymore. We might be staying here a while—the diner needs a swing-shift waitress, and there's a room to rent within walking distance."

"Are we moving here, then?" I thought guiltily about my postcard, pushed it out with thoughts about home, wondered if it was safe to ask more directly how long we were staying for.

"Not really. Just laying low for a little while. I want to figure out which end is up."

I had found my mother's green card before, in a desk drawer with my father's birth certificate: her gap-toothed smile looks nothing like mine, her cream umber skin darkened as she aged. When I first found it she wouldn't tell me what it was, why she didn't have a birth certificate, and my father had explained that it meant that Ma was "off the boat." And I hadn't known much more than that until I asked her, sitting in the car in the turn-off near the West Virginia border just after the cop knocked on the car window, where my grandparents lived. Somewhere between breakfast and the town where I'd thought we wouldn't be staying, she started in on that story.

In 1970 her parents emigrated, messily, from a little farming village in Sicily; she'd been six years old. Her mother's father—my great-grandfather—had traded his stonecutting skills for U.S. citizenship, and only moved back to his own father's hometown when he'd saved enough to start a family, but even with her inherited citizenship it had been difficult for my grandmother to bring her family across to America. An elegant woman with a degree in fashion design, she had been forced to take a factory job sewing men's shirts in New York for the lowest legal wage; my grandfather worked construction, then started a business of his own. My mother and her brother had been left in a Catholic orphanage in Palermo for the six months it took for their parents to save their money, rent an apartment, and sort out all the papers that would let them stay in the country. Ma wouldn't explain why her parents hadn't left them with family instead, why an orphanage had been the solution they'd fixed on; it wasn't until later that I found out that my grandmother's parents had thrown her out and my grandfather's had disowned him, and that none of their relatives would speak to them at the time, let alone volunteer to take their two kids.

When Ma arrived in the States her language marked her out: a rural, southern dialect that other Italians barely understood and held in contempt. The Americans she met didn't care; all wops were the same: filthy, immoral, stinking of garlic and barely more than animals. She learned Spanish before she learned English, from following her father to building sites and listening to the foreman's shouted instructions. Most of her English she learned from the secondhand TV her parents bought to keep her and her brother company on the long nights when they were locked in the apartment together, both parents working overtime.

As the language came to her she waited to feel like she fit in, but even when she had learned to diagram sentences and could recite entire scenes of Shakespeare by heart, she never did: she did not know how to act American. She did not even know how to act female— her mother had been at her place on the factory floor for hours by the time Ma woke up, and so for years she went to school with her stockings run and back to front, her brassieres the wrong size, her hair tangled, no packed lunch and no money to buy one. It wasn't until she met my father that she learned the difference between scrambled, fried, poached eggs; she never stopped wildly mixing her metaphors.

She learned to blend in, to fade into the foreground, killed her accent so that she didn't stick out, but every new English word took her farther from her parents and the country where she had been born. She wedged herself into an in-between space: not American, despite the social security number they gave her in her late teens; not Sicilian, despite her green card; but eternally other, so that she could only be comfortable when no one expected her to belong.

CHAPTER II

The apartment was above a little grocery store, with a porch and a staircase up to it out back, beside the dumpsters. It was one room with cheap pressboard furniture: a kitchen table with chairs, an awful couch, and a bunk bed; there was a hotplate in a corner and no TV.

Ma started work the next day, walked down the gravel road in the dark and birdsong to serve truckers and other lost souls oily coffee and comfort food from four a.m. until twelve noon. I woke when I wanted to, which was earlier than ever before because of the hollow feeling her absence gave the apartment. That emptiness made me crazy, so I laced up my boots while my toast browned, guzzled milk from the cold-clouded glass bottle until I stopped being hungry, and stepped out into the half-light of daybreak.

On that first morning I stood for a while in a beam of syrupy light on the porch, looking up the slope of the mountains in front of me. I catalogued everything I'd left behind, the almost friends that I almost missed, the toys and books and half-finished projects, wanting some reason to stay in the empty apartment, because I

16

didn't want to step out into those woods alone. It felt like a vacation, like I'd be back to normal life in a few weeks, and that made it easier to not want. We couldn't be staying here forever. As soon as Ma got over her angry or her sad or whatever it was that had made her finally walk out we'd go home and everything would go back to the way it had been.

It was mid-May, a month away from the end of school and from my fourteenth birthday, and the woods were green with the mist of moss and lichen and budding plants, rich with the cold damp smell of decaying leaves and growing things. I felt the breath of it settling in my body and I stepped down onto earth, then slowly walked into the woods, stopping every few yards to look back. Then the apartment and the grocery store under it disappeared from sight, and I was freed from the fear of getting lost because I was lost. I wandered, up and down rough hills and through bottomland oozing like a scraped knee just beginning to heal, until the sunlight poured down the mountain that hid the eastern horizon and cut through the trees in heavy beams. Here and there the bones of the earth poked through, jagged-edged boulders and looming cliffs that begged to be climbed and which I did climb, not through any desire for conquest, but for the deeper stillness I found while perched on a crag, looking out over the rippling cloud shadows on budding treetops, not thinking of anything until suddenly I realized that eventually I would have to get down, and I wasn't sure how I had gotten up in the first place.

After a few days I stopped wondering when we'd

go home, hoped even that we wouldn't leave until I had missed the last of school, maybe even gotten through the long, lonely summer without having to spend days sitting on the front porch of our house admitting that I had no friends and nobody liked me enough to talk to me when they didn't have me in their face every day reminding them I existed. Then came a day that Ma did not return home at noon.

I had started to grow confident in my ability to navigate the mountain, comfortable in the silence, and so at first I thought that I had just gotten home early. But I sat on the top step with my legs dangling in the sunlight, and still she did not come. Then I wandered down to the front of the grocery store beneath our apartment and saw that her car was gone, and I wondered if she had gone home without me, or gone on without me. If she had found out about the postcard, and abandoned me because I couldn't be trusted. I ran back up to the apartment: her clothes were still there, but she could buy new ones. Then I ran my hand under the mattress of the top bunk, and found that our bankroll was still in place, a thick pack of cash wrapped in a sandwich bag that she didn't want to carry around. That was only so comforting.

I waited, counting my breaths, until I heard the hum of her car and the grate of tires on gravel. She cut the engine and came around the corner of the store carrying a large cardboard box. I was so relieved that I nearly threw up.

"Where were you?" I asked, trying not to sound accusatory but not quite succeeding.

"The Baptist church down the highway was having a book sale. You weren't back when I came for the car, but you can come with me next time."

"Oh." I couldn't think how to tell her about my overwhelming fear without sounding like an idiot, so instead I helped her haul the books inside. It was only half past one.

"You didn't have to wait for me to eat," she said, and I noticed the paper sack of diner food on the table. My fear melted into embarrassment.

Tucked into the box of paperbacks was a map of the United States, like the one that hung in the back of my seventh-grade classroom, except less colorful and with the major highways picked out like veins showing through thin skin. After we ate, she quizzed me on spelling words while she sat before the unfolded map on the floor, searching the wide page carefully, her pen hovering, before marking little stars.

"Whatcha doing that for?" I asked.

"It helps me wrap my head around things."

"What kind of things?"

"Places I've been. Places I might go sometime. Places where people I know have gone to."

While I worked through math problems she scribbled notes in black next to the stars, her writing tiny. I pretended it didn't interest me.

The days began to bleed into each other. I spent mornings wandering the woods and getting lost, but never so lost that I wasn't waiting to greet my mother at a little past noon, or rather to greet the bag of leftovers that she brought from the diner: old chili or mashed potatoes or meatloaf, cheaply made commercial food we warmed in a frying pan and wolfed down without dishing it onto plates. Sometimes, after eating, she went with me into the woods, where she named the plants and birds and we stuffed wrinkled sandwich sacks with the mushrooms that she knew were safe, to sauté them in butter and pile them on toast. But eventually she'd give me the Look, and even if I washed up and swept the entire apartment it couldn't be put off forever, and we would settle at opposite ends of the table, she with a book and me with my schoolwork. When I lost my way she would stare, unblinking, at the text, until memory gelled and she could explain the equation, the part of speech, the chemical reaction, that had given me pause, but mostly I plodded on as she read, in a papery, comfortable silence, shaped by the scratch of my pencil and the cry of birds and the brush of wind and the rattle and voices of the people in the store below. I lost track of where we were in the week, in the month, what month it even was, so that I felt as though I existed outside of time, in a never-ending summer.

On the days that she didn't work we threw food and water bottles into our rucksacks and wandered the mountains, until our legs and hips grew hard. More rarely, she drove us into what passed for civilization, to the thrift store to poke among other people's memories, or to the Baptist church's weekly book sale to replace what we had already read. It wasn't long before these trips filled me with the same trepidation that I had felt on that first morning, staring down the mountain. I was forgetting how to be around other people. My words were drying up.

She picked up every extra shift that she was asked to, stayed late and arrived early with the understanding that she might have to leave at any time. The less she said to her co-workers about why she might have to quit town quickly the more people imagined, so when, nearly three months after we first turned up, the sheriff's deputy in the brown cruiser came with photographs of her and me and my father, her boss shoved her out the back door with her pay in cash and a kiss on the forehead, and promised to keep the deputy talking for as long as he could while we made tracks.

When my mother left by the back door of the diner I was ranging across the face of the mountain, wandering from one band of heavy August sunlight to the next, feeling it stir my blood and bring my selfness to the surface, and I heard my name in her voice echoing at me off the rocks.

I imagine now that she stood on the porch hugging herself, or paced on the gravel by the car with a cigarette between her fingers, thinking, weighing her options. She'd run away on an impulse, I know that for certain, and maybe if she'd been given enough time hidden away there in the mountains she'd have gone back home on impulse. But the arrival of the fuzz forced the choice. Maybe if I'd taken longer to come when she called for me, or else been quicker and given her less time to think, she would have chosen differently.

By the time I got to the apartment, having made as

direct a return as possible, she had piled our books into a plastic milk crate—permanently borrowed from down-stairs—bundled our clothes into our backpacks, and crammed our food and cooking things—a pan, a spatula, an electric kettle, and two plates with cutlery—into a heavy canvas bag, and stacked it all in the middle of the room. The map, her map, was folded into a clear plastic freezer bag on the table along with all the money, and she stood pensively on the tiny porch, chain-smoking cigarettes and dropping the butts onto the lid of the dumpster below, waiting for me.

We stuffed all of our things into the car in one trip, locked the apartment door and left the key with the grocery clerk, and set out south, her hunched over the steering wheel, me leaning back in the passenger's seat, the zip-lock full of map and money on my lap. My conscience was pricking—I couldn't know that it had been my postcard that was setting us on the run, but I felt guilty.

I held my peace for a few hours, watched Ma suck on cigarettes and wondered what she was thinking. We went south for a good while, and I could tell by the map that we were running parallel to the West Virginia border—not the folded map that Ma had marked up, but the road atlas that she'd pulled out when she'd gotten in the car and left opened to the correct page on the dash in front of me, in case she got lost. Then we dipped back into Virginia, and I crossed my fingers that we were going home—we were, I guessed, quite a way south and west of it, but in our part of the state the best way to get to a place was often to go in exactly the wrong direction, at least until an interstate showed up, because taking the mountain roads could take you forever.

But the farther south we went the less faith I had in that theory, and when the green sign with *Welcome to North Carolina!* whipped past I had to admit to myself that Ma hadn't decided to save the sheriff's deputy the bother of dragging us home. The sky had clouded over, and a slow rain was falling, the drops fat. The sound of it hitting the car and the way it greyed and hazed everything outside the windows made it feel as if we were in a cocoon, made the smoke-and-candy-smelling inside of the car feel safe in a way that the nerves in my stomach couldn't accept was real.

"Ma?" I began. "Where are we going?"

"South," she said, and her voice crackled on the vowels. She took a drag on her cigarette like she didn't expect me to say anything else, but as she let out the smoke she reached down and turned off the radio, which had only been on quiet, so that I knew that she knew that the time for a little explaining had come.

"How far south?"

"As far as it takes to get somewhere where no one expects us to go and no one knows us."

"How come?"

She took another drag on her cigarette, kept her eyes square on the road. Her hair was tied back tight for work, and I couldn't tell if the bones of her face were standing out stark because she was tired or for some other reason.

"I've been thinking about that for a while now. When

23

we left I just wanted to get away, didn't care where to. And when we got there I wanted to keep our options open, earn some money, not be findable until I wanted to be." She gave me a sharp glance then, and I thought about the post-card and felt the back of my neck blaze hot. "There are places I've been meaning to go back to, loose ends I should have tied up, that I've been putting off for years now. Since I met your dad, really. And now that moving on seems like the wise choice, I can't see a reason not to get it all done."

I let the quiet hang on for a few miles.

"Why not go back home?" I asked, and I could tell from her silence that it was the wrong thing to have asked. I waited for the coldness to wear off, then said, "So we're going to visit some people for a couple days?"

"Not quite, kid. There are some things to sort out first, people I need to get in touch with. Guess the cops couldn't have turned up at a better time—school will be starting in a few weeks, and you need to be in it."

I made a face at that. "Do I have to?"

"Oh, hush. It'll probably take me until next June to get the money together. What else is there for you to do all day?"

I listened to the rain a while, then dropped the map onto the floor and kicked my feet up onto the dashboard.

"What kind of loose ends?" I asked.

She pulled a cigarette out of the packet with her lips, cranked down the window an inch, lit it one-handed without taking her eyes off the road, then let out the first plume of smoke. Then, to my surprise, she started telling me.

*

24

Some families just don't work out. Ma's family happened to be one of them.

Her father was a black sheep, disgraced and turned out by his parents for differing reasons depending on who told the story: an argument that ended when he stabbed a cousin; money stolen from a brother; the police coming to their home in search of smuggled food, pilfered truck parts, missing livestock. All of the stories about him that her aunts and uncles and cousins had told her were probably true, or not far off the truth.

He was passing through town looking for seasonal work when he met my grandmother, fresh from the big city with her new degree and planning on making something of herself after one last summer at home, cooking for her brothers and making dresses for her mother. He fell for her; her parents knew he was no good; they had a little romance in secret. It was the oldest story ever told, but with a twist: when he asked her to marry him, she said no. She wouldn't go against her parents.

So he shot her.

It was with a small-gauge bullet, barely larger than the BB gun my own father had as a boy, in the fleshy part of her leg, and even though it bled and scarred into a thick raised keloid that my mother remembers running her finger over when she was little, her life was never endangered. But she had to go to a doctor to have the bullet dug out, and the doctor called the police, and the police took my grandfather to jail.

When he was released on bail he went to see her, asked her again, would she marry him? He was sorry about her leg, but he'd been forced to it: he would be tried, and she, as the only witness, would have to testify, would have to tell the truth, would send him off to prison for years and years. Unless—wives could not be asked to testify against their husbands. She could fix it, or she could have his imprisonment on her conscience.

Whether she bowed to this logic immediately or was slowly worn down, the result was the same. She married him. Without a witness, the case was thrown out. And when they found out what she had done, her parents threw my grandmother out.

CHAPTER III

We stopped only for coffee, to refill the gas tank and, once, to coax a suspicious counter boy into giving us the battered key chained to a block of wood that unlocked a reeking unisex bathroom. The sun set and the road emptied but we continued south, passed through cities that were nothing more than constellations of lights in the dark, then back into the nothingness of the countryside, time suspended.

The night felt too thick for talking. But then a song that Ma didn't like came on, and she fiddled the tuner up through the 100s and around to the low numbers again before clicking the radio off. She settled her shoulders back against the car seat and when I had stopped expecting her to speak she began, in a slow quiet voice, a story about her life before that might have been for me or might just have been to keep herself awake.

The first Laura Ma met lived across the road from her from when she was nine until she was twelve. She was a short, plump girl with mouse-brown hair and an astigmatism that meant she had to wear glasses but constantly tripped into things anyway. She was Irish, but since they went to the same church, confessed to the same priest and received the Host together they were permitted to be friends.

Their Church believed in early confirmation—most of them would be married by sixteen, grandmothers by thirty-six—so at the age of eleven they talked at length about the implications of being recognized as adults in the eyes of God, wondered how they would be treated differently by friends and relatives, tried to think of things to confess that were more sordid than staying up late to watch *The Dunwich Horror* and stealing dimes for sodas from their mother's purses. These discussions were usually held while they smoked stolen cigarettes behind the yew hedge at Our Lady of the Sacred Heart School, where they both wore uniforms and were taught by aging nuns. Laura was older than my mother by less than a year, but it was enough to make a difference. She had read more, she could imagine more, while my mother could only repeat what she had seen elsewhere, and in their make-believes my mother always felt that she was at a disadvantage. Laura painted a future in which, the moment they were confirmed, all nagging would cease, everyone would be stunned by their beauty and maturity, and they would develop passionate but chaste relationships with attractive young priests, who would see them as the women that they were, hear the confessions of their hearts and understand them like no one else could.

When they were finally confirmed it was not by the handsome, young, sympathetic priest that they had imagined, but by an old, half-deaf one, who couldn't remember their names and smelled of menthol cough drops and age.

They were annoyed with him for not conforming to their fantasy, for not being the young attractive man with whom they wanted to share the innermost workings of their minds and who, more importantly, they had been depending on to instantly recognize the inherent wonder in the innermost working of their minds. Laura was the one who met Father Luke, and took my mother along to chat with him in the empty science classroom during lunch. He wasn't really a priest, he wasn't ordained yet, just a seminarian that had been brought in to teach trigonometry when Sister Marceline broke her hip, and he was still in his twenties and as handsome as a sallow young man with pimples and a harelip can be. The pretense, at first, was that Laura and my mother were concerned about some things that they'd read in Butler's *Lives of the Saints* and how it matched up to what they'd been taught in class. It seemed, Laura said, that an awful lot of girls had died to preserve their purity, but wasn't suicide a sin? When that question had been hammered out, they asked him if they could be condemned to hell for impure thoughts, and how impure the thoughts would have to be to constitute a mortal instead of venial sin, and if it was a sin to read the sort of books that encouraged those thoughts, and if dreams were sinful if they really couldn't control what they dreamed? My mother mostly just went along with this, since Laura was the true mastermind, and they both found the discussions as thrilling as their weekly confessions with the mentholated priest failed to be. They looked forward to their lunches with Father Luke, explaining to each other regularly that there was nothing unseemly about the meetings, since after all neither of them was alone with him and he was instructing them in the ways of purity. But that was not the view that one of the nuns took when she walked in on them conducting a very hands-on discussion about what a girl should and should not permit a boy to do, and how she might react when he persisted in putting his hands in places where they did not belong. Father Luke was packed off at top speed, and there was quite an inquiry into who had influenced whom into doing what, in which the good old appellation of 'foul temptress' was trotted out at least once.

Ma paused in her telling to light another cigarette and smoked it thoughtfully, as if the story had come to an end.

"You went back to playing together like normal when it all blew over though, didn't you?" I prompted her.

"No, we never really got the chance to."

"How come?"

"Well, my father made some crooked deals with crooked men right about then, and when he figured it was going to catch up with him he threw us all in the car in the middle of the night and moved us out to Oregon with no warning."

I waited for the punch line, but when it didn't come I asked, "Seriously? Grandpa did that?"

"It didn't really do him any good. They caught up with him before the year was over—it was just a huge-ass mess. The cops got called. Your uncle and I got popped in foster care—I think that was the second time we were put in a home since coming to the States. We were in for the better part of a year—it took my parents that long to get themselves sorted out. Once they got us back and got the money together we moved back to the east coast to our old street. Not our old house—the landlord took everything we'd left behind for the rent your grandfather didn't think to pay while we were gone. And while we were gone, Laura's family moved. Just like that, she went from being my best friend to being someone I could only remember, someone I had no hope of tracking down."

As rain began to rattle against the roof my eyes closed. I heard the engine on the other side of my dreams, felt the car move, but it was easier not to be awake. It wasn't until we stopped and I heard Ma put the parking brake on and cut the engine that I opened them again.

She was leaning her elbows and wrists on the steering wheel, holding a lit cigarette between her fingers but not smoking, the mumble of the radio cut off like she'd closed a door on the lonely singer. The sky was white over a whiter beach and even whiter breakers, all tinged a faint blue from the tint of the windshield glass. Out of the dark, foaming ocean a sun was rising, massive and red. It balanced on the black line of the horizon and spilled its blood across the sky, tore the scudding clouds with pink and caked the wet sand, and for a moment I wondered if, in the course of my sleeping, we'd made it to the end of the world, where the sun rose out of the ocean like a newborn thing in the way I'd always imagined seeing but never had.

"Where are we?" I asked.

"Florida," she said.

"Oh."

She failed to volunteer further information.

"What happens now?" I asked finally, as the ash of her cigarette lengthened and she continued to stare at the waves rolling over themselves to reach the tideline.

"Whelp," she began, and took a long drag. "First, I get some sleep. Then we go find some place to stay on more comfortable lines than the inside of this car. Then I find a job, and we find out how to get you back in school without catching hell for the time you missed."

She leaned her seat back and closed her eyes, and for the first few minutes I watched her as her body sank deeper and deeper into sleep and the muscles of her face relaxed, but as her eyes began to flick beneath their lids it became too intimate, my intrusion into the closed space of her dreaming, and I quietly opened the door and stepped onto the sanded parking lot and into the smothering weight of August heat, stood for a moment by the car and looked around me.

The waves rolled irregularly onto the beach, a moving mass of grey that seemed to be alive and breathing. The dunes blocked out the view inland, so that I felt trapped in the narrow margin of wave-smoothed sand. I toed off my boots and left them, sweaty nests for raveled socks, under the shadow of the front wheel, and began to walk.

My mother was still asleep an hour or so later when I returned, her head lolling against the torn headrest, face relaxed but body still tense, muscles clenched. I felt like I'd never really seen her before, like I'd held onto a shorthand image of her that was one half how she'd looked when I was six and the other half the idea of "mother," which wasn't too different from the idea of "God" when you thought about it. And like God, I'd never really thought about her as a person, instead paid attention to what she could do for me, what the fallout of her wrath might be. Something had changed, in the car near the North Carolina border, but I wasn't sure if it was in who she was, or just who I thought she was.

While she slept I sat on the warm sand in front of the car and stared at the water. I wasn't listening, wasn't really watching, and so was surprised when a handful of teenagers wandered from the parking lot and onto the beach. They were a few years older than I was then, a few decades younger than I am now, and they talked too loudly and laughed too much, moved with a long-limbed grace and touched each other with a calculated nonchalance that betrayed attraction. As I watched them I became slowly aware of a place low in my belly and between my hips, a strange hungry place bone deep that felt oddly tight and prickling, as though my pelvis needed to sneeze.

It had been months since I'd seen people my age. In West Virginia I kept a weathered ear out, made sure that anyone else wandering the mountain never caught sight of me. The clerk in the grocery store below our apartment was middle-aged or older, as were the manager and the staff and the patrons at the diner where Ma worked and where she took me once or twice for a hot meal; the ladies we'd run into at the thrift store and at the book sale had been anonymously motherly, beige ciphers I barely noticed. Something had happened to me in those months alone, something that I'd been warned about at school and at home but only recognized in retrospect: my sap had begun to rise, my brain to flood with chemicals and skin thrum with impulses I'd never imagined before and wasn't able to put a name to. When we'd left home other people my age were there to ally with, ignore, or avoid; on the beach I was unexpectedly made aware that there was a fourth option.

I picked up handfuls of sand and crushed them against my legs, concentrating on the soft-rough feel of the grains, watching and not watching and wishing that I were one of them, wanting to receive an electric burning touch.

The car door cried on its hinges, her feet crunched on the sand, and still I watched the surfer kids, fully dressed but feeling more naked than I'd ever been. She stretched, her shoulders and hips making a scrape-click sound as they settled into place, then sank down to sit on the sand next to me. She breathed deep and I did too, taking in the smell of salt and decay, ozone and seaweed: the strange, intoxicating, iodine-laced breath of life.

The ocean is the lover our species never got over.

We crawled out of its arms to stumble and stand on solid ground, and have pined for it ever since. It's the tragic romance to end them all. And the ocean hasn't forgotten, hasn't forgiven that abandonment—try and climb back into its bed without due precaution and it will kill your ass.

We didn't speak, but I felt that my mother was reading my thoughts, knew what I had been wanting even though I couldn't name it, and shame burned through me.

"When are we going home?" I asked.

"What is home?" she asked back.

"Our house."

"But what if our house is empty?"

"OK, then you and Dad and me in our house. Making blintzes on Sundays and going stargazing from the porch roof and playing cards when the power goes out. Borrowing each other's clothes. Arguing about chores. You know. Home."

"That's a time, not a place. And time only goes one way."

I sat quiet for a few minutes, watching the waves climb up the beach and fall back, then tried again.

"Think you'll give talking things out with Dad a shot sometime?"

"Kid, you don't know how many 'shots' I've given your dad already." She rose up, smacked her ass to knock the loose sand from the seat of her jeans. "Talking things out? No. Talking? Maybe. Sometime. C'mon, it's time for us to get rolling again."

*

We found a sad-looking apartment complex with *Pay by the week—move in today!* on a cheap banner under the sign; Ma handed the clerk a folded bundle of green bills thick enough to cover the first month in exchange for a lease and a key. We carried our milk crate and backpacks up two flights of rusted white enameled stairs to a room that smelled like old cigarettes and disappointment, smaller than the place over the grocery store. A sagging sofa, old TV, and a kitchen table with mismatched chairs indicated that the front half was a living room, with nothing to divide it from the bedroom—a bed, night-stand, and closet—in the back half. A door behind the sofa led to a kitchenette barely large enough to turn around in, and a door beside the bed led to a bathroom that wasn't much larger.

When we had piled everything into the middle of the room, Ma kissed my forehead and left me to unpack as much as I felt like, and I had a second of anxiety that she wouldn't come back. It didn't last, and I hung our thrift-store clothes in the closet, put away our food and pan and kettle, stuffed the plastic bag of money under the mattress. Pulled the bag out again, removed the folded map, put the chain on the door, then spread the map out in the middle of the vomit-yellow carpet.

It had been folded and refolded along all of its creases, like she'd looked at it several times since she'd bought it. The stars she'd drawn scattered the map, clustering more thickly on the east and west coasts, thinner in the center of the country, the notes that went with them even-edged blocks of print written in uncannily straight lines. Despite their neatness, I had to read them over and over before they began to make any sense to me. They were notes she had written for herself, the most important crumbs of the places they marked, and given the kind of language she used I guessed that she hadn't considered anyone but her would read them. The recurring *Group Home* and *Foster Home* written by the red marks were sometimes accompanied by modifiers: *Where I learned to drive, Crazy Laura, Kissing Laura, Dead girl found in bathtub.* Notes by the green stars spoke to an entirely different flavor of experience: *Free love commune* in Oregon, *Den of prostitution and overpriced wine* in Nevada, *Brainwashed broodmother* in Texas, *Cocksucking motherfucking son of a syphilitic whore* in Michigan. A trail of yellow highlighter—the way she marked our route for road trips when we took them—ran along the branching arteries of highways, from Georgia up to Michigan, back down to Mississippi and across the country to California. Then the yellow went north through Washington and to the edge of the map, ending in an arrow pointing to where Canada should be, with the name beside it in thick black capital letters: *LAURA*. That looked, to me, to be as close to an ultimate destination as I could ask for.

For a few minutes I tried to match up the stories she'd told me to the notes without much success, copied the path in rough ballpoint on the inside cover of an Agatha Christie Ma had already read, then refolded the map along its creases and stashed it back with the money.

She was gone five more hours. Every time I considered pulling the map back out for a second look my brain conjured the sound of her engine, her footsteps rattling the loose metal staircase, her key in the door. I could have copied out the entire map and all of her annotations in the time she was gone, but instead I caved to my nerves and read one of the paperbacks from our stash.

When she finally reappeared I was so absorbed in the book that I heard neither her engine nor her footsteps on the staircase. The door smacked to the length of the security chain, and I had to skitter up to let her in. She tossed first her keys, then a grey brick that it took me a few moments to realize was a new cellphone, onto the little table under the wide front window, then fell back onto the bed, starfished, and moaned, "Goddamn, it is hot out there."

"You got a new phone," I observed.

"Had to—you need a phone number to put on the job applications. Got an offer to work at a sports bar, and another bar, though I'm not sure if I'm going to take one or both." She took a breath. "And I registered you for school."

"What?"

"You start eighth grade in a few weeks. I managed to get you out of phys ed. You're welcome."

She tossed me a sheaf of papers: Spanish was mandatory. Oh, joy. Then I realized what else was in the sheaf: my social security card and birth certificate.

"Hey, Dad's name isn't on my birth certificate," I said.

"Nope," she said.

"Is this fake, or has it always been like that?"

"Funny story," she began. "We had a blowout fight when I was simply enormous with you, and I walked out. Drove around town all night long trying to stop being angry, and around breakfast time the next day realized what I was feeling wasn't hunger cramps. Went to the hospital. When they asked me if I wanted to call anyone to sit with me I told them there wasn't anyone to call. Sixteen hours later they handed me you, and dangit if I still didn't want to kill your father. And that is why his name isn't on that birth certificate."

"Are you making that up?" I asked.

"It wasn't just that I was angry with him," she conceded. "I couldn't see myself living out of my car with you only a few hours old, but I figured that one day I'd want to leave again, and if I did I wouldn't be leaving you behind. And if your dad wasn't on your birth certificate, then he couldn't really stop me from taking you with me. After I got home I told him what I'd done, told him he could get it changed, get his name put on if he wanted, and he said he was going to. But you know, fourteen years and he never once got around to it."

I put the papers on the table, weighted down with her keys. I wanted her to be making it up, but it sounded like something she would do; it also sounded like something my father would do, or rather fail to.

"So, is this home for now?" I asked.

"Home?" She looked pointedly around the room. The

air-conditioning unit kept the room clammy and made it smell, the wallpaper was water-stained in one corner up near the ceiling, the blankets were scratchy, and even after hours in the car with no relief the bathroom had given me serious pause. "Nah. Home's a long way away still. But we'll get there."

CHAPTER IV

The first couple of weeks in Florida I thought I would go out of my skin. I was on my own for long stretches of time, the same as I'd been in West Virginia, except now whenever I stepped outside our door, instead of being in the cool, silent woods I was in a loud, reeking city, and I couldn't stand it. I'd forgotten how to be around other people. So just before sunrise and just after sunset I went down to the beach, scudded my feet in the sand and breathed in the fresher air and wished for the day that we'd get on the road again, get on with the loose-end gathering that Ma seemed so set on so that we could get back home.

After the day we arrived—most of which she spent asleep, trying to recover from the drive—I barely saw her. She took both jobs, and took every shift of both jobs they would give her, so that when she wasn't working she was sleeping or showering or just getting ready to split, and half the time she was in and conscious I was out; I'd never lived so close to the ocean, and I didn't plan on wasting it.

The day before school started she surprised me with

new clothes—jeans and a plain black T-shirt—and a new backpack with the pencils and notebooks and calculator and things they expected you to drag along. I'd been hoping that she'd lost track of the days, forgotten about school.

She eyed me up as I looked at the clothes, then said, "You should probably put on some deodorant tomorrow morning as well—you've started stinking like an adult."

"I do not!"

"Trust me, kid, you do. And you need to either commit to using a comb on the regular, or you need a haircut."

I opted for the haircut, sat outside on the second step down and let her snip out the matted tails that I hadn't realized had become more or less permanent due to the daily application of saltwater, pare it back so that it hung just to the bony knob where my neck met my shoulders. I wouldn't let her go any shorter than that; my hair grows more out than down and is curly enough that if it's cut too short I look like a dandelion until it grows back.

Now that she mentioned it, I noticed the smell—I spent enough time in the ocean that it wasn't a constant funk, but after a few hours in the sun I usually started smelling something like onions and sour that I hadn't realized was me. And I'd started sprouting hair, not a bunch yet but little isolated ones almost the same shade as my skin so you could barely see them, popping up in my armpits and groin and on my legs and even one or two in the bumpy halos around my nipples, like they'd gotten lost on their way to my eyebrows and stopped to ask for directions. And my nose had gotten longer, the

Roman bump at the bridge that I'd gotten from Ma grown bigger. I was not particularly happy about any of this.

I had hoped that, even with haircut and new clothes, Ma would forget about school by the time I had to leave for it, but when I got back from my beach walk the next morning she was waiting with breakfast and a determined look that said I was going even if she had to carry me there over her shoulder. I was still scared enough by her—or not scared, really, but whatever it is that makes kids do what their parents tell them—that she didn't have to resort to this.

Whether it was my unremarkableness or their apathy, I didn't seem to register on anyone's radar, teacher or student. No one called me out for being new, or gave me a hard time about my loose, plain clothes, or tried to trap me into admitting whether I was a boy or a girl. I suppose I was forgettable, came across still as whichever gender a person expected to see, and I was thankful for it even as I worried that this was the last year I'd be able to skate by so easily, that eventually someone would make an issue of my careful androgyny and I'd have to choose my side in the war, make up my mind as to where my allegiance lay, whether I identified more with my mother or my father. Because in my mind that's what they were asking: do you want to grow up to be like your mom or your dad, Alex? And I still wanted to know why I couldn't be both, why it was an either/or situation.

Though I was grateful for this indifference, it also stung; that was new. I had always been perfectly happy on the fringe, occupied with my own fantasies, with books

43

and one-person imagination games and just a little bit contemptuous maybe of the sort of person that took too much notice of the people around them. But something had punctured the smooth wall of my inner world, infected me. I noticed it for the first time on the day we'd turned up in Florida and I'd sat on the beach and watched those teenagers; once I was surrounded by other people my age I couldn't deny it anymore. My peers had become unexpectedly tantalizing.

They seemed perfect and delicious in a way I hadn't known they could, and I wanted to touch them and taste them and smell them; I didn't have to pick a gender alliance to know that I was attracted to all of them. I glanced at arms and legs and the backs of necks, the way they walked and how their lips moved when they spoke and all the little unconscious gestures. I limited myself to glances, fearful of how I might give myself away were I to take a full look. I couldn't imagine that anyone else was having these cravings, these urges. And I didn't have friends who could disabuse me of my misconception.

After school I trudged slowly through the sadder part of town back to the apartment, locked and chained the door behind me in case one of the neighbors realized I was alone and decided to help themselves to our stuff, ate an apple, glanced at my homework, considered going down to the beach. Then, with boredom and frustration prickling under my skin, I climbed under the stiff blanket on the too-firm bed and slipped my hands into my clothes. There was no one to see but it felt like the cheap prints on the walls, the water stain in the ceiling, the blank eye of the television were all watching my every action. I closed my eyes and let my hands drift down to my thighs, looking for the tingle that had shamed me on the beach, trying to set it free but untutored as to how. I thought about the people I couldn't stop looking at, imagined the feeling of their hands on my skin and my hands on theirs, stripping each other slowly naked like we were in a bad made-for-TV movie—and was overcome by the unlikeliness of this ever happening, my own unloveability. The tingle fled, and I gave up.

Ma met her third Laura when she was fifteen and living in a group home in south-eastern Pennsylvania, the kind of place where a dozen kids that weren't cute anymore were watched close enough that no one got pregnant or seriously hurt, not so close that life was boring. My uncle was still cute; he had been sent elsewhere.

This Laura had sleepy eyes and brown hair that never grew past her jaw because she cut it instead of cutting her skin when life got bad. She had narrow hips and small breasts and was exactly four feet ten and three-quarter inches tall. She wore kids' shoes that velcroed closed and secondhand everything in impractical colors. She didn't understand my mother's putty-green ranger boots. They came from different philosophies.

Laura made prison hooch and bathtub gin, secured the permission of the house mother to bake brownies for Valentine's Day and successfully spiked one of the three pans with Purple Kush, took my mother on the wrong bus back from school and got lost on the edge of the county, found sticks of opium in the watch pocket of her jeans and shared them liberally, found a way up to the roof so they could smoke cigarettes after lights out. And Laura was charmed—she never got caught. She was more careful than she let on, but the staff thought that she could do no wrong. And for a tripped-out, magic chapter of her life my mother was carried in her wake.

Their friendship was an accident, Ma said. They both arrived at the same time, were assigned beds next to each other, and while they were stowing their stuff in the girls' dorm Laura had told her that they'd be going dealer hunting that afternoon, because every town had a dealer if you knew where to look. And Ma could have said no but instead she went along with it. They asked for permission to go shopping for tampons, not the kind that were kept on hand but a special kind of high-absorbency biodegradable hippy tampon because the normal scented ones made Laura break out in a rash so that she couldn't sit, and Ma needed to go with her for safety and solidarity. They found the tampons, but only after trekking to a stretch of rocky beach by the river to light up bitter-smelling buds in the company of the guy named Keith who had sold them. Ma didn't say much. She wasn't at an age where she did say much, even when the weed starting getting to her.

I'm pretty sure Ma didn't realize that she loved Laura until the night they played strip poker. There was gin in Dixie cups, and a little plastic camping lantern so they could see, and two beds pushed together and a deck of dog-eared, faded cards mixed from three partial packs. Six or so of them crowded onto the dead mattresses, with the anorexic light of the toy lantern filling the crater that their thin weight made, barely bright enough to make out the suits. And off came socks and belts and cottony layers as the drink burned into them brighter than the lantern light, and discarded clothing carpeted the floor around the bed until they all sat in their panties and bras—long legged, long bodied, short and gangly, knobs of hips and spine jutting out or smoothed over, olive and milk and oak and cherry-wood colored skin, heavy breasted or boyish. A cabal of young women, smooth and crouching, perfect in the half-light. And then my mother was out of clothes: what to give next? So she bet a kiss, and someone squeaked. Quietly, they didn't want to get caught. A kiss, and my mother lost.

Their mouths were thin, or soft. She remembers them: toothy, full of biting; one girl with lips like an overripe plum; too wet; shrinking and hesitant. But Laura's mouth sent electricity over her skin: firm and warm and tasting deep purple. A perfect kiss, or, rather, the kiss perfectly suited to my mother's taste, because everyone craves a different perfect.

They went to bed soon after. Revision: they fell asleep like puppies in a warm, naked, tipsy heap on the two beds, and even though my mother's kiss had led to the slow exploration of all of their mouths, of the strange intimacy that is kissing, in the morning it had mostly been forgotten. Except by my mother, who woke to dreams of Laura's mouth, that purple kiss.

She angled for one, asked for one, hoped that each time they drank together afterwards it would magically all happen again, but the second kiss was a kiss goodbye. Her parents had gotten their life straightened out enough for her to go back with them, at least for a while. She was bundling socks into her backpack when Laura came into the dorm, pulled her down so as to reach, and gave her a second kiss, longer this time, then left the room without a word.

Maybe it would have ended differently, if they had been older, had met three or four decades later in human history. But they were fifteen years old and it was 1979, and they had a first kiss and they had a last kiss and in between got lost and got high and talked about their sex dreams and pretended they couldn't hear when each other's beds creaked with the rhythm of longing in the night. Maybe there was romance, in another reality.

The time I didn't spend on the beach I spent in the apartment, clammy with the air conditioning, sometimes watching the flickering TV but more often combing through our secondhand books looking for dirty bits, reading the dirty bits over and over, and then climbing under the blanket on our bed so as to feel hidden while I thought up dirty bits of my own and fumblingly explored my body. I'm still not sure if it was more due to hormones or to boredom, but even the black-and-white diagrams in the medical encyclopedia we'd somewhere acquired got me excited. As that failed to satisfy I shed layers, until I found myself one afternoon in the middle of the floor, the cheap carpet rough under my back, naked and trying to touch my entire body with one hand while the other worked away at its Sisyphean task. I had become an absolute pervert, and it tortured me. I was the only being on earth so obsessed and controlled by such strange and strangely satisfying cravings. I decided I was going to hell if I didn't stop. Then I found the superintendent's collection of dirty magazines, and decided that I'd better make going to hell worthwhile, because I would never be able to excise the obsession.

As the months passed my wanting grew more intense, more confused. I was bored, and I was lonely, and nothing seemed to hold the power to captivate me anymore. The things that had kept my attention so well just the year before had become as riveting as my baby toys, so that I found myself pausing mid-action, preoccupied by the kids at school, by the teenagers at the beach, images of them conjured by my mind's eye to dance across the world in front of me.

God knows how I paid attention long enough to learn anything that year.

I hung on like death to the knowledge that we wouldn't be staying there forever. This was just a season, a gathering of resources before our next big push. Ma couldn't have left home for this: a one-room squat where we could hear our neighbors hitting and fucking each other through the walls, where all the food came in a can or smelled like grease because we didn't have a real kitchen, where Ma came home at odd hours and collapsed on the bed in an insensate haze, her feet bruised from standing.

She smelled of other people's cigarettes, of stale beer, of lipstick, exhausted from too much of the fake friendliness she had to slather on to earn her tips. Sometimes, when she came home in the morning and hugged me as I went out the door to school, she smelled of what I assumed to be Man: a baritone sweat that wasn't hers, a spiciness to cover it, a clean, flat, mineral scent I tried not to interrogate. She didn't say that she was seeing someone; she didn't say she was spending the nights that she didn't work in some other bed. I didn't know, and I knew, and I didn't want to know. She worked hard; she barely slept while we were in Florida, slowly gathering in the wrinkled tips that would eventually, hopefully, be enough to get us out of there. And no matter what she was doing, I figured I couldn't hold it against her: I was a person and she was a person, and we both tried to kill that bastard, time, in similar desperate ways.

We were poor enough for me to get free lunches—and free breakfasts, if I got my ass to school early enough. I didn't think much at the time about how Ma fixed it all; I took it for granted still that she'd keep the machine of daily life running. I was grateful for the breakfasts, but free lunch meant that I could no longer give up eating and squirrel away the money for something I needed more. But I had light fingers, and rich kids aren't careful. I stole what I needed a dollar at a time, small amounts that people could have dropped or miscounted. When I had enough—a little over $220, which took me from the second week of school, when I had the idea, until the first week of March to get my hands on—I wrote a note to the principal that I was getting some bad teeth taken out, signed Ma's name and dropped it at the office, then bought a bus ticket to Alabama.

If cops showed up at our door, it wasn't going to be my fault this time.

CHAPTER V

The bus left at four a.m., stinking of people that hadn't slept or showered or got much hope left. I sat near the back and wrote a letter to Dad in my marble composition notebook—it seemed like a long way to go just to send a postcard. I wasn't running away, I just needed him to know that we were OK, that I was coming back one day. Maybe going to Alabama was overkill, and I just needed to go to another city, somewhere not where we were living but still Florida. Or maybe I myself needed to go to Alabama, to get out of my mother's reality for a bit.

Dear Daddy—it went,
I'm just fine. I haven't sent this from ~~home~~ where I am though, because the last time I did cops turned up and we left in a hurry. Mom's all right, too. She seems to have a plan—or I hope she has a plan—so I'm going along until it's finished, and then I'll come back. Please don't move; I need to be able to find you again. I'm still in school and I take care of myself, so there's nothing for you to worry about.

After that I didn't know what to write, but I felt like I had to write something, so I remembered all across the page until the heat and the rocking put me to sleep and when I woke up we were passing through Ozark and my pen had left a dripping snail trail of blue at the end of a closely packed page of text.

I couldn't save my school lunch money, but I could save my lunch, so I had bruised apples and clementines and sandy sawdust brownies and dry sesame bagels in my backpack, and I ate enough of them that I could pretend that I wasn't hungry. The air at the bus stop was slick with diesel fumes and made me almost throw it all up again, but I kept it in because I didn't have the money for food.

Part of me thought that I should look around, make the most of being in a place I would probably never see again, but the essential part of me went looking for a blue U.S. Mail box, then wrote our address on the envelope in careful block letters, put on two of the stamps that I'd gotten from the English teacher's desk, the extra one just in case the letter turned out to be heavier than standard, and pitched it into the darkness. Then I went back to the station and waited for the bus to Florida, got in line, put my hand in my back pocket, and found that my ticket had wriggled out and run away.

I had a vague idea that hitchhiking wasn't advisable—you could get kidnapped, have your internal organs stolen, or get picked up by a serial-killing cannibal druggie and never be seen again. Boy, girl, young, old, it wasn't safe for anyone; the kind of person that stopped was exactly the kind of person you didn't want to be alone with in a confined space, not when they were in control. But I couldn't walk back to our apartment in Florida, not from southern Alabama. So I walked to the on ramp of the highway south, tried to look as harmless as possible while still giving the impression that I could protect myself, and stuck out my thumb.

The first dozen people didn't stop, and I started getting worried that the police would show up—I was standing right by a *No Hitching* sign. I could have given up and walked, or found a cop to take me home, but at that point I was still clinging to the idea that if someone stopped for me I might make it back before Ma missed me, might tell her that some friends had built a bonfire on the beach and I'd fallen asleep on the sand. There was a chance she wouldn't get in until tomorrow night.

Then lucky number thirteen came, a youngish woman driving a dented sedan that rolled to a careful stop a few hundred yards past me, and I trotted over like a grateful dog and hopped in the front seat.

"I sure am glad you didn't keep going," I said.

"My sister has a kid your age, I couldn't leave you there," she said. I realized then that she only looked youngish: she was probably about fifty and careful, freckled and tanned with her dark hair streaked brassy from the sun, the kind of sun you only get from being outside and too busy or excited to remember a hat.

"I'm not as young as I look," I said, trying not to sound too cocky about it.

She pulled back onto the road.

"Where you headed?" she asked.

"Back to Florida." I hadn't thought of a story, but it came together as I talked. "Got the bus up to visit my grandma, went to go home and found out that I'd lost my ticket back. So I'm stuck hitching."

The woman made a sympathetic noise. "Couldn't your grandmother get you a ticket?" she asked.

I shook my head. "No, ma'am—she's in prison."

"Prison?"

"Yes, ma'am, she stole a whole bunch of gem rings from some fancy department stores, waltzed right in and got a nice young clerk to take a bunch of them out for her to see, and when she was finished looking and had tried on almost everything she walked out with one of them on her finger. She walked in with her hands just full of rings in the first place, so the poor clerk didn't notice till too late, and no one suspects a little old lady is there to rob them blind. So now Grandma's in jail and I have to get the Greyhound if I want to see her."

"I didn't know there was a prison in Troy."

"No, ma'am, but there is one in Montgomery. I thumbed it this far hoping to get home before my mama notices I'm gone."

"You've come all this way and your mother doesn't know where you are?"

"I saved my school lunch money to buy a ticket. Hoping that I can get back before anyone notices, or else I'm in some serious hot water."

I hoped that my story would tempt her to take me

farther than she'd originally planned to drive, but her reply let me down quick.

She sighed, and said, "I'm pretty reluctant to set you back down out there, but I've got a dental appointment in Dothan, and that doesn't land you far. By rights I should take you straight to the police station. Better to be in hot water and safe than not back at all."

"I'll be all right—I've done this before. And I never take rides from men on their own."

Both halves of that statement were a lie. When she set me down outside of Dothan and gave me a fiver for a sandwich I stuck my thumb out again, and the first person to stop was a man on his own. He let me be, just played talk radio, but we only got ten miles or so before he turned off the highway and I hopped out.

With the next fellow I ran out of good fortune. I had my eye out for police cruisers, figuring that I was pushing my luck, so when an ugly brown Oldsmobile with tinted windows stopped for me I went for the passenger door before I even looked at who was driving. We rolled back onto the highway as I buckled my seat belt; I looked up to say thank you and saw that he had his dick out and wiggling at me, stiff and veiny purple like a deformed thumb. I looked away quick, stared out the windshield and pretended that I hadn't seen it, like that would make it go away. We were going about sixty, maybe seventy miles an hour by then, and even though I knew that something bad was about to happen I didn't like the odds that jumping from a car going that speed onto a freeway offered. It wasn't like he could kill me with his dick, and as long as he had one hand on it and one hand on the steering wheel he didn't have any hands left to reach for a gun or a knife or anything I needed to really be worried about. I wondered first if he'd pulled it out because he thought I was a girl, then wondered if it was because he thought I was a boy, then figured it didn't really matter to him what I was; he just wanted to wave it at someone who wasn't expecting it and couldn't make him stop.

"No one in life is entitled to a free ride," he drawled, and it sounded like the politicians on television when they're talking about immigration or social welfare. He rubbed his hand up and down as he spoke, slow and lazy, like he didn't realize he was doing it. The smell of the cinnamon gum that he chewed was overwhelming. "Least of all people your age, who haven't paid back any of what their parents and society have so generously given them."

His voice had a hypnotic quality to it, and even though I didn't want to I slowly turned my head to watch what he was doing. I'd never seen a full-grown man's dick in real life, just in magazines. Time went all like silly putty, so I could make out real clear the smooth head and the slit across it, the angry purple skin with angrier blue veins like expensive cheese, the nest of coarse, straight hair that sprang from his open fly. It looked like it couldn't belong to such a clean, neat, pale-skinned person, like he'd sprouted a scorpion's barb between his legs. It looked ridiculous, unfinished, an afterthought stuck on because there had to be some way to tell men and women apart. I almost thanked him for the show even as my heart ka-thumped into my gut, because I knew without being told that, like a loaded gun, a naked cock meant trouble for someone.

"Now, you've got to the count of ten to figure out how you're going to be paying for this ride," he continued, "and then I'm taking you to the nearest police station and telling them to charge you with vagrancy and solicitation."

He began counting, but before he'd gotten to two I had both hands on the door handle, shoving as hard as I could, trying to get out. He let go of his dick then, mashed down on the auto-lock button with one thumb, flicked the signal stalk with the fingers of his steering hand, and slid over towards an exit ramp.

"Hold up, hold up, I'll be good," I said, and my voice sounded more panicked than I felt. I knew in a far-off way that I couldn't let him stop the car. His hand kept time, up and down, and as slowly as I could I unbuckled the seat belt, leaned over the gap between our seats, and licked the smooth, rubbery end of his dick. It tasted like pool water, and trouser lint, and overly yeasted old bread dough, and he moved his hand to nest in the short curly hair on the back of my neck.

"See now, you're a smart kid. Not half the ones I've picked up on this road have been this smart. Most little shits don't know when to shut up. Now you keep going."

I pulled my head back enough to say, "I keep going

as long as you keep driving," and even though he chuckled as he pushed me back down, the hand on my head made something in my chest flutter.

He was silent as I sucked, and my jaw ached immediately and he smelled of crotch sweat and cinnamon, and I thought that it was funny that after so long—or so it felt—aching for sex this was what I got.

I was still fixed on getting back, hadn't been thinking about what I might need to do in order to make it back before Ma missed me, hadn't thought that some of the steps that might be required to do that might not be worthwhile in the final analysis. If you asked me what I was more scared of, my mother knowing I'd run off or the man with his cock out, I would have said Ma, even though I couldn't have said exactly why, or what I thought would happen to me if I didn't get home before she figured out what I'd done.

I didn't have any idea what I was doing, besides keeping my teeth to myself, but eventually figured some of it out. The taste improved as my spit washed away the film of sweat from his skin, but the chlorine burn in the back of my throat never went. I drew him out slow, as slow as I could without pissing him off, and it felt like we'd been driving forever when he pulled over into a private, wooded area to finish. I had no way of knowing how long it had been—the only things I could see were the weave of his trousers and the brush of his hair—and I kept my mind blank as I could because I knew if I started thinking about what was going on I'd probably start freaking out completely and there was no telling what he'd do if I did that, and time passed even slower with his dick in my mouth than it had when I was seeing it for the first time.

He finished fast and hard and when I wasn't expecting it, and I choked on the thick white fountain and some of it came out my nose, while the rest burned the back of my throat and ached my teeth and tongue like I'd drunk vinegar and then sucked a mouthful of old pennies. He pushed my head down as he did, but as the spurting let up his grip went loose and I pulled away, coughing and gagging with my eyes streaming. I got one hand on the door handle and the other on the strap of my back-pack, couldn't decide if it was better to jump out and run or stay where I was, wasn't sure if I could make myself run if I had to. He leaned back against the head-rest, closed his eyes and breathed out hard, and when I thought he'd fallen asleep he sat up straight and turned the key in the ignition.

"You're a good kid," he said. "I'll take you a couple of miles further." He didn't seem to notice the hunk of slime on his trousers. Instead he started telling me about his wife, who was a frigid cunt who'd left him and taken his two kids with her, and now expected alimony out of him. She hadn't even left him for someone, she'd just left to spite him, after all he'd done for her, and how did I like that? He asked how I liked things a lot, but I didn't answer. I scrubbed my face dry with rest-stop napkins from the glove box. My throat burned. When he dropped me on an off ramp I walked a mile to a gas station and rinsed out my mouth and throat and sinuses with sink water until the clerk threatened to call the cops on me for truancy—it was a school day, after all—but I couldn't get the penny-lint-chlorine burn out of the back of my throat.

CHAPTER VI

For a few moments or hours the need to continue on warred with the need to go to ground, to find a hidden place where I could cease to be until I could trust myself to be let loose in my own body again. But my feet won, bullying me back to the highway and dragging me along the green part, behind cover of the thin trees like over-mascaraed eyelashes. With every step forward I felt myself sucked back as though the earth before me were being stretched; even as I moved towards home it was pulled farther from me.

Then a college-aged girl in a white pickup stopped and shouted at me to hop in, and her skinny sunburned little sister squeezed over so that I could fit, and time suddenly began to drip and bleed in the more normal way again. They didn't ask questions but told stories instead, talking over each other until their voices blended together in a counterpoint of contradiction. They pulled off the highway for greasy bacon cheeseburgers, and I realized how late it had gotten, how far I still had to go, but even so the food and the rocking put me to sleep.

The girls let me out when they turned off the highway, and I thanked them before stumbling sleepily into the roadside brush. It was time to call it quits for the day: I had been up since before four, and none of the sleep I had had while moving had made any impression on the heaviness that pressed like limp pastry on my eyelids and shoulders and muzzed the inside of my head. I stumbled farther into the brush, crawled under a mass of greening forsythia whips bound together by kudzu, and pillowed my head on my backpack.

And, of course, because I had chosen to give chase, sleep stuck its thumb out, leaving me still on the hard ground, listening to the hum of cars go past.

My mind wandered restlessly, took strange turnings as I looked but didn't see the wavering leaves, the birds that perched and flew as the shadows lengthened and melted together into night. I thought back to half-remembered conversations, interactions years before, looked ahead and daydreamed improbable heroics, invented friends and admirers and people who would adore me simply because I was—thought about everything, in fact, but the man in the car, which I avoided like a sore tooth which might not be sore anymore but which isn't worth the risk of pain to test.

It had been an exchange of resources, a milestone reached in an unusual way, an odd moment stretched out and filled with an awful mineral taste. It was over. I hadn't told him to let me back out, that I'd get a ride with someone else; I'd gone along with it. Nothing bad had really happened. But I did not have those thoughts until later. Instead that night I played in the maze of childish dreams until the angles of my body wore comfortable spots in the firm earth, and I could sleep. But even in sleep the odd feeling remained, the quiet need to cease existing, just for a little while.

The sky was pearling with four a.m. when I decided that I could not lie still anymore, so I gathered myself and broke the crust of morning. It felt a violation to be awake and moving in the darkness, to breathe too deep, to make human sounds, even though the birds were raising hell all around. But I had been gone for twenty-four hours, and with each minute that passed the chance that my mother had noticed my absence became more of a certainty.

At least I was getting close: there had been signs for our city counting down the distance in painful increments that seemed to have no direct relationship to the rate at which I traveled. I wanted to break off towards the coast, follow the rolling breakers home, but that would add miles, and miles meant time, and I had to be home, like Cinderella's princeless doppelgänger, by evening, while there was still probable doubt, when I could have been out living it up instead of run away or kidnapped. Logic escaped me: I could have found a pay phone, called the bar or my mother's cellphone, told her I'd been out all night doing something appropriate to youth and high spirits but not ridiculously dangerous or stupid. Perhaps she would have come and picked me up even—I was at that point not so far from home. But I was fixated on the idea of getting home before she realized I had left, though when I began to agonize over it, as I put one foot sorely in front of the other, trying not to shatter the morning with my humanness, I realized that her random comings and goings were not so random, matched up with changing shifts at two unreliable jobs plus a few hours here and there spent in ways I had no more right to question or judge than did she my personal recreations. She was never gone for more than thirty-six hours at a time, popped her head in sometimes on her way from one job to the other, kept me in weather-appropriate clothes and fresh fruit and granola bars seemingly by magic. The absent, preoccupied mother I had assumed would not miss me when I stepped onto the Greyhound became in my mind, as I walked, the embodiment of the panopticon, conscious of my every movement, of all of my plans, knew that I had skittered off and waited, knowing, for me to return so that she could hand out judgment and castigation.

I kept to the brush; the miles melted beneath my feet, and anxiety melted my stomach lining. The hours melted by faster: in the late afternoon I came to the edge of what my long walk had made in my mind "Our City," and I wasted nearly an hour misreading bus timetables before I found a line that would take me to the central hub and then out to our general neighborhood. I was leggy and skinny and very fourteen—a birthday had passed, blessedly unremarked upon, while we were living in the mountains—but still prepubescent looking, big eyed and non-threatening. I asked women with kids for bus fare, people that looked like they would sympathize with whatever parent was waiting for me. The tears that overwhelmed my lower lids added to the poignancy of my request, and I fell asleep in both busses in part to escape the searing embarrassment of begging.

I didn't recognize the gas station that I passed every day on the way to school until we turned the corner and I saw two of the kids from social studies walking home. At the next stop I stumbled out, legs stiff from sitting and sore from walking. I didn't care now what Ma said or did to me, all I wanted was sleep. Sleep and a hot shower. And food. French fries. Doughnuts. Scrambled eggs and roast turkey and macaroni and cheese and potatoes and everything hot and thick and filling that I could shovel in until the soft warm feeling of it made me fall asleep at the table. These images dragged me to the motel: our car was parked at the foot of the rusting white stairs. Fear leapt in my empty stomach.

The railing rocked under my hand. I fumbled out my latchkey, leaned into the door, and was dragged off my feet and into the room by my mother's blind, grasping hands. I saw her white, terrified face for a moment before she crushed me to her chest so tightly that I couldn't breathe. She put it away before she let me go, but I had seen it, had seen that her fear, waiting in that room for me to get back, had been so much greater than my own.

She warmed up leftovers on the hot plate while I leaned against the tiled wall of the shower and thanked God I lived in an era that featured water heaters. She asked if anything had happened to me, and between forkfuls I said nothing had, because in my mind, at the time, it hadn't. No one had knifed me, drugged me, kidnapped me, or touched me in any of my personal places: nothing had happened that was bad enough that I had to tell her about it. Then she asked the harder question: what the Sam Hill had I done, anyway, that took me away for two goddamned days and left me as hungry as a fasting Pentecostal?

I started to tell her that I'd gone beach walking and just kept going until I ran out of beach, but that didn't wash. She had called the school only hours after I left— the pre-four a.m. exit was the tip-off; I was never up that early of my own free will—and been apprised of my situation re teeth extraction. She had covered for me and asked to pick up my homework assignments later that night, figuring that the forged note was proof enough that I was just being an idiot rather than a kidnap victim.

She watched the stories I wanted to tell her be born and die on my face: a free concert in Jacksonville, an all-night rave, a bonfire party with all the friends I did not have, a really long trip on some drug I'd never tried but she probably had and would recognize the moment that I tried to describe it that I had no idea what I was talking about. I was too used to telling people the truth they wanted, or the truth that they didn't want but were more likely to believe than the actual way of things—reality is so often complicated and far-fetched to the point that most people are quicker to believe a lie. For once she waited until the real truth came to the surface.

"I didn't want Dad to worry but I didn't want them to know where we were. So I took the Greyhound to Alabama and sent a letter from there. But I took longer than I should have getting back because I had to hitch-hike since I lost my ticket."

Her face flickered in a way that I couldn't understand, but now that I've passed the age she was then—and realized just how young she was—I recognize the retro-active horror. She had, apparently, given more weight to my natural reticence and tendency to obey without ques-tion than to the determination that we shared to make it through at all costs, taken it for granted that if I made a bad choice it would be of the stay-up-too-late-eat-too-much-candy variety. And her misassessment scared her: while her back was turned I'd stopped being a child, despite my occasional tendency to childishness. I was, unexpectedly, old enough that she didn't have to worry about me wandering off with strangers anymore, but that didn't matter because half the things I might get up to of my own volition could get me killed. She couldn't protect me from the world anymore and she knew it.

She let me eat in silence after that revelation, drawing a paper towel through her fingers like beads in a rosary, then screwing it tightly around her thumb, then picking it birdlike into shreds, her face flickering all the while with unspoken words. I slowed in my hasty forking. Something was up.

"Don't worry about your dad," she said abruptly as I was spreading the last of the mashed potatoes out on my plate and dragging my fork tines through them, in imitation of a Zen rock garden. "I've been talking to him, off and on. Promised I'd keep you in school and let him know how we were doing every few months if he'd stop trying to find us."

"Why didn't you tell me you called him?"

"I did—you didn't seem to take much interest in it."

"No, you didn't!"

"Same way I never tell you anything, right?" she asked, and I felt myself go red. She'd taken to doing imitations of me that were intensely embarrassing, even though there was no one there to bear witness to them: in her own voice, announcing she was going somewhere or about to do something or asking if I wanted to eat dinner at the bar; then, with her hair in front of her face in fair imitation of me, a sullen grunt of acknowledgment, followed by an equally fair imitation of my wail, "You never tell me anything!" I was aware that she often spoke to me while I was preoccupied with books, television, or my own sticky daydreams, and I brushed her off, but try as I might I couldn't break the habit, and I'd figured anything as important as having spoken to my dad would warrant a little more effort on her part.

I squashed potato and didn't look at her, still suspicious that she hadn't told me she'd talked to Dad, but knowing that it was pointless to argue.

She offered an olive branch. "Well, I got your attention

now, so listen good—we're clearing out at the start of summer."

Given the amount of school that still stood between me and summer, this seemed like a date so woefully distant as not to be worth contemplating.

"By the time classes are over I should have enough cash to get us to the end of the road, if we're careful how we spend it. Won't know exactly when we're leaving until closer to the time, but be advised—it is happening."

In the interest of honesty, let the record stand that I managed to retain this information for exactly as long as it took me to finish eating, investigate the household dessert situation, and get ready for bed; the next morning I once again took the eighth grade, that beach, and our residence in Florida wholly for granted. My mother had a point about both my attentiveness and my tendency to remember important details.

As I scraped the plate clean she asked who had picked me up as I went, who I'd met, what I'd told them. So I made it a story, stringing the people and places together until I felt my father's slow, honeyed voice buzzing in my own chest, and my mother asked me no questions, just listened. But I did not tell her about the second man, the one who had punished me for my youth and help-lessness, the gall of my outstretched thumb, and for his own self-hatred. Shame, possibly, was why I left him out, or guilt. I didn't want her to know what I had done, as though by refusing to describe my degradation it was somehow undone. She guessed, probably, not then but after, that I had left something out in my telling. Luck is finite, and everyone, sooner or later, meets a bully from whom they cannot run.

She never asked, though, probably could not even trace the blank in me to that event; she did not know what question to ask, and if she had I did not know how to answer, not until I was older, had learned to borrow other people's words to fill in for the things I could not say.

Though our habits while we remained there didn't change we were more aware of each other in that time, of the rhythm of coming and going, and I was more aware of her giving me my space, letting me ease into and suss the shape of my growing self. Perhaps she came home less often with the scent of strange men clinging to her skin, though I doubt it. I did not want to think then that that was her third means of employment, making men like her, take her home, pay her to kill their loneliness and keep their vices secret. My light-fingered-ness, and the willingness to use it, must have come from somewhere. She was probably proud of her skill for survival, as was I.

My strike out into the wilds of the world could have made me more adventurous, more willing to explore the city, make friends. Instead I became more preoccupied with the world inside my own head. My erotic fantasies grew elaborate, absurd, surreal, only tangentially related to normative sexuality, barely probable or biologically possible, but the more wild my desire and outlandish my thoughts, the more likely I was to be suddenly over-whelmed by the smell of warm man and cinnamon

71

chewing gum, the feel of a rough knuckled hand, the taste of salt and pennies.

Then I would stop abruptly, mind blanked with shock like falling into cold water, frightened, ashamed, over-whelmed by something I did not quite understand. There was no real cure for this; once it happened the rest of the day was done for, spent in restless shifting irritability, preoccupied with nothing and tender as a skinned peach. The only thing for it was to wander down to the beach and fling myself into the water, which was likewise saltily reminiscent but nonetheless burned me clean, blank my mind and swim against the current until I was too exhausted to think.

On one of those days, lying on the burning sand after, rash guard feeling like it was painted on and my muscles stretched-out rubber bands dripping lemon juice, without the energy to drag myself to my feet and walk home, a boy in his mid-teens stopped and bent over me.

"You OK, squirt?" he asked, and I dragged my face, one half crusted with sand, up enough to squint at him.

He was golden: hair bleached tawny, skin burned caramel, so that if he lay down face first on the sand all you would see would be the electric blue of his swim-ming trunks and the paleness of his untanned palms, as though he cupped handfuls of salt. The others were behind him, different shades of tawny, cinnamon, dark sienna browns, their scraps of clothing—bikinis, trunks, shorts—bright on them. I recognized them as the group I'd watched on the morning when we'd first arrived, realized that this was their beach, that they'd probably been coming to this selfsame spot since before they could walk.

"Yeah, I'm OK," I said, but didn't get up. My limbs were full of lead, immovable after the magical buoyancy of the water.

They had surfboards.

"Want a drink?" he asked.

My throat was full of salt. He pulled me up.

"We saw you in the water. We were placing bets on whether you were trying to drown yourself or just stupid."

"I swim all right," I said in between sips of the water, which was so cold it hurt my teeth. A few of them had gone out, just beyond the breakers, stood with their palms on their boards watching the water roll as if they were scrying in its oily, foam-ringed surface. "Maybe I do want to drown."

"Don't say it and it won't happen," he said. "You all right now?"

"Whatcha guys doing?"

"Surfin' a bit, if the right wave comes."

"Teach me."

My balance was bad, my courage slightly lacking, but I was willing—so long as they promised to pull me out of it if it looked like I was drowning—and they found me endearing, or just entertaining, so by the end of the week I'd become a sort of mascot. They thought of me as a kid, probably took it for hero worship when I stared at their tight, sunned bodies.

When I was in the water time ceased to matter, the hours sliding past like quicksilver. On evenings when the weather was good and we didn't have school the next morning we lit bonfires, roasted cheap hot dogs and ate them rolled up in slices of Wonder bread, drank beers that had been stolen from parents' garages and refrigerators. On those nights the others grew bolder, laughed louder, tickled and play-wrestled and teased each other across the sand, and I felt myself growing too tight for my skin; I thought I could smell sex in the air.

It was after one of those nights, indistinguishable from all the other times I'd walked home smelling of bonfire smoke in the pale half-light in the hour before sunrise while fabricating an elaborate fantasy with which to get myself off, that I realized as I drew close to the motel that the car illegally parked at the foot of the rusted white staircase was my mother's, and that the trunk was open. Our front door was as well; all of our things were in boxes and bags in the center of the room, and she was sitting on the bed, an unlit cigarette between her first and middle finger, looking over the road atlas.

"What are you doing up?" I asked. She was dressed in her jeans and undershirt, boots on her feet. "Aren't you going to work today?"

She smelled like ginger and coffee under the cigarettes. She smelled like herself again. She wouldn't get any tips dressed like that.

"Nope. Gave my notice two weeks ago, kissed

everyone goodbye last night. We've got enough cash to get us where we're going, and the entire summer to get there."

"Where are we going?" I asked, bewildered by exhaustion and need. I refused to believe that she wouldn't be putting on her short skirt and heels at any moment, that she wouldn't be leaving me and my imagination to ourselves.

"Get your good shoes on. As soon as I'm done with this thing we're rolling out."

"Can I wash the salt off first? My skin itches."

"Make it quick. I want to get out of here before sunrise."

"What about saying goodbye to my friends?"

"I told you months ago that we'd be leaving when school let out, and I told you two weeks ago that move-out day was June fifth—you should have done it before."

"No, you didn't!"

She gave me a flat, dead-eyed look that was the equivalent of a bucket of ice water in the face, and I dropped it.

I locked myself in the bathroom and turned the water on as hard as it would go. For a moment I leaned my forehead on the tile and felt the water flowing down my back, sleep fuzzing my brain and desire tingling other places.

My mother's knock startled me awake.

"Move it, Alex. We've got to get going, you can sulk in the shower later."

"Almost finished!" I shouted, but I had only just

decided to indulge the more expedient craving when she knocked again.

"I mean it, Alex. If you don't get your ass out here in the next three minutes, I'm coming in there and I'm taking you out myself."

"Fine!" I bawled back, annoyed. I squirted a glob of shower soap into my palm and rubbed it into the salty mess of my hair and down my body and legs, let it rinse off, and stepped out unsteadily, everything from my navel to my knees pulsing, throbbing, aching. I toweled off, then wrapped up in it, carrying my dripping swimsuit and rash guard. "Did you pack all my clothes?" I asked.

"They're in the top of the duffel bag. And put some underwear on, kid. It's OK to forget for a day or two, but we're not going to be washing jeans for a while, and those are going to get nasty."

She took the first load downstairs, and I dropped the towel and began throwing clothes on as soon as she was gone. There wasn't enough time, but I was still tempted to try to finish, was convinced that I would go crazy if I didn't, but she was back before I'd found my socks.

The urgency gradually abated, but the ache remained as we pulled out of the parking lot, and I sat in cranky sullenness. Ma didn't seem to notice. Or she was ignoring me. I sulked more pointedly, stared out the window with my arms crossed, trying to make my silence project "not talking to you." But I could only resist the effects of a day of swimming and a night awake for so long. My eyes closed before we hit the city limits, and I dreamed naked people, naked me, and hands all over me, all the way to the Panhandle.

CHAPTER VII

Ma met the second Laura in a group home in New Jersey when she was fourteen. She'd been put there by Social Services just after—and if she recalled correctly, to some degree because of—her running away for the sake of a long walk along the Appalachian Trail. Laura was already living there when Ma showed up, had been living there for a while. She was dark haired and dark eyed and grim faced, didn't speak so much but would shriek out of nowhere like someone had pinched her, ate off plastic and was given crayons to write with because she threw things, indiscriminately and without warning. But Ma didn't know that when she first arrived; it wasn't until later that the other kids told her that Laura was crazy and a liar and swore that little green aliens had kidnapped her when she was a baby, that people came into her room after lights out and felt her up, made her do things.

"Because everyone is just dying to touch up a psycho—you think you're so hot that no one can keep their hands off you? Come the fuck on, you'd be so lucky."

They all ate together at a long table, and on her first night there the place that was left empty was the one next to Laura at the far end. Ma didn't think anything of that, took the seat without asking questions. As the plates were being passed Laura leaned towards her, whispered into her ear, "Hey, what's red and bad for your teeth?" Ma had barely registered that she was being spoken to, barely registered the question, when Laura continued: "A brick."

Ma was tired and overwhelmed and taut with apprehension at the newness of the place, new rules to learn, so when the joke hit her a few seconds later she broke, doubled over with her face on the table, laughing so that she couldn't breathe. Of course, no one else had heard the exchange, had even noticed that anything had been said to my mother, so it just looked like she was a little nuts as well.

They became a matched pair, the screamer and the laugher, and for once Ma didn't really care what they all thought of her. Odd as she was, Ma really liked Laura, so much so that she didn't care that Laura was paranoid and a liar.

And then she found out the hard way that Laura wasn't paranoid or lying.

She had climbed into Laura's bed one night so that they could whisper in the dark. They were still girls, still enjoyed the things that make girls' lives exciting, so they were pressed tight together and telling secrets, half asleep, when the door creaked open and she felt Laura go stiff and silent against her. They weren't supposed to be in each other's rooms ever, let alone after lights out, but this wasn't an about-to-get-caught panic.

79

Ma was on the far side of the bed to the door, reacted before she thought and rolled to the edge, lowered herself silently onto the floor so that the spill of comforter and the darkness hid her. She heard the door eased closed, footsteps crossing the room, and then a creaking protestation of springs as the edge of the mattress was put under the stress of an adult's weight.

"You've been waiting for me, haven't you? There's a good girl," someone said in a voice too rough with whispering for it to be recognizable.

My mother stayed there on the floor, silent, unseen, until the person left. But she wouldn't tell me what happened, what she heard happening.

In the morning Ma found herself unable to speak a word. She looked up at the faces of the teachers, the kitchen workers, the custodians. It had been dark, the voice distorted by the harshness of whispering, she hadn't gotten a look at the person's face, had no real sense of height or breadth or shape. It could have been any of them.

Laura didn't ask if Ma believed her now. They shared a look, the quiet dark look that made people say that Laura was crazy, and the teachers asked Ma if Laura's aliens had come for her as well and stolen her words while they were visiting.

They traded everything they could—candy, cigarettes, dirty pictures—for money, stole long-life food from the pantry, planned and prepared as well as they could. The tension of need—the longer they waited the more resources they had, but the sooner they left the less likely it was for their stash to be discovered—drew them tight.

When they finally made tracks it was unplanned, a day like any other, except that they both decided during breakfast that there would be no more waiting. They weren't kept locked up, were allowed out and about town in their free hours, so when they said they were going to the library that afternoon, had their backpacks with them, it didn't seem out of the ordinary. Except the bags were full of food, and instead of going into town they hopped the first bus in the other direction.

They made it to a city, a not-so-big place whose fortune was on the downward trend but still big enough that they wouldn't be found so easily. There was a choice of abandoned buildings, and they pried away boards over windows and made a nest in one of the empty offices, piled up blankets and cardboard against the cold and made their own world. They begged and busked and stole and slept together under the mound of dirty comforters that other people had thrown away, and all was well for a while. Other people joined their little kingdom, down-and-outs with nowhere to go that didn't want to risk it alone; they had nothing and they shared it all. Winter came and they begged more, added layers to their clothing, and handfuls of the people that had joined them disappeared, either dead or given up and gone to a shelter or to prison or back to wherever it was that they'd been running from.

Then one night Laura didn't come home, and my mother curled alone in the mound of clotted cloth and tried to suppress the terror that churned her gut. The next morning the boards across the windows splintered

81

away, and the rest of them were taken. My mother didn't even try to fight.

The minister who conducted Bible Study at the home twice a week had recognized Laura, had walked past her twice to be sure as she sat cross-legged in the sun in one of the city parks, shaking a cup and smiling at everyone she saw. He had called the cops to have her picked up, take her to the police station. She had told them about the squat because they accused her of kidnapping and murdering my mother.

They were almost properly arrested, for vagrancy and solicitation and breaking and entering and underage consumption of alcohol and tobacco and everything else that the cops could think of, but then their reasons for running away and how young they really were came to light. Laura, who was slightly older, was sent to a women's shelter; Ma was pitched to the next group home, where she met another Laura and had her first kiss.

I asked her then how she crammed all of this running and living into such a short span of time, how she got through school. She didn't answer at first, sucked on her menthol until the tip burned red like the eyes of the damned and her cheeks sunk in, peered at the dark road and let the smoke slowly out her nose.

"You can pack a lot of living in if you try. And it feels like longer than it is, when you're young. Time moves slower."

When I woke up we had crossed over into Georgia. There was a bag of trail mix and a bottle of water open in the gap between our seats, and Ma was smoking slowly, tapping her fingers in time to the country on the radio. It was like we had never stopped rolling, like we had just left the mountains and the diner and the apartment over the grocery store. Nothing had changed, except for me. I wasn't the passive kid anymore, going along with my mother's plans, because I knew now that she didn't have a plan as such, that she let things happen and pushed back against them just as much as I did.

"You mad at me?" Ma asked finally.

"What makes you think that?" Which in my family always more or less meant yes.

"You're in a funk. And I always thought you were my kid, that you wouldn't mind the moving around, moving on. But you're your dad's kid, too."

"No, I'm glad we're on the road again." And I was. It was comfortingly familiar, and at the same time overwhelmingly full of possibility. And as much as I wanted to see my dad, I wanted to see where we were going more. "I just feel kinda shitty. Been feeling kinda shitty for a while, really—one day I want to cry and the next I want to punch people, and the only thing that helps is wearing myself out." I didn't mention my extended sessions of five-finger solitaire—some things are just too private.

"Sounds like hormones," she said. "They'll settle down in a few years. Or decades. Or else you'll learn to deal with them. I'm sorry, and I know adolescence sucks complete ass, but all you can do is ride it out."

I rolled my eyes at her miserably.

"And keep the attitude in check so that I let you live that long."

"It's better when we're on the road," I said. "There are too many other things to think about."

"I guess that's good. We're going to be on the road for a while."

"What about school?"

"Hopefully not that long, but if things don't go to plan . . . It's not like you'll be able to learn anything right now. Makes more sense to let you keep to yourself until your body and your brain start settling down. And anyway, I picked up some textbooks at the last garage sale I went to. If we haven't found a place to stay put for the winter when school starts up again, you'll be able to keep up on your own."

"Why are they all called Laura?" I asked.

"Say what?" Ma said.

"Is that a code name, so you don't give away who they really are? Why do all the women in your stories have the same name?"

She'd been quiet for a while before answering, so I wasn't sure if she was inventing a cover story, if I'd been right in guessing she'd rechristened them all to make the remembering easier, or if she was trying to determine herself why it was that so many of the women who had had a lasting impact on her were named Laura.

"First of all," she said, "they're not all Laura. You're conveniently forgetting everyone else. My girlfriend who ran off with the preacher wasn't named Laura. Second, when we got to Florida you were complaining that every kid in school was named Jason or Brittany—it just so happens that when I was born everyone was naming their daughter 'Laura.' And third—" she paused for a drag on her cigarette—"well. When you're eight or nine, say, and you make your first best friend, they're the greatest person in the world and you know that you'll be friends forever. But one day one of you moves away and they leave a vacancy. And then you meet someone with the same name, and because you're eight part of you thinks not exactly that they're the same person, but they were made from the same block of clay, maybe. And you try to get the new Laura to fit into the hole the old Laura left. And when you get older it doesn't matter that you know things don't work like that, because your ears will be primed and your heart will beat faster at the sound of that name. It will stand out to you and make something inside you go soft, and since it stands out you'll pay more attention to them, and if you pay more attention more often than not you wind up being friends with them, until you look back when you're forty years old and realize that you have a long string of Lauras behind you who were all important, and it isn't just coincidence but the eight-year-old you trying to fill in the hole that the first Laura made."

We stopped only when we absolutely had to, marked time by the journey of the sun across the sky measured in hand spans rather than minutes. By the late afternoon the landscape had changed: we were somewhere in the rural part of Georgia, hot and dripping with green. She pulled over often now to look at the book of road maps, but each time it only confirmed that she remembered correctly, or almost correctly. She could read a map well but there was some interruption of the signal when it came to applying the ink-and-paper guide to the landscape around her, so she handed me the book and asked me to confirm her turnings. The part of the map we were on was mostly nothingness, a road or two through a blank.

The sun was wallowing low behind the trees when we swung onto a long driveway, the rutted dirt overgrown with weeds. We had to stop twice to move fallen branches, clear enough space for our car to inch farther along the dark track. I could tell that she was nervous, and that made worry bubble up in my own stomach, worry of what we would find, of what was putting her off when so little did.

The trees ended suddenly and we rolled out into open late-afternoon light at the bottom of a small, bare hill. I had to lean forward to see the house at the top: wooden, the paint peeling, with a broad, low, wraparound porch and dark, hollow windows.

The place skeeved me out.

"Are they expecting us?"

"Nope." She cut off the engine and leaned her crossed arms on the wheel.

"Are they going to be happy to see us, or are we, y'know, going to get chased out of here with shotguns and dogs?"

"Don't think so."

I didn't ask which possibility she was referring to as being the unlikely one.

She got out of the car and I followed a few feet behind as she trudged up the hill. The house was incongruous, a chip of suburbia set down in the middle of the woods. A few yards from the front door she veered away through the sparse, baked grass, and strode around to the backyard.

She took the bucket that was wedged under the downspout at the corner and emptied it. The house had a wide screened-in porch on the upper level, and she stood the bucket on its end to give her a boost up enough to step onto the knob and then the frame of the back door. She clung with her toes and fingertips for a moment while I listened for dogs, then pulled herself up. Her fingers fumbled with a corner of the screening, then pushed an entire section in, so that she could somersault herself through the hole. I heard her boots on the boards of the porch floor, then the scrape of a window opening. I started counting, decided that if she didn't come back by twenty, fifty, one hundred, I was going back to the car, going to hide in the trees, getting out of that creepass place.

The back door shrieked open on unoiled hinges.

"Settle down, it's just me." She took my arm and pulled me into a mudroom that smelled of old rubber and musty raincoats. "You didn't half scream."

"What if they come home while we're in here? What if we get arrested or shot or they just lock us in their basement for the rest of our lives?" I locked my knees and tried to break her grip on me as she pulled me farther into the bowels of the house.

"For Pete's sake, Alex. They aren't coming home. They're dead."

CHAPTER VIII

I didn't scream again, but it took her a while to convince me that we wouldn't be finding any dead bodies.

"They died more than a year ago. They're safe and buried, I promise. Somewhere else! Somewhere else! I didn't mean under the floorboards, you morbid nutcase. We wouldn't be here if they were still alive, trust me."

The house was frozen in the fifties: the wallpaper and refrigerator, the radio in the living room, the curtains that no one had bothered to draw when they left. I followed her slowly, quietly, from room to room as she ran her fingers through the dust on the furniture, stood for a moment in seemingly random spots and corners and let out sighs that she might have been keeping in since she was last in the house. There were framed photographs on the wall running up the stairs, all of them black-and-whites of groups of kids, and in the background of most of them a man and a woman with serious faces and white, white skin, whose clothing looked cheap and uncomfortable, like it had been made out of polyester bedsheets. As I went up the stairs the couple got older, began looking more and more like each other. She didn't look at the photographs as she went up, kept her eyes on the heavy railing like she expressly did not want to see them, but when she got to the landing she stopped and took a picture off the wall.

We paused at the top of the stairs: five closed doors. She looked at them, not as though she were guessing what was behind each but as if she knew and could not decide which to face first.

We began on the left, her moving slowly, me following a few steps after. The first room was closed up neatly, like a cosmetics case or a paint box: two sets of bunk beds flanking a high, heavy-sashed window, a chest of drawers on either side of the door. It had a dormitory feel to it, as though it were intended to sleep whomever was passing through and had failed to gather the imprint of any one child's psyche. She went over to the window frame, poked at the left side a moment, then took out her pocket knife and pried a slab of wood out of the skirting board.

"Whatcha looking for?" I asked from the doorway.

"Something someone else took a long time ago. But never mind. They probably needed it more than I did."

"Who was that?"

"I'll tell you later."

She went back out to the hallway and opened the next door, and a flutter of moths came out. It was a closet with linens still folded and piled neatly. She went down on her knees, sunk her hands between the sheets under the bottom shelf, then pulled them out into a tumble on the hall floor, stretched out on her belly to get a better reach into the back of the closet. I heard wood scrape on wood, and then she handed a panel of chipboard out to me that was painted white on one side, and wriggled farther in so that only her legs from the knees down stuck out into the hallway. Behind the back wall of the closet I heard her sneeze.

"I used to fit my whole body in there," she said as she backed out. "You could get two of us in, if you really wanted to." She had a cigar box in her hands, one of the deep, narrow ones, and her fingers had left trails in the thick dust that coated it. I waited for her to open it, but instead she hefted it in her hand, shook it a bit to hear it rattle, then put it down next to the picture, which she had left on the floor by the top of the stairs, propped with its face against the wall so the children couldn't watch us.

"What's in there?" I asked her.

"Things."

She paused in front of the fifth door, skipping the third and fourth altogether.

"Are you sure that we aren't going to find any dead people, and no one is going to show up and arrest us for trespassing?"

"Yes."

She pushed the door halfway open but stood stuck on the spot.

"If there aren't any dead bodies, why aren't you going in?"

"We aren't allowed in their bedroom," she said.

The furniture was ugly veneer in a dull color that had probably been the thing to own when it was first bought.

Ma hung on the edge of the room, her hands behind her back, remembering another time. We stood there for a while, so silent that I could hear the birds outside, the sough of wind through the trees, the creak of the house settling around us.

"Hey, I need you to do something. I thought I'd be able to but I'm not so sure now," she said, and I gave her the eye. "There're some plastic packets sewed to the underside of the mattress—I need you to wiggle under there and get them out." She fished in her pocket, pulled out a folding knife that I was pretty sure was over the legal length, and handed it to me, and I only hesitated a moment before getting down on my knees and crawling under the bed. I figured I was immune to whatever it was that was bothering her.

The room smelled musty and old in that way that makes your throat close up, and the underside of the mattress was about as pretty as you'd expect, but I found what she'd told me I would: three squareish bundles done up in vinyl sheeting and stapled closed, sewed on all four edges with huge stitches to the underside of the mattress, lumpy in the center with things I couldn't see. I lay on my back like I was working on a car, picked at the dark thread with the point of the knife—misjudging and having one drop on my face only once—and tossed them blindly out to her one at a time.

She looked at me gratefully when I'd wriggled out, then collected up packets and picture and cigar box before backtracking to open the third door. I'd been expecting another bedroom, but it led us out to the screened-in back porch: two metal bed frames were set up there, heads against the wall and only a narrow gap between their feet and the screening. A folding card table and a pair of chairs stood at the far end of the porch, and as I sat down I could see into the room behind the fourth door, the one that we hadn't opened: another dormitory-like bedroom, dimmed by the old glass.

"What's in the packets?" I asked.

"Old things. Jewelry, pocket watches, some money. They were worried about thieves, so she sewed it to the underside of their mattress. I think I'm the only person that knew they were there. I hid under the bed before I knew we weren't allowed in that room."

"Can we open them?"

"Nope, they aren't ours." She sat back and slid open the cigar box, and a strange look came over her face. I leaned in to see, but she snapped it shut.

"Nu-uh, you have your secrets, I have mine. Now let's fetch in our junk—we're sleeping up here tonight and I'm famished."

Before we went down she stretched the screen that she had popped out to climb in back into place and carefully pressed the rubber strip into its channel to hold it down. When she was finished you couldn't tell that it had ever been pulled away.

We dragged two mattresses out to the bed frames on the porch and laid blankets over the top of them, then went down into the backyard to dig out a half-overgrown fire pit Ma remembered from before. We must have stopped at a store while I was asleep: there was a yellow tin of lighter fluid and kabobs to roast.

"It's later now," I began. "Wanna tell me what's going on?"

We had settled in to wait for the flames to die down enough to cook over, and she was sitting across from me, knees drawn up and not seeming inclined to start the conversation herself.

"When I was here I got to be friends with one of the other foster kids, and when I left I kept up with him. He wrote me a couple months before you and me left Virginia, to let me know our foster mom had died—her husband kicked it a few months later. Their kids are in Canada and New Zealand—one's some kind of doctor and the other one teaches. They never want to come back here, just waiting for the damn house to fall down so they can sell the land it's on. I said I'd stop by, pull together the stuff they might want, mail it to Tony so he can send it on to them. They're perfectly fine with us being here, so stop being jumpy about someone turning up."

I began balancing kabobs over the coals. There was probably more that she wasn't saying, but I kept quiet while dinner cooked.

"So why do you hate this place so much?"

"What makes you think I hate it?"

"OK, hate's the wrong word. But you were walking around inside like you thought all the pictures were going to come to life or something."

She rearranged the skewers before answering. "This

was the first foster home I landed in, after we came to America. Didn't have my brother. Didn't understand the ways of Americans or Baptists—which I still don't—and got smacked quite a bit for it. They really believed in 'spare the rod, spoil the child.' I was eight years old and I hadn't figured out how to get on in homes yet, how to forget about whatever rules there'd been in the last place because the new place had different rules, how to make friends. And I was completely terrified because none of the adults would explain what was going on. My parents and my brother could have been dead, for all they told me. Guess it left an impression."

"Why'd they keep sending you different places, if they could've just put you back here where you already knew people?"

"My parents moved a lot. Either my dad was looking for a new job or the last job was backfiring on him—sometimes they needed to cross state lines to keep the cops from finding them. And the social workers thought that was the best way to do it, back then. Move the kids around a bunch so the people taking care of them don't get attached. The system's changed a lot since then."

We ate dinner as the sun went down, the dying coals still hot on our faces. I watched Ma and Ma watched the memories playing out on the inside of her head, until it was dark and the air had cooled. Then we raked through the ashes and took ourselves to bed.

There was a breeze on the porch, gentle and fresh and perfect, but I was still wide-awake from my daylong nap.

It was dark and we didn't have a flashlight, so we groped our way to the beds, rolled into them carefully, eyes still dazzled by the dying fire. It was a long time before I fell asleep, and I knew from her breathing that, even after driving since sunrise, it took Ma a long time to fall asleep as well. I wondered what she was thinking about as she lay there, wondered what she was remembering.

There were stories that she couldn't tell. Everyone has them; most people pretend that they've been forgotten. How you dropped your baby sister down the stairs and she nearly died. How you got into a fight that got out of hand and were nearly sent to juvenile detention. How someone did something to you that you still think is your fault, no matter how much you know that there wasn't anything you could have done to keep it from happening. There were stories that moved behind her eyes that she hadn't told me, that she couldn't tell me because the words to get them out just didn't exist. I knew because I had stories drifting in the same way behind my own eyes, like dust and pollen spinning on the current of dark water. But they were her stories, and if she told them it was her right to decide when and who and how. If she had been a different kind of mother she might have insisted I tell her mine, said that she had the right to know, and I am eternally grateful that she never did, that she let me choose my own time and place for things.

Even if I had been able to say those words, I would have never been able to get them all out at once, to describe every facet of the experience. Memory is slippery, not even like a fish but like an eel, like an ice cube, like a clot of blood whose membranous skin can barely contain internal shifting liquidity. It's something that, the firmer you try to grasp it, the weaker the hold you have on it, the less trustworthy it becomes. But it doesn't matter what really happened, does it? Reality matters less than how it is perceived, that edge or feather or scale that you catch onto as it flickers by. And after a year or ten in a dingy pocket who can say if it was a lizard's scale or a dragon's in the first place?

CHAPTER IX

When I woke up the next morning, Ma was already sitting at the little table at the other end of the porch, sipping at a steaming cup of bad instant coffee and poking gently through the cigar box.

The morning air was light and cool, but there was a thick feeling at the base of my skull that meant that it would probably rain later. The pale leaves glowed, casting dappled shadows across my legs, and I lay there for a bit, sinking deeper and deeper into the mattress and wanting to never stand up again. Then my hips started getting twitchy and I had to.

"Good sleep?" she asked.

"Once I actually fell asleep, yeah." I stretched. "Is there breakfast?"

"Trail mix and apples—that's what we've got until we hit civilization again."

I sat down across from her and picked up the photograph she'd taken down yesterday. You could see the shadow of the photographer on the grass and up the children's legs. There were five of them, three girls and two boys arrested in motion, their hands on each other's arms like they had just been play fighting, or were scared of being pulled apart, with the bared-teeth smiles of children that haven't learned how to appear happy on demand. The youngest looked six, the oldest twelve, with my mother in the middle. She looked straight out, eyes serious and big, and at first I didn't recognize her. All of the girls wore smock-like dresses, and I wondered if they were all taken from their homes too quickly to pack their own clothes.

"Why'd you pick this picture?"

"It's got Anthony in it." She reached over and tapped the boy standing close to her. "I don't have any pictures of him." She killed her coffee and stood up. "Come on, there's breakfast and work to get on with."

We found a wooden crate down in the kitchen and she filled my pocket with trail mix, and as I munched I followed her around. The contents of the house were more scant than minimalist, all of the furniture cheap and warped, the floors uncarpeted. It looked like all of the money they owned had been spent buying the land and building the house, and then it had been finished and furnished from a refuse heap: free to a good home. But there were a few nice things, and these she took and put into my crate: a stained-glass butterfly hanging in front of one of the downstairs windows, a statue of Jesus made from cherry wood, a woven wheat-straw cross from over the kitchen door. Some of the things she took were less logical. All of the oddly shaped magnets on the antique refrigerator. The large wooden cooking spoon that, for some reason, sat on a sideboard in the living room next to a mass of resin angel figures, rather than with all the other utensils in the kitchen. A plastic snow globe with half the water dried up from the windowsill over the sink.

We went up to the master bedroom last, and there she hung in the doorway, pensive, arms crossed and one leg wrapped around the other. She took a step into the room, then stepped backward, pulled out a cigarette and played with her lighter.

"I can get things, if you tell me what to get," I finally suggested, as she showed no inclination to enter the room.

"Good idea. Start with the pictures on the wall."

Her voice was hoarse as she guided me through the dresser drawers, through the shoe cupboard, through all the little places a person could hide something important. There wasn't much, but even so, I went through each drawer, over each surface, picked out the things that my mother told me to and added them to the crate, even slipping my hands into the shoes in the closet and disturbing the array of pantyhose and girdles in one of the shallow pressboard drawers, just in case something had been hidden there. Through it all Ma stood in the doorway, turning the cigarette in her fingers, tense but not impatient. When I had finished she told me to peel the patchwork quilt off the bed and fold it up, leaving cheap cotton sheets through which the blue stripes of the mattress showed, and when I stepped out of the room with my arms full she closed the door firmly behind me.

Then we went back through the house a room at a time, taking down all of the photos and piling them on the large kitchen table. There was a dated wedding photo, the dress cheap looking and the groom ugly, then pictures of the young couple with a first baby, with groups of people, black-and-whites of previous generations. And, of course, the series that trailed up the stairs. Many of the children appeared in only one photo, while others appeared in handfuls, and the two that I took to be the natural children remained in all.

We sat at either end of the kitchen table, prying out the staples that held the photo backboards in place with butter knives, piling the cheap frames together in one stack and the backing material in another, separating the photos with waxed kitchen paper and sliding them into a large Manila envelope Ma had found marked ~~TAXES Documents 1973~~ HOUSEHOLD RACEETS. The packet slid neatly into the crate with everything else we had collected. It seemed sad that a couple could have left so little worth taking.

"Oh, wait a moment," Ma said as I picked up the crate to take it to the car. She scurried to the dining room and shuffled about, then came back again with a thick Bible— the only book I'd seen in the whole place—its covers floppy and corners worn. "If they want to burn this, they can do it themselves." She wedged it into a space in the jumble.

We carted our own stuff and the things that we had collected down to the car, wedged it all in the trunk, then sat for a bit on the back bumper while she smoked a cigarette and stared contemplatively up at the house. Dark clouds had gathered overhead while we were inside.

She flicked her cigarette butt away, and breathed deep. "There's only one way to do this," she said, more to herself than me, then rummaged in the back seat of the car and strode purposefully up to the house, a familiar yellow tin in her hand. I followed at a trot, but she didn't seem to notice that I was there.

We went back in the front door, up the stairs and paused again in the doorway of the master bedroom. She let the door swing open, leaned as if to go in, but kept her feet rooted to the carpet of the hallway. She held the tin out, red nozzle first, at the full length of her reach, and flicked her wrist to squirt neat ribbons of clear fluid across the floor, the bed. It made looping lines on the white sheets, seeped through so that the blue stripes on the mattress became clearer, so that rusty-brown stains began to show. She put down the tin carefully, checked her hands and arms for drips, smelled them to make sure.

Then she pulled out a cigarette and placed it between her lips, bent her head to her cupped hands and lit it with one stroke of her lighter flint, and dragged deep. The tip glowed. Then, like a girl at a county carnival throwing laundry pegs into milk bottles, she lined her toes up with the carpet seam that demarcated the border between the bedroom and the hall, leaned her body forward ever so slightly and tossed the cigarette onto the middle of the double bed. We stood there, watching as the tip glowed, and then the cloth began to smoke and blacken. Then came the lick of flame, and the lighter fluid caught with a snap like wet fabric in high wind. She crouched to pick up the yellow tin, and turned away.

"Time to make tracks, kid."

We thundered down the stairs, and she locked the front door from the inside and pulled it closed after her. I was still fumbling with my seat belt, not sure of what I had just seen, or the implications of what I had just seen, when she flicked on the engine and pulled away. It wasn't a panicked sort of urgency, but an intense desire to be gone, to not be there anymore, and as it drove her back down the pockmarked driveway I twisted in my seat, trying to get another look back at the house, to be sure of what had happened because, even with the remove of just a few minutes, I was questioning my memory.

As we pulled back onto the main road it came into view: a column of dark smoke, small but growing, hard to make out against the gathering clouds. Ma glanced up at it, then settled back, let up on the accelerator for a bit.

"Didn't you want to watch it burn?"

"No. Just didn't want to have to wonder if it was still there for the rest of my life."

*

It was when her parents came back to Sicily to take her and her brother to a city full of immigrants in a country whose language they didn't speak that Ma started running away in earnest. Before then she had often wandered away, gone up into the hills around their village early in the morning to swim in the abandoned Roman baths and play hide-and-seek in the olive groves with other local kids, rarely coming home before dark. Something about coming to America, or the time in the orphanage before she came, changed her.

When she told me about the group homes and the foster homes, places she'd been and things she'd done, I asked where her parents had been, why she and my uncle had been taken away.

"My parents were horrible at life. We kept getting evicted or having the lights or water shut off because they forgot to pay the bills. Not that they couldn't afford to, but that they forgot. The winter Danny was seven I stole shoes for us because ours had worn out and neither of them could get it together enough to go to the store and buy new ones—they never noticed that we had new shoes. They forgot to feed us, they forgot sometimes that we existed, didn't come home for a day or two and just left us there like cats. And their English was bad and they didn't understand how America worked—there were so many times that if they'd known what to say or what to do or asked the right person we wouldn't have been taken. Then, when I started running away and actually getting somewhere with it, not being dragged home by neighbors in the evening but actually going missing for a while, the social workers got involved. So from when I was fourteen it was my fault, really."

Somewhere around when she was seventeen or eighteen her parents vanished from the stories, so that "home" became the front seat of her battered station wagon, the sound of radio music fading in and out, whatever cigarettes were cheapest that week. I asked, once, where my grandparents lived now, what they were doing now, when she'd seen them last. She'd been silent for a few minutes, then said with an exhale of smoke, "Don't know," and turned the radio louder.

We turned our backs to the chapter of my mother's childhood that was going up in flames and continued on the road north, taking a slow pace by the back roads, crossing into South Carolina and then North Carolina. We stopped there at a campsite, still some hours before dusk, and pulled into the trees away from the water hook-ups for mobile homes and the handful of people already in situ. Ma was quiet, more quiet than normal. She built a fire and then told me to keep an eye on it while it burned down to coals for cooking; she needed a walk so that she could clear her head.

A few minutes after she walked away I heard again the crunch of her feet on the dirt: she went to the car and pointedly dug out the cigar box and tucked it under her arm, then walked back into the woods before she could see me blush. Finding the box in the jumble of the trunk had been difficult, and I'd just started poking through the oddments inside when I'd heard her returning footfalls and jammed it back into place.

The box contained a pewter figure of a knight about one inch tall and bent crooked on his base, so that when I stood him up he listed to the side as if he were drunk, or walking in high wind. There was also a red silk ribbon of the kind that my mother liked but never wore, and a handful of different marbles stuck together by a half-used lipstick (the end of the tube said it was "Nutmeg Dust") that had popped open and gone melty on them. There was as well a thread bracelet, a scattering of old coins, a picture of a young couple (who I assumed to be my grandparents since I recognized the two kids with them as my mother and my uncle from other pictures I had seen), stones and shells and stamps and single earrings, and a badly carved wooden elephant; a slender plastic periscope that telescoped neatly in on itself to become pocket sized completed the flotsam. I couldn't imagine why she wouldn't want me looking at what was apparently a collection of childhood treasures, wondered if she were trying to pique my curiosity about the box as a way of keeping me from looking for other, more important things that she'd hidden among our varied cargo.

We hit the road again early the next morning, and for a few dozen miles I held the irrational half-hope that we were going back to my father, even though I knew from the map that our path passed home and continued towards the Great Lakes and the unknown. I used to have the same hope when we passed the strip mall with my favorite ice-cream parlor on the way to do the weekly grocery shopping; even though we never turned into the parking lot, there was always the possibility that we would, up until its neon sign whipped past and I needed to stretch to see it out the back windshield.

She was in a hurry now, not an excited hurry but the deadly dogged kind, the get-this-over-with-before-her-nerve-failed kind. We drove through the afternoon and past dark with no stops except for gas, and even then Ma threatened to leave me behind if I wasn't back from the bathroom by the time she put the gas cap back on. She didn't tell me where we were going, or any stories that would let me know what to expect when we got there, but drove hands gripped tight on the wheel, eyes fixed ahead, a muscle in her jaw dancing. This, I guessed, was a destination for unfinished business.

When her eyes began to droop she pulled off the highway and catnapped in rest-stop parking lots, and I woke up through the night as she stopped and started and stopped again. It was early afternoon when we crossed the border into Michigan, and I could have killed to get out of the goddamned car. My body felt like a stale pretzel. We had driven nearly twenty-two hours, and my stomach knew it. I remembered still the notation that Michigan had on her map—"*Cocksucking motherfucking son of a syphilitic whore*"—wondered if it was there because that was where we were going, or because it was a place to be avoided.

It was full-blown summer, even though to me, coming as I was from Florida, the air was as mild as lemonade. There were people on the sidewalks and smoking outside of the bars that we passed, legs showing under the ragged hems of cutoffs.

"Isn't it a Tuesday?" I asked quietly, my eyes fixed on a laughing woman, skin the pink of new sunburn, about to spill the bottled beer that no one seemed to care she'd brought outside.

"Every night's a Friday night here," Ma said back just as quietly. "There's fuck all else to do of an evening."

She turned off suddenly down a side street, making me slide in my seat, pulled into an empty lot sandwiched between tall buildings where the raw grass burst up through the blacktop like a rash and the *Violators will be towed* sign swung upside down on one rusted bolt. She snapped the ignition off and tossed the keys into my lap, then reached between her feet for the plastic bag and began counting out bills.

"Whatcha doing that for?" I asked.

"I owe this guy some money, that's all. You wait here, this shouldn't take me long."

"That looks like a little more than 'some money,'" I said. Her fingers flashed too fast for me to keep count, but I knew she was past one thousand.

"Never you mind, just keep your ass in this car. We might need to leave quick."

I waited as Ma stalked across the parking lot and down an alley, then I slipped out of my seat as quietly as I could, pocketed the keys, locked the car, and followed her at a distance back onto the main street. She was tense, preoccupied, and I'm certain she had no idea that I was trailing behind. We swam through the milling crowd of people, half of them drunk and most of them smoking, so that I lost and found her a dozen or more times before she ducked into a tattoo shop. I hesitated outside the door as she strode right past the kid—gauged ears, pierced face, bad hair, maybe twenty years old—at the front desk, who wasn't fast enough to stop her.

There was a middle-aged white guy laid out on a padded table in the back half of the room, getting something big and bloody drawn on his upper thigh, and the tattooist with a face mask and blue gloves on a stool beside him, the gun buzzing in her hand. Ma ignored them; her attention was on guy number three, who half sat, half leaned—in the too-cool-for-my-own-skin way I'd only ever seen in movies and high schoolers—on a table against the wall. He was leggy and charming looking, his long but neat hair and goatee frosted with grey. When we walked in he had been flicking through one of the design books that littered the table; he saw Ma and marked his place with a finger.

"Hey, Fletcher. Remember me?" Ma asked.

"You're going to have to help me out a bit there," he said, and his tone made it clear that he was only talking to her because she hadn't given him a clear reason to throw her out yet.

"Maybe it'd be easier if I took my clothes off and busted my face up a bit," she snapped. "Unpaid bookkeeper extraordinaire and 1984's sidepiece of the year. Remember me now?"

It took him a moment, but when he did you could see it on his face.

"I wasn't expecting to see your ass around here again, princess," he said.

"That's not my name, you motherfucker."

"And that's no way for a lady to talk. Did you return to my place of business after all these years just to cuss at me, or is there something else you wanted?"

"I'm here to give back what I owe you."

He was looking at her with an amused expression on his face, like she was a cat that had done something cute. Even though he was slouching, she had to tilt her head back to look him in the eye.

"Here's the cash you think I took." She smacked the money on the floor at his feet. "And here's what I owe you for thinking I took it."

And she punched him, clean and hard, in the face.

The tattooist and the bare-assed man on the table didn't move, but the front-desk kid flinched as Fletcher's head snapped back, blood spurting from his nose.

"And I owe you a fuck-ton more of the same, but let's call it even." Ma shook her hand like she was shaking water off of it, blew on the splits in her knuckles, then turned to leave. When she saw me standing in the doorway an expression passed across her face, fear and fury together, but she didn't do anything more than grab me by the front of the shirt and pull me after her as she went by.

CHAPTER X

There was a fourth Laura, who wasn't mentioned until after we'd left the east coast behind. Ma was on the move at the time, so that even when she had just slept she looked tired and when she had just showered and changed she looked travel-creased, but she was seventeen and still springy-souled, still believed in the goodness of things.

This Laura found my mother sleeping rough, waiting for the energy to push onwards. She saw this Laura as an old woman, but when she looked back to tell me the story she realized that Laura hadn't been that old at all, had just seemed old to the girl that she was then. She was too tired to be suspicious of the platinum-haired woman who offered her food and a place to sleep.

Laura drank absinthe out of red crystal glasses, and spent three-quarters of her time in the conservatory at the back of her house, painting. Not sipping and daubing like a rich lady, though; she went wild with a palette knife, stiff brushes, bits of card, her fingers, then became perfectly still for a moment or two, assessing, then continued, her pace gradually slowing as the work became more detailed. Her paintings were a marriage of photo realism and surrealism, the colors she used shocking and vibrant up close but blending to mundanity when you drew back enough to see the figures. They even sold, though she didn't need the money: she'd romanced oil barons and arms dealers as a young woman, if 'romanced' was the right word for what sounded like an opportunistic blend of good old-fashioned gold digging and even older-fashioned prostitution, and had the lucre of two dead husbands in the bank. My mother didn't believe her, entirely, when it came to the more fantastic details, but that didn't change the fact that Laura had Money.

Ma lounged around the house in patches of sun reading books and regaining her strength, or posed naked to be painted with wasp's wings sprouting from her back and briar thorns growing from her arms. Artists and people who wanted to be artists and people who were willing to settle for being around artists came to dinner, and there were séances and more strange liquors and sometimes acid and my mother would wake up just as the sky was fading from black to blue naked but covered in a woven rug with the edges tucked around her to keep her bare skin from touching the cold stone of the conservatory floor, curled around the legs of the stool where Laura perched and scraped madly at her canvas, one last drink still in her hand.

The parties and the wild permissiveness appealed to her, the strange things she tried were alluring, but as her energy returned so too did her minute sense of responsibility. She wouldn't go back home for its own sake, but she had two years of high school to finish, and she was sensible enough to know that her chances of getting along in the adult world were greater if she dragged herself through them.

Laura didn't argue, let her pack her few things and put on her own clothes, but as my mother turned to walk out the front door she got up from her canvas and fished her keys out of a kitchen drawer, led my mother to the garage and unlocked a periwinkle Cadillac that had not once been resurrected or alluded to during the course of my mother's stay, pulled out the registration and the title.

When my grandparents came home the next day they found my mother sitting on the kitchen counter of their apartment in New Jersey, forking up cold green beans from a cereal bowl and listening to the radio. They weren't as upset as they could have been because she'd gotten back before school started, so no one of an official nature had come looking for her and found that her parents had lost her, again. When they asked, she said that she'd been doing drugs with artists in Middletown, Connecticut, so they didn't believe her. They also didn't believe her when she said that the strange car parked out front was hers, but their not believing it didn't make it any less true.

We found a low wall outside of some ugly municipal building to sit on. Ma was shaking still but her steps were long and purposeful, so that I had to skip to keep up as she dragged me after her through the crowds. She may have remembered the place, or led us there by chance, but when she stopped she let go of my shirt so I could fold down onto the sidewalk with my back against the wall. She snapped out a cigarette, ignited it with a loud, ragged breath, then spit on the sidewalk.

"Damn, that felt good," she finally said, and there was a raspy little chuckle in her voice. "Gotta quit this, though." She flicked at her cigarette, inhaled and made the cherry glow. "Maybe when we're settled in again."

"What just happened?" I asked as I handed over her keys.

"Cleared an old debt, was all."

"Well, I got that much from the conversation."

"When you're older."

"I am older!"

She dragged deep.

"Fletcher owns the tattoo parlor. He also owns the club upstairs. The second floor is just a nightclub, but on the top floor there's table dancing. And it's the kind of place where if the guests are rolling or the dancers want to take someone in the back for a little special treatment, he doesn't make a thing of it because he's making extra money in either situation, if you know what I mean."

She paused to drag again, fracturing her narrative, but I waited, worried that she wouldn't go on if I pressed her. "I came up here when I was twenty to spend the summer after my second year of college rooming with

114

a girl I knew from school and working for her uncle, but two weeks into it she kicked me out and moved her boyfriend in, and a week after that her uncle fired me because seeing me every day at work made her feel awkward. I didn't have the money to leave, and the first thing I could find that paid was working at Fletcher's. I started off washing floors and collecting empties, but after a while he got me dancing. He was letting me crash for free, so I didn't want to tell him no. And then, since I was there all the time anyway and knew what I was doing, he got me to start helping on the office shit, doing paperwork and balancing the books and stuff like that." She settled on the wall, ashed her cigarette. I squinted up at her, watching her mouth shape the words.

"I did what he told me to because I was too tired to figure life out for myself. I wanted to feel safe for a while, wanted to know that I'd have a bed to come home to, and I hadn't been able to do that on my own, yet. And he let me into his stash when he was feeling generous, and we hooked up off and on. Don't tell your dad—he says he doesn't want to know that part."

"You told him about all this?"

She nodded, blew out gusts of white. "He wanted to know, but he got so upset that I never got around to filling in all the details. No sense in making both of us feel sick about it."

"But you're telling me."

A cop car turned into the parking lot behind us, then a second later two of them turned out of it onto the road, the sleek, fast ones that get used for car chases, and I wondered if they were looking for us, if they might not stop and talk to us even if they weren't looking for us, since we looked just as shady as we always did.

"You asked. And you watched me punch the bastard. If I don't tell you, you'll fill in for yourself. Or go digging through my private shit again.

"Anyway. One night I fell asleep in the office, the way I usually did. I'd either been smoking or drinking, I don't remember, but I passed out pretty hard, and when I woke up an entire weekend's take was missing from the desk drawer.

"For a day or so I thought I'd just moved it, put it down somewhere in the room and then couldn't remember where that was. It was in one of those blue zippered wallets, waiting to go to the bank, with a deposit slip and everything in it. I tore the room apart, and then I tore the rest of the building apart, and then Fletch wanted to know what I was looking for."

Another police cruiser rolled by, but the man at the wheel had his eyes on the road, didn't even glance at us as he passed. It made me nervous.

"His brother had been staying with him for a few weeks, and that night he'd hung out with me, brought me drinks and kept me company while I worked on the books, but I didn't guess that he might be responsible until after I'd given up on finding the cash. There were other people in the building, but no one else who could have gotten into the office without someone

116

saying something or me noticing them, no one else who knew where the money was kept. The guy was a deadbeat—more so than the rest of us, I mean—fresh out of jail on a robbery charge. Except family is family. So Fletch decided that it was my fault." She flicked away the cigarette butt, pulled out and lit a fresh one.

"I thought he was going to kill me for a little while. When he got done expressing his dismay I almost wished he had. He made it pretty clear that I could work it off or face the consequences. Then I found out that I was already in his debt, for the space to crash and everything he'd done for me before—he'd just been keeping the balance sheet to himself. And, not that I'm in favor of perpetuating the misconception that women's sexual behavior exists primarily as a form of currency, it did piss me off that none of our hooking up seemed to be factored into how much I owed.

"So I danced more, and worked longer hours, and I tried to pay him back, but I kept getting deeper into the red. And we went from being buddies and sometimes lovers to me being his punching bag, and I didn't punch back because I was too scared. But I didn't wise up until he suggested that I start making back-room offers to the guys that bought dances. Then I realized, fuck him, this was just as much his fault as mine. So I packed up, wrote him a letter swearing that I'd pay him back when I had the money. Whenever I earned anything I sent him a bit, but the worry that one day he'd come after me never completely went away. So when I found myself with the cash and the time and the backbone . . ." She dragged deep. "I paid him back."

She stubbed out the end of the cigarette and jumped down from the wall. "Now, I'm bushed as shit, so why don't we find someplace cheap to bed down for the night, and somewhere else cheap to food up first, eh?"

She pulled me up, wrapped her arm around my shoulders, and for the first time I realized that we stood eye to eye.

"There more stories like this that you haven't told me yet?" I asked.

"Plenty. They'll come up when they come up."

"I dunno what to say about this one."

"'Nothing' works just fine. It's over and done with now. We're just giving it an epilogue."

We began to stroll towards the center of town, the throbbing beat of bass. The sky was a pure, eternal dark blue over our heads, paler at the western horizon.

"We sticking around this place a while?"

"Here? Naw. If I had the juice to leave tonight we would."

"Where we going next then?"

"Harrison County, Mississippi."

Back the way we'd come. I groaned. "Can't we just go straight to wherever it is that we're going?"

"Alex, you seem to have some fundamental confusion about the nature of the Quest. What if Sir Gawain and all them had just . . ." She trailed off there. We'd gone down the alley and popped out in the lot where we'd left the car. A tall, square-shouldered figure was fast-walking towards us from the entry we'd driven in by; he could have been in a hurry to get to his own car but I knew that wasn't the case even before I recognized his clothes and the goatee. Ma grabbed my arm, wheeled around, but the front-desk kid from the tattoo shop was already coming towards us down the alley.

"Thought I'd give up if you sat outside the police station long enough?" Fletcher asked. The kid had stopped, blocking the mouth of the alleyway, but he was still coming towards us, walking casually with his hands in his pockets, like he just wanted to have a chat. He was bigger than I'd realized.

Ma shoved me downwards, and I was so surprised by it that I hit the ground, the blacktop cutting into my palms and knees. I looked up in time to see her reach into the back of her jeans, saw her pull out what I thought at first was the cap pistol my dad's parents had given me for a birthday, which Ma had hidden before they even left. Except it was too heavy in her hand to be a toy, too fake looking and at the same time too real. I wondered for a moment when she'd gotten it, how I'd not noticed that she had it. There was a metallic snap far above my head, like someone breaking a toothpick, that I guessed was the safety coming off.

"Dude, just let us get out of here and there'll be no problems." Her voice was steady, which scared me even more. I could feel the gravelly surface of the parking lot through my jeans, the sharp edges imprinting themselves into the skin of my palms.

"Damn. Would you really shoot me?" he asked, as if he were asking her for the time. "'Cause that is not the way you want this to go." He held his hands up, as if he were just gesturing to emphasize the "not." I agreed with him.

"True, but I can think of a million worse ways it could go."

"So you're, what, going to do it right in front of your kid, or march me someplace out of sight like an SS officer? Listen, I just want to talk. Can you aim that thing at the ground or something? It's making me nervous."

"Guns never made you nervous before," she said, but she pointed it at the ground, and I heard the click again as she put the safety back on. "Can't imagine what the fuck we'd have to talk about."

I shifted into a more comfortable position, saw that the kid was hugging the wall now, like he didn't particularly mind witnessing what was happening but was fully intending on making tracks the moment the gun went off. Everything felt fuzzy and underwater, and a distant part of my brain decided that I must be panicking.

"I'm curious, about why you came back is all. If I'd realized you were this wound up I would have just let it lie."

"I can't imagine why I would be 'this wound up' as you put it," she said.

"Was I that much of an asshole, you figured you needed to bring a gun with you?"

She gave him her are-you-kidding-me look, the one I got way too often.

"It's been twenty years," he said. "You thought I was still pissed off about it?"

"You seemed pretty pissed off when it happened."

"Yeah, well, I might have had a bit of a habit of over-reacting back then. I'd forgotten about it—and you—until about an hour ago. You didn't think, when you never heard back from me, that I'd decided to let it slide? That it didn't matter that much to me?"

"Well, it mattered to me. For a few years I was mad that you'd given me such a raw fucking deal. Then I had a baby and I got scared, because I realized you'd been able to make me do anything you wanted, were still making me do things even though you weren't there, and that lasted a long while. But the whole time, from the moment I left, I wondered if I'd look up one day and you'd be there. And I wondered what you'd do to me, do to my kid, and I couldn't stand it. So I wanted to know for dead certain that I didn't owe you jack."

"I never knew you saw me as that much of a monster."

"You didn't give me much reason to see you any other way."

She was still holding the gun, stiff armed, aimed at the ground, and Fletcher still had his hands out, and the kid was still in the alley. I felt sick. I wanted to know how this ended without living through it; I wanted to skip ahead a few pages. Pity you can't do that, in real life.

"So did it feel good to punch me like that?"

"Oh, real good," she said. "If I thought I could get away with it I'd have done it a few more times."

"So would you say we're square now?" he asked. "I don't have to worry about you turning up again and smacking me around in public?"

"You're one to talk," she snorted. "Yeah, if I don't have to worry about you coming after me."

He offered his hand, and as she reached out to shake it I felt a stab of fear, the conviction that she was about to shoot him in the face—she still had the gun, in her left hand—that there was no way that she was going to walk away from him, after the story she'd told me, without getting revenge.

But they just shook. He leaned in close and whispered something into her ear, and she stepped back, laughing.

"Be honest," she said. "You loved having a live-in bookkeeper who worked for free, and a regular lay that didn't kick up a fuss when you fucked around with other people—the only thing you loved about me was that I was both in one."

"One way or another, I never did manage to replace you," he said, and then backed up slowly until his shoulders were against the brickwork of the building that hemmed the parking lot. He waited there as Ma pulled me up and handed me into the front passenger's seat, then slid in herself, and as we pulled onto the road he gave a nod to the rearview mirror that I'm not sure she saw.

We'd barely gone a mile before Ma had to stop so I could puke on the side of the road. My stomach did not appreciate adventure.

CHAPTER XI

The last Laura was tall, and curving: she carried her weight in her butt and hated it; Ma confessed that she went out of her way to follow her up a flight of stairs.

My mom hadn't intended to go to college. College was something other people did. But her social worker didn't agree. He pushed her to write applications to any school she thought she could get into, and even though she was sure that it was less that he believed in her than that he wanted to look good to his superiors, she did what she was told. When she was given a place—at Hood College in Maryland, which was still women-only then—she was glad that she'd applied, since once she finished high school she couldn't think of anything else to do.

She saw Laura for the first time during freshman orientation, here and there and everywhere, still with the leggyness of adolescence and always smiling, laughing, and my mother wanted to know her. Maybe it was fate, or else what she'd told me about the way a name can charm was true; by the end of the year they were companions in studying and stoning and dancing during midnight underwear parties on the roof of the gym.

When she came back from Michigan, a year later than she should have, Laura started crying when she saw her, ran up and held her tightly.

"I thought you were dead. No one knew where you were, no one had heard from you, no one could tell me anything."

That shook Ma up. She hadn't realized that anyone cared, that the way she felt about Laura—the blood-fierce fondness not so different from the way she felt about her brother, spiced with a romantic longing that she tried to deny—might actually be requited.

They both had two more years to go, Ma for psychology, Laura for a five-year dual degree in biology that she wanted to follow with a few years studying technical drawing and a lifetime of illustrating textbooks and research publications. Laura had plans, my mother did not; Laura's plans were quickly revised to include taking care of my mother to the extent that she was allowed, and in that time Ma did not wander. She spent term time in the lab, in other women's rooms drinking wine and writing papers and feeling normal, the summers waiting tables for as many hours as she could get and sharing an apartment with Laura, who seemed determined not to let Ma out of her sight again.

They graduated; Laura moved an hour south to Washington for even more school, and Ma went with her. Laura was seeing a midshipman from Annapolis who they had met in their second year, when he was bussed in with dozens of his kind for a school dance so the girls wouldn't have to dance with each other. My mother was waiting tables and seeing my father, who she'd met during the summer before their final year while she was slinging coffee in a diner. And every few weeks, when it looked like work or boyfriend was about to devour one or both of them, Ma would kidnap Laura, drag her into the front seat of the periwinkle Cadillac that she kept running possibly through will alone and drive them to strange places, new towns or beaches or woods where they could forget their responsibilities, find balance again.

My mother, I think, could have gone on that way forever, but Laura finished school and got married and moved to California for her husband's profession because her work could be done from anywhere. Ma couldn't afford D.C. rent on her own, didn't know anyone she could move in with—except for my father. Laura left in May of 1989 and the next June I turned up, and they could no longer afford Washington. That was probably what the fight that made Ma walk out the day before I was born was about: he wanted to go home to Lynchburg, Virginia, where his parents could babysit and the living was cheaper; she probably wanted to go anywhere but. My debut forced the issue, and we lived with Dad's parents for the six months it took them to get back on their feet, find jobs and rent the house that Ma carried me out of in the middle of the night thirteen years later.

Maybe she hoped that being with him would satisfy the odd craving that arose when she thought about Laura kisses and Laura curves; maybe she was still denying that it existed. I guess that after I was born she decided that maybe she was the kind of deviant who would never be satisfied, that she should stop her restless searching and settle into normal life. The resolution wasn't entirely unsuccessful: she lasted through thirteen years of silent longing before she finally cracked.

She wouldn't tell me when she'd gotten the gun, or where.

"Were you really going to shoot him?" I asked.

She didn't answer.

"Did you really figure you needed it?"

"I figured it was better to have it and not need it than vice-versa. And I figured you'd stay in the car, so that whether I needed it or not you'd be safe."

We moseyed south, rolled down all the windows and stayed on back roads between massing ranks of corn and grain; everything was green. I could almost pretend that she was taking me strawberry picking, that we were on the way home from a not-very-successful day trip, that everything was normal. The trees, the birds—everything looked like home still, but slightly different, like aliens had built us a terrarium so they could study us but, even though they'd got the idea of trees and birds right, they hadn't paid enough attention to the little details, to leaf shapes and flight patterns. It was completely familiar and completely not all at once.

The farther south we went the more relaxed Ma became, leaning back in her seat, leaving her cigarette pack pinched between her thighs instead of dipping for a new one as soon as she'd jettisoned the previous butt, even smiling a little to herself and mumbling along when a song she especially liked came on the radio. I wanted to know more, I wanted to ask about the gun again. I kept falling asleep.

Ma shook me as we passed the little green sign telling us that we were now in Harrison County, Mississippi. It was early evening on the third day after we'd left Michigan, and I blinked myself awake slowly and tracked our progress as we grew closer and closer to the coast. We were almost out of road according to the map when she parked up behind a laundromat, locked the car and set out on foot down the quiet streets with me following. She seemed to know where she was going, but in a half-remembered way, like she had dreamed the place, or not seen it in a long time. We found the bay, and then we found the quay, a collection of boats bobbing on the water, fancy powerboats and rusting pontoons, sailboats and dirty fishing vessels. Ma wandered a little while I sat on the edge of a dock with my legs hanging over, looking down into the terrifying black water and watching tiny jellyfish flash and sink like coins tossed into a shopping-mall fountain. Then I heard Ma's voice: "Excuse me? Could you tell me who owns that boat?"

A rusty voice answered back, unintelligibly, and I pulled myself up and scrambled towards them. She couldn't be planning on buying a boat. What did she want to do, sail to Cuba?

I found her as she was stepping off one of the fishier-smelling boats, the older man standing on it squinting

127

at her retreating back. There was a piece of paper in her hand.

"We've probably got just enough time before sundown," she said as we walked back to the car. She shuffled in the back seat for a map, paged to the index and began looking up the address.

"What are we doing?" I asked.

"Looking for someone," she mumbled as she flipped back through. "Someone that might not remember me anymore, but it's worth a shot."

I followed her back down the winding streets of the town, staying just a little behind, nervous, not sure if we weren't going to have a repeat of Michigan. The houses were small, battered looking and dirty, every bit of metal red at the edges. It was beach season, but it didn't seem like a beach place, a vacation place. No tat shops, no trinkets, no restaurants with barkers on the sidewalks calling tourists in to try their fried medley. It was a fishermen's town.

I nearly walked up her heels when she stopped, abruptly and in the middle of the street, to study three of the little houses, tight in a row and all the same size and general design, just like all the other little houses on this street, like they'd all come out of a candy box, a matched set made of the same chalky stuff as Conversation Hearts, lawns cluttered with seashells and crab pots and bits of metal so rusted that you couldn't tell what they'd once been, the cement shells of the houses painted pastel green or pink or yellow, worn awnings stained orange-red in places. All the same, except these three were missing their numbers. They were bracketed by numbers 9 and 36; number 62 was directly across the road.

"Middle for diddle," she said after staring for a moment, walked up the yard to the solid grey door of the pastel-green house and knocked, leaving me on the sidewalk, frozen with nerves. After the previous stop I wasn't so eager to follow where she led.

She chatted cheerfully for a moment with the older woman who opened the door to her knock, then thanked her and skipped back to the road.

"Good guess, wrong house. Come on." She took my hand this time and, ignoring my reluctance, dragged me to the house on the left, pale pink and just as empty-looking as all the others.

This time an older man answered her knock.

"Can I help you?" His accent was thick, his curly pure white hair making his tanned skin look even darker.

Ma answered in what sounded to me like Spanish, but with an odd inflection to it, not quite the accent I'd heard in the classroom in Florida. He nodded, opened the door wide so that we could come in and I followed close behind her, itching with shyness.

The house was packed with photographs and trinkets, but neatly arranged, like a treasure box. He waved us into a living room and onto a sagging, ancient blue couch that tried to eat me as soon as I sat down, and while they talked I looked around the room.

There were photographs in nice frames and photographs in seashell-crusted frames and photographs tucked into the edges of the frames of other photographs or taped to random surfaces with Scotch tape so old that it had turned yellow. The people in them resembled each other, wide mouthed and slightly squint eyed, though that could have been from all of the staring into the coastal sun that they did. There were several pictures of the old man with his wife, so that I could recognize the younger versions of them by following the iterations back in time: pictures of them together when they were teenagers, at their wedding, holding a baby, holding a slightly different baby, corralling small kids, dwarfed by their two grown sons and then slowly giving way to time, gaining a comfortable thickness about the middle. Taped to a little statue of Mary in a plastic grotto like the end of an upturned bathtub was a picture of them together not so long ago: she was wearing a hospital gown, and her scalp showed through her thinly curling hair, but they were grinning at each other, that squint-eyed grin that little kids get when they're so overwhelmed by happy that they can't take any more.

There were signs of her around the house, but no her, so I guessed with a sick feeling that she was dead, and I didn't want to imagine it but couldn't help it: someone being around all your life, being there even when your parents die and your kids leave and your aunts aren't speaking to you. And then one day she's gone, this person that you've been with longer than you've been without, longer than you were with your parents, longer than you've ever been with anyone. And nothing will ever bring her back. It doesn't matter that you had plans, that there were things that you meant to say to her, or things that you wanted to tell her about. It doesn't matter that you really need her to be there, really want her to be there. It's final.

I caught maybe one word in ten of their conversation as my butt sunk deeper and deeper into the couch and parts of my brain went to sleep. Tonino was mentioned several times, and I gathered that they meant Anthony, the Anthony that my mother knew from the foster home that we'd burned down. Also family and boat, bread, water, wine, the woman, but it could have meant beautiful boat, or the mother, or the Madonna; that was as far as my middle-school Spanish class could take me into their conversation.

They gestured at me once or twice with smiles, and I smiled back, but otherwise my role was to sit still, shake my head to the coffee he offered us, and study the room until my back teeth and my left butt cheek fell asleep. I had zoned so far out that Ma had to prod me when it was time to go.

"Come on, kid, we have an errand to run real quick."

I followed her out of the house, shaking the pins and needles out of my left leg, and hoped that there was about to be food.

"Dinnertime yet?" I asked, but she didn't seem to hear me. "Ma? Can we eat something now?"

"There's granola and apples in the car if you're hungry—we've still got stuff to do."

"I mean real food. The kind you have to let cool

before you eat it. With a fork. On a plate. Sitting at a table. You remember what I'm talking about, don't you? Failing that, a burger or something wouldn't be that bad, either."

"If you see a roach coach you can get something, otherwise we're on a mission."

Even that sounded good, though I didn't know what a roach coach was until she wandered over to a white truck parked on the side of the road, paid with a crumpled wad of bills and coins, and handed me something greasy in a football of bread. It filled a longing that was probably just my stomach but felt like it dipped into my soul, and by the time we made the car again I was licking oil off my fingers.

"Looks like you weren't hungry after all," Ma observed. "Get on in, we have to go somewhere before we go to see Mr. Panagopoulos again."

"That's the old man's name?" I asked.

"Don't make fun. His mother was Puerto Rican and he married a Puerto Rican and if you ask him he says he's Puerto Rican, but his dad was Greek. Anthony still swears that one day he's going to change his name. Hand me the map."

She drove slowly with it open in her lap, circling round the same piece of block several times, twice almost making wrong turns down one-way streets. I was starting to feel sick when she slammed on the brakes in front of a bunker-shaped building, the peeling sign on its front lawn declaring it to be an official United States Post Office, for all it looked like the headquarters of Doctor Doom and his army of world-dominating robots.

"Go get me what's in postbox one eighty-three." She unclipped a heavy brass key from her keyring and tossed it into my lap.

"What?"

"Just get it, Alex, we're in a bit of a hurry."

So up I marched to Doctor Doom's inner sanctum, tugged on the door hoping it would be locked but found that it was not only unlocked but recently oiled; the door might have hit me in the face.

There was a metal mesh pulled down in front of the teller's counter, but the mailboxes were unguarded, ranks and ranks of them. I plodded to 183, jiggled the key in the lock, and was showered with an explosion of paper. The box was clotted with envelopes, fliers, coupon books, and I took off my overshirt and bundled the pages into it in creased handfuls, then tied the sleeves together and hauled it out to Ma.

"You didn't need to bring out all the junk—all we needed was the white package."

"You could have told me that. It's in here somewhere."

"Did you relock the postbox?"

". . . Maybe."

When I got back to the car for the second time she had the bundle open on the passenger's seat and was stuffing leaflets for community yard sales and Al Anon meetings into a plastic grocery bag. A white cardboard box was propped on the dashboard over the speedometer, where she was also stacking the bills and hand-addressed

133

envelopes. I shuffled the mess into my lap so I could sit down and helped her sort junk mail until my shirt was empty, then as I put it back on and buttoned it over my undershirt she shoved the envelopes and box from the dash into my lap and pulled away.

"Why are we in such an all-fire hurry?" I asked.

"I don't want him to change his mind."

"Is it likely he will?"

"I don't think so. Color me excited. I made this promise a while ago—didn't think I'd be asked to keep it."

"What promise?"

"Tell you later."

"It's later. What promise?"

She sighed.

"Anthony and his family don't talk to each other anymore. Or see each other. I know them, though, and they liked me, when I was around here. So Mr. P doesn't mind too much helping me do something that isn't really legal."

"Are we going to kill someone?"

"No. We're going to put someone to rest."

"That means kill someone, doesn't it? We're going to shoot some guy and the old man is going to help us dump him into the Gulf of Mexico, isn't he?"

"Good guess, Alex, that is exactly what we're going to do. Then we're all going to get matching gang tattoos done by a blind excommunicated priest using nothing but a sharpened crucifix and the ashes of a holy book moistened with the blood of our enemies. And then go into hiding in the Bermuda Triangle until it all blows

134

over." She was quiet for a moment, then, "I'm in a hurry because we have to beat the sun. I promised that I'd do it at sunset."

"We're doing black magic then, aren't we?"

"Just shut up. You'll find out in a bit."

CHAPTER XII

We wove back through town to the quay, left the car illegally parked half on the grass beneath the U.S. and Mississippi flags. She plucked the box off my lap, tore it open and pulled out two little canisters. They looked like the kind of thing expensive tea came in, both covered in nubby paper decorated with gilt fans, one red and one black. She put them on the dash carefully and pulled out a sheaf of lined paper written over in slightly smudged pencil, skimmed each page, then grabbed the canisters and hopped out of the car, leaving me to follow or stay as I chose. I followed.

She trotted down the quay, the wood rattling under her boots, stopped at the battered boat that she'd spotted when we'd come by earlier that day, the one that had led her to Mr. P. It looked to me like a toy, the general shape of a rowboat, but larger. There was a tall, narrow pilothouse in the front end with a hard, flat canopy coming back from its roof to shelter most of the deck. She called out a greeting, and the old man called back and stepped out of the pilothouse, hatted and jacketed in spite of the heat, moving slowly and just a bit

136

reluctantly. She hopped down onto the deck without hesitation, then looked back to see if I was following. I stepped onto the boat with hands tight on her arm for balance, and immediately felt the rising tide of panic as the deck moved under me.

"Sit here, don't move," she said, and pushed me onto what looked like an upside-down wooden box in the middle of the deck, which I guessed was the covering to the hold, or the engine, though given what I knew about boats it was just as likely to be a handy gateway to hell. I was facing backwards, but I didn't care; I had no inclination to shift around.

Ma unwound the mooring rope and the old man started the engine, and we pulled slowly away from the quay, the wood beneath me rumbling with the motor. The boat was of a simple design—if it hadn't been for the thick metal crane that rose like an arm from the deck about halfway between the pilothouse and the stern and its worn but efficient-looking block and tackle I'd think that the thing was just a pleasure boat, a little toy that someone had built in their backyard to tootle about the bay on a lazy weekend.

Ma and Mr. P continued to talk, in short, edged sentences that sounded like directions, or like they were making and dismissing suggestions back and forth. The way they stood and moved and spoke made it seem as though they had done this together a hundred times before. As we slipped past the moored boats and out into the bay the buzz of the motor intensified, throbbing up through the wood and into my bones. I clung to the edge of the box and tried not to think of the dark, crushing void below us, the finned and toothed things moving through it. I loved the ocean, but only in that moment did I realize that I was terrified of deep water.

We moved into the Gulf with what felt like excessive speed to me, but which seemed like no speed at all when I considered how little the coast changed minute by minute as I watched it recede. Once away from the protection of the bay the wind picked up; I could feel it in my thighs and chest, on my face like a thick mask, and I didn't know how Ma stayed upright when she stepped out of the pilothouse, strode to the very back, and looked out at the land and buildings we were leaving behind. She stayed there as they slowly disappeared, stiller than I had ever seen her before. Every moment I thought we would stop, that we must have come far enough, but we continued on with the sun falling down into the ocean on our right-hand side—and I realized that I'd never seen the sun set into the ocean before.

The land behind us was a caramel-peanut-butter smudge when we cut the motor, hazed by water vapor. Ma dropped what was probably an anchor though it looked nothing like one into the water, then stood again and stared out at the horizon. For a few moments we stayed as we were: the old man in the pilothouse with his hands still on the wheel, Ma with her feet planted wide, arms folded, bare skin goose bumped but ignoring the wind, me hunched and confused. Then the man said something to her; she called back, "I know," but still stood by me. The sun had floundered and half sunk into the water, poured itself out in a long, snaky stream towards us. This was what we were waiting for, but why?

She went forward to the pilothouse, brought back with her the two little canisters, one in each hand, and stood at the side. She faced into the setting sun, and now I could see there were tears on her cheeks. The old man came out also, leaned against the metal crane, and watched her.

"Well." She seemed to be talking to the sun, or to someone in her own head. "I never thought I'd have to make good on this, you wonderful nutcase. I guess we're as close to sunset as we're going to get." She sucked her finger and held it up to check the wind, then put one of the canisters down on the ledge and held the other, the red one, in her hands like an offering. "I guess I should say something, but I never did know what to say. We loved you, and you loved here. Don't forget us, wher-ever you are. We're going to come find you one day." She paused for a moment as if she were looking for more to say, then gave a little that's-all-I've-got shrug, and carefully unscrewed the lid of the canister. She held it still for a moment at arm's length, and then let the lip dip down, and the breeze carried the pearly grey powder like a comet's tail over the water, towards the dying sun. She didn't turn it out entirely, though, but kept a bit back in the bottom that I saw when she put it down and picked up the second container.

"Baby doll, I never knew you, but if I had I know I would have loved you. Keep your mama safe. She don't know how to be at peace—she hasn't had your practice at it."

This tip was more abrupt, and the dusty streamer had far less volume. She stood for a moment watching it drift away, then went back to the pilothouse and returned with a plastic bucket on a string. She threw it off the side, waited, then pulled it back up and very carefully poured a small amount of seawater into the two vessels. The old man queried her, briefly, and she answered, "He wanted it," in a way that showed that it wasn't exactly what she would have thought of.

We stayed watching the setting sun for some minutes, our silence thick, until the old man turned to go back to the pilothouse. So he did not see Ma empty her pockets onto the deck with quick scoops of her fingers, step out of her shoes and toe off her socks, and then one two onto the ledge and three, throw her arms back and then forward and then arc herself into the dark water with a great noise but hardly any splash.

And in the moment of my panic I was with her in the dark, the weight of the water above me nothing to the eternal, unseen depths below, and I felt the burning in my lungs and eyes from the salt and tasted it in my nose. And I knew we were going to drown. Then she shot to the surface in a fountain of spume, and I knew we would be all right. The old man shouted to her, and she waved and called back nonchalantly, but instead of coming close to be pulled aboard she lay back in the trail of the dying sun, its blood clotting in her clothing, arms and legs and hair all spread out like an anemone.

I wanted to be the sort of person that would dive in after her, the sort of person that welcomed the unfathomable depths without needing to understand them. I wanted to be my mother, in that moment. I knew that I was not.

She finally curled in on herself and disappeared beneath the swell, and I held my breath until she surfaced again, swam neatly over to the side, and carefully pulled herself back into the boat.

Her clothes were sodden, her shirt hanging off her oddly and her jeans clinging. Water beaded on her freckled collarbones and salt clotted her hair, but even though the old man did not sound happy in his words to her while he started his engine, the look on her face was one of pure peace, and I knew that I had never seen it there before.

Her first year of college she hadn't known that they wouldn't be allowed to board over the summer. She found this out only a few weeks before classes broke up.

"Why didn't you just go home and live with your parents?" I asked.

She shook her head. "That wasn't an option anymore. And I didn't feel like I knew anyone well enough at that point to tag along home with them. I liked a lot of people, but I didn't trust them yet."

For five days she lived in her car, going around to all the shops and restaurants looking for summer work, considering moving on to look elsewhere but worried what cash she had wouldn't last long enough for her to find something. Then she got the postcard that called her south.

She and Anthony had found each other again some years before, kept up by letter and occasional long-distance phone call. She had told him that she was being turfed out at the end of the school year; the postcard suggested in tiny pencil writing that she come down to Mississippi and run his grandpa's crab lines with him. She hadn't even phoned first to make sure that he wasn't just joking but looked up the route in her road atlas and headed south the very same day.

"And then what happened?" I asked.

"And then we crabbed all summer for Tony's grandpa and I went back to school in the fall with money in my pocket," she said.

But there was more to the story than that.

She was nineteen, he was a year or so older, and when she got to Mississippi it was like they'd last seen each other the day before, that the years since they'd been face to face didn't count. Except for one thing: Marisol.

Her name meant "bitter sun" and she lived with her mom and dad and older sister near to where Tony was staying with his grandparents—Tony and his grandparents were still speaking to each other then, even though at the time he wasn't speaking to his parents, aunts or uncles, or most of his brothers and sisters, half-siblings and stepfathers.

Tony and Marisol met the week before Ma showed up, so when she got there late in the evening, found the house, bounced up the steps and into Tony's arms, Marisol was just behind him. The women could have behaved like lions circling the kill, like leopards contesting territory, old friend against barely legal barely girlfriend, but Ma didn't like Tony that way.

She slept on the couch that would try to eat me a couple of decades later, surrounded by photos and Madonnas, was shaken awake long before dawn the next morning, wandered down to the water with Tony to find Marisol waiting for them, cast off into the Gulf of Mexico and learned the other way to catch crabs.

Tony's grandfather owned five hundred and forty inkwell-style pots, and they let them out in strings of sixty, baited and marked with a buoy. Every morning the three of them were down at the boat before four, motored out into the bay and pulled up each string—this was where the metal crane came in—piled the crabs of keeping size in the ice hold and tossed the small ones, re-baited the traps and dropped them back into the water. It took them until six in the evening, sometimes later, to sort through every single trap, and even though they were all Catholic they went out on Sunday as well, went to Mass and took communion on Saturday evenings to gain absolution for spending the Lord's day on the water.

It didn't take them long to find that Marisol was crazy. Break-the-law-and-then-sweet-talk-her-way-out-of-being-arrested crazy. Try-and-kidnap-someone's-dog-because-it-looked-lonely crazy. Strip-naked-for-no-reason-at-all-and-dive-into-the-ocean-miles-from-land crazy.

Happy-one-day-and-down-the-next crazy. And she liked Ma, who was going through one of her stoic phases then, didn't talk much but from time to time whipped out barbed observations that would have been cruel if they weren't so funny. The Gulf rotted their clothes and locked their hair, and when they thought Ma wasn't looking Tony and Marisol would pause for long, wet kisses on the far side of the pilothouse, and Ma would roll her eyes at the seagulls and pretend that she didn't hear them.

Theirs was a very religious community, so Ma was also there the first time that Tony and Marisol had sex, not there on purpose but because it was the only chance they'd gotten and they didn't know that she was awake.

They'd taken sleeping bags and Thermoses out into the fields away from town to watch the Perseids, and it had been assumed by the adults that with my mother there everyone would stay out of everyone else's drawers, but Ma fell asleep, and what woke her up was the sound of zippers being undone and she wasn't sure what she should do but she knew she didn't have it in her to jump up and put a stop to the festivities.

When the end of summer came they didn't want Ma to leave. They made a pact that they'd come back to the Gulf one day, alive or dead, and if one of them died the other two would lay him or her to rest in the setting sun if it was the last thing they did; this last part was Marisol's idea, but the other two agreed that it was probably as badass a funeral as any of them could manage.

144

She kissed them both goodbye, the money she'd earned a fat roll in her pocket, and headed back north to start school again. She'd guessed that everything would go on as before, hoped that she'd be able to go back the next summer and work the water alongside them again.

But six weeks into term she got a phone call from Mr. Panagopoulos: had she seen his grandson? She was understandably confused, and the old man explained that Anthony and the neighbor girl had both disappeared a few days before, and everyone wanted to assume the best, that maybe they'd decided to come visit her and hadn't bothered to mention to anyone that they were going. But Ma hadn't had anything but a letter, two weeks before, with the usual news, nothing about leaving home or going anywhere.

Three weeks after the phone call from his grandfather Ma received a letter from Tony, and she was so relieved that she opened it while standing in the mailroom.

The first line asked her to keep all that followed to herself, that the parents and grandparents and etcetera had been told that the two of them were OK, and the rest would come out when it was the right time. They had gone to Canada, were working the water off Nova Scotia, and Marisol was pregnant. They'd been wanting to leave Harrison County for a while, but the baby was what had actually made them go: she couldn't get rid of it, she couldn't tell her parents, she wasn't quite eighteen yet. They wanted Ma to come up and visit when it was born, when summer came around again and she could get free. She read their letters eagerly, pinned the photos of Marisol with her slowly growing belly to the cork board in her room, woke up at three a.m. when Tony called to tell her it was coming, and then at four a.m. the next week when he said that this was really it. He called again at a more reasonable time the same day: the baby really was coming this time, but the doctors were worried; something was wrong besides the fact that they were a few weeks early.

It was a girl. She lived for three hours.

Ma went to visit quite a while later, after Michigan, and that was when Tony told her the details, how Marisol refused to let go of the still, blue body, how she screamed at the doctors that they'd killed her baby, how they'd had to sedate her. They hadn't even named the child yet, hadn't been able to agree on who it was being named for, so the little casket of ashes they'd given him had been marked with Marisol's family name.

They'd tried to keep going as they had been, even tried for a second baby—the mistake that had made them run away from home had become a blessing that they desperately wanted. Marisol hadn't been able to handle it. About a year after the baby died, Tony came home to find a letter on their kitchen table and all of her things gone.

They'd both gotten occasional postcards from Marisol over the next decade, supposed that chapter of their lives was over and she'd be OK from then on. She'd gotten pregnant again, three or four years after I was born, and everyone involved had held their breath. There wasn't really a dad in the picture; she'd wanted a baby, not a boyfriend. This time it lived, thrived, was sent home from the hospital with a clear bill of health, and they let that held breath out. Everything had seemingly fixed itself.

Then one morning Marisol let her three-year-old go outside to play, had been about to follow her out to keep an eye on her but had paused to pour another cup of coffee, had dropped the coffee and paused to make another pot. She'd known there was something wrong because of the silence, went outside and found that her daughter had drowned in the rain barrel under the downspout. She'd dropped a plastic truck in and in trying to fish it out had slipped head first into the water and hadn't been able to pull herself back out. Her mother dragged her out, called the cops, stayed calm as they tried to resuscitate the girl, gave her statement, went to the hospital. She'd stayed calm, and when they brought her back home she made herself a cup of tea, wrote some letters, washed her hair, then went into the bedroom and killed herself.

Her daughter was given to its father's family to be buried, but Marisol had requested cremation for herself in one of the letters, which she'd addressed and left on her kitchen table, pinned down by the freshly washed coffeepot. She had also requested that her ashes be sent to Anthony Panagopoulos. The letter that went with them contained nothing but the chorus from a song that had come out the summer they spent together, that they'd heard over and over until they caught themselves humming it as they sailed into the Gulf at sunrise, that they'd sung at the top of their lungs the night they drove out of town to watch the meteors; it reminded him of every promise he had made to her.

CHAPTER XIII

We gave the old man a ride back to his house, and though Ma walked him to his door, told him goodbye, gave him a hug, he seemed absent, detached, as though now that we'd done what we'd come to do we didn't really exist anymore. We returned to the fast-food truck and bought far too many burgers, then drove out of town a ways until we found a stretch of empty field where we could pull over just past a yellow-orange glowing streetlight and spread out for dinner. We took our shoes off, even though the grass was dry and prickly under us, spread our knees wide to let the orange grease drip between and onto the crisped earth. There was some sunlight still, the sky dark almost completely except for the nail paring of indigo at the western edge, the stars like freckles spreading to flaw the blackness.

"We used to do this a lot, at the end of the day. Eat cheap food at the side of the road and watch the stars come out."

"Was this a happy place, then?"

She finished a burger and swallowed thoroughly, washed out her mouth with bottle soda before answering,

"Yeah, it was a happy place, once I learned to be happy here.

"If I could do one thing for you, kiddo, I'd make it so you didn't want. Not that you had everything that you could want, but that you never felt the feeling of 'want.' That you could get along without it."

"Life would be boring then."

"It would also be pretty close to painless."

I mulled that over for a while, but before I had an answer I heard her soft-edged snore, the one that she made when she was really asleep. It was a rural road; we'd been passed by maybe one car, two cars, in the whole time we'd been sat there munching, so I didn't know whether I should wake her up so that we could go find a real place to sleep or if she was planning on sleeping right there in the half-dead grass, well onto the shoulder but nevertheless still on the side of the road like a bum. I didn't have much time to think about it; I fell asleep too before long, the grass tickling the back of my head and the heat of the earth seeping up into my hips.

Sometime in the night she must have woken up, wrestled my limp body into the passenger's seat, kept going west until she found someplace for us to park just off the road. I only found this out though when—déjà vu—a cop knocked on her window around 6.45 in the morning. It was a much more civil exchange than the one we had with the cop on the second morning of our liberty. This one was more concerned than anything, welcomed Ma's explanation that she'd started nodding off at the wheel and had pulled over to rest rather than cause a car crash—or a cow crash, as was more likely in that location. I wrestled on my shoes as he asked her if she felt safe at home, whether she would be interested in the addresses of some local women's shelters, and I thought how different I was from the last time a cop had stopped us, how much older I felt, and not just because we were only a few days shy of my fifteenth birthday. I was more sure of myself than I'd been then. I'd stopped being scared. I'd stopped being a kid. I was still being dragged on my mother's wild expedition, but when I told myself that it was only because I wanted to, that I could leave at any time and go home to Dad, I believed it.

We cleared life with the deputy—and asked where to find something decent but cheap to eat—and started up again, our backs to the slowly rising sun, me with my boots on the dash, Ma with her cigarette trailing a fine streamer of white behind us, the country singer on the radio playing us out of Mississippi.

Welcome to St. Tammany Parish flashed by on a green highway sign, and I wondered why they used the God-awful worst shade of green in existence. A while later came *Welcome to Louisiana* in English with French beneath it and a fleur-de-lis between them in case the two versions wanted to get frisky. We rolled through construction on highways that didn't look so different than the highways in Virginia, except the trees still looked odd. That was I-12: trees and trees and buildings here and there and billboards saying you should stop for a burger or something, on and on and on. As we passed through Baton Rouge I realized that we were no longer following the highlighter path that she'd drawn across her private map when she'd first bought it in West Virginia. We should have started heading northwards, shooting for California on I-49; instead she was continuing west, towards Houston and central Texas on I-10.

It was in one of those wild places where we passed into Texas. I almost missed it. We were crossing the Sabine River, and Ma had turned off the radio for the sake of telling me about the Rape of the Sabine, which I wasn't sure if she was making up or not. Still green, still hot and somewhat tropical looking, still not so different to home. Nothing looked that much bigger to me. I dozed through Houston, woke up as we were driving through a scrubby nothing place, grass and some trees, now and again a billboard, a low-slung house, power lines. It was a lonely place, and I was glad that I wasn't the one doing the driving. It wasn't unlovely, but the flatness bugged me.

Ma's mood had perked up; I could see the happy on her face and the weight was rolling off her shoulders like stones, a destination at a time, and it looked like she might start singing at any moment. If she'd been the kind of person that sang. Really, she'd be more likely to start spontaneously handing around shots of tequila as an expression of happiness, but singing sounds better.

Time felt funny then; maybe it was the constant forward motion. I felt like we'd been in the car for years,

152

not days. Maybe it was like being in a rocket, aging at a different rate to everyone on earth. The blacktop rolled away under us and I felt time rolling away with it, diffusing into nothing. Minutes and hours had no meaning anymore, even though Ma had entrusted me with the copiloting, told me to take out the road atlas and keep us going in the general direction of Three Rivers, Texas. I could measure the distance with my fingers, calculate our average mileage, figure out how far it was, but we had lost the blind urgency that had driven us. When we hadn't stopped for bathroom breaks before we now stopped for sunsets, fresh vegetable stands, flea markets and jewelry shops even though we never bought anything, restaurants that looked really good even though we could have kept going for a while, so that what should have been a pretty direct under-taking turned into a multi-day wander, and I didn't care. I hadn't had any privacy since we'd left Florida—not the kind of privacy that I'd gotten used to while we were living there, at least, but though I still wres-tled with strange dreams of a night, was still hit now and again with an acute awareness of my more sensitive parts and an overwhelming desire to do something fun with them, I'd learned to ignore them, just like I'd learned to ignore all of the other primal desires that had to fall by the wayside when we were on the move—like being able to piss whenever I needed to, or sleeping stretched out flat with a real pillow, or not being constantly just a bit hungry but also just a little nauseous. I wonder if that's how all the great explorers felt, hungry and a little sick and just hoping that they could find some land so that they could get that boiling-hot, fit-your-whole-body-in-at-once bath they'd been madly wanting. For the time being my senses were sated in other ways—the hugeness of the sky, the saturation of color, the heat, the landscape.

We had odd, drawn-out conversations around the songs on the radio: I'd say something during a commercial break, and then neither of us would speak while the music played, and a man left his wife and a wife found her husband and a dog did any number of doglike things, and then in the next break or if she got tired of the song Ma would respond, one sentence, and then a few minutes later perhaps another sentence would follow, and then eventually I would get around to answering.

She was being cagy about why exactly we were in Texas, and I was wondering a little bit if the gun would be making a reappearance. We were off the highlighter path, but according to the map there was a *Brainwashed broodmother* somewhere near the middle of the state. But she seemed too cheerful to be on her way to deal with anything as serious as brainwashing, even if she was a bit preoccupied, a bit meditative.

"We going to stop here for long?" I asked in between songs.

"Don't intend to," she said. "I'd like to make this as quick as we can."

"Make what as quick as we can?"

"I'll tell you when I know—I haven't made up my

154

mind completely as to what we're going to be doing. Depending on how things pan out, we might have some company for a little while."

That was when fate—or God, as we would later be insistently told—intervened.

Rural Texas was rolling by below us and above us and to either side of us, and the warm breeze through the open window made my head feel thick and the sun made me feel sleepy. We were both quiet, Ma driving slow and not smoking or drinking coffee for once, me leaning my head against the window half asleep, something relaxed and instrumental on the radio. Then I saw a wheel roll off like a thrown hulahoop, on a break towards the horizon and freedom. I had enough time to think, Hey, that looks like one of our—before there was an almighty bang, the front of the car pitched forward, and the world started to shake apart.

We grated to a stop on the sandy shoulder of the road and sat for a terrified minute, breathing deep and too surprised to talk, the music going on quietly in the background like nothing had happened.

"I think it was just a flat," Ma said. "A big flat."

"Nu-uh," I said, "I think the wheel came clean off."

"Don't be silly. How would the wheel come off?"

She climbed out and walked around to the sunken corner—my corner—to see, and I followed her out her side because my door wouldn't open.

The wheel was gone. The axle had bent sharply when

it hit the highway, and the nose of the car had cut a rut in the dirt as we scraped to a stop.

"Alex, where did you see the wheel go?"

I walked back along the road to the point where the drag marks started, found the rut the escaping wheel had made and followed it out until we found it on its side in the dead grass. We stood it up on end and rolled it back to the car. Two of the bolts were missing, the rest had sheared off.

Back at the car Ma stood for a few minutes leaning against the trunk, thinking, looking at the wheel that wasn't where it needed to be. There was no using the spare, not with a bent axle and no bolts.

"Get your backpack, kid. We're going to have to thumb it for a bit."

She shuffled around in the trunk after her own bag, and I saw her stick the gun down her pants. The wheel got shoved in the back seat; she pinned a white T-shirt in the window to indicate distress, then joined me on the shoulder with her thumb out. I was scared now, maybe of what might happen to us or of what might happen to whoever picked us up if Ma decided to use the gun, but I didn't need to be. A purple eighteen-wheeler with *Jesus Saves!* painted on the doors and mudflaps and pretty much every inch of the front and back in reflective white rolled to a stop just beyond us, and the long thin man in the driver's seat leaned over and opened the door so that we could climb into the cab.

"In a spot of trouble, missy?" he asked her, and you couldn't get offended by the "missy" because you could tell that was what he called every woman he'd ever met.

"Are we ever—lost a wheel."

"There's a mechanic's a ways ahead, I can give you and your—" he looked at me a moment, settled on—"kid a lift. There isn't much else around here."

"If you could put us down there, I'm sure we can figure it out. They tow, don't they?"

There was gospel on the radio, but I kept my hand on the door latch just in case. Even holy rollers can have psychotic breaks. Ma seemed comfortable, though, chatted about the picture of his wife and kids on the dash, asked how he'd gotten into trucking, putting him and herself at ease until we saw the sign for *Ted's Tow, Trucking, and Repairs* and glided to a stop on the side of the very much not-busy road.

Ma thanked the trucker extensively while I stood awkward on the shoulder, then she hopped down and slammed the door. The air fell quiet as the sound of his engine faded, and our feet crunched too loudly on the gravel as we walked towards the mechanic's. I was still nervous, even though we had nothing, really, to worry about: nowhere to get to, no time limit on how long we could take getting there, probably enough money in our pockets to get us out of this fix quick and easy. But I didn't have the child's blind trust in the omnipotence of parents anymore: I had eaten the apple, knew that Ma was no different from me, that she probably didn't know what to do right now anymore than I would, that her only advantage was a rapidly narrowing gulf of experience.

A bell over the door jangled as we went into the mechanic's lobby, but there was no one behind the counter. It was a small room, the walls dingy and the countertop chipped and yellowed from the sun. Three plastic chairs were lined up with their backs against the wide front window, with two more facing them, flanked by a vending machine with half its spaces empty and a hot-drink machine on an overturned milk crate, with a coffee table covered in old magazines and eviscerated newspapers in the middle. The ceiling fan rocked on its mooring, made a tak-tak-tak sound as it spun. I hung back as Ma wandered first behind the counter, then through the back door into the shop, calling out a careful "Hello?" as she went.

They were in the garage, one under a dented sedan up on a lift, the other filling in paperwork at an oil-stained worktop. The one under the car came forward, shook her hand, led us back to the front office and got her a cup of coffee from the little push-button machine before asking her what the trouble was.

He nodded slow as she explained about the wheel flying off, then said, "I can haul it in for you, easy, but if the axle's bent it might cost more to fix than the car's worth. Might be best to trade it for parts and start clean."

"I can't afford a new car, not right now." Ma's voice had gotten thin and high. "We're living on savings till we get to my sister's in California."

This was news to me—I assumed that she was making it up.

"I've got a used station wagon out back just waiting

on a radiator, should be turning up Wednesday, Thursday. I could have you out of here Friday afternoon the latest—probably the best offer you're going to get unless you plan on hitching the whole way."

We slid into the front of the tow truck with him; on the ride back Ma was silent, thinking, about what I wasn't sure but I hoped that she had a plan for getting us out of there. I didn't want to spend the next four nights camped out beside the mechanic's, living off our peanut-butter crackers and dried fruit.

The car looked even sadder when we came up on it like that, heeled over like a drunk, the paint flaking in places from salt and sun and too many rides. The man hooked it up and cranked it into the bed of the tow truck, took the white shirt from the window and hung it off the back end, commented, "Y'all sure make the most of your trunk space" as he started up the truck again, but still Ma was quiet, thinking, and I was worried that she wasn't going to get us out of this, that it was Florida all over again and she'd be waitressing in sports bars for the next year while I struggled through school and tried not to die of boredom.

At the garage he left our car on the tow truck, went inside with Ma and filled in forms, looked over her registration, took her out back to show her the station wagon, then finalized things while I sat holding my breath in the lobby. At some point it had gotten to be mid-afternoon. I was hungry but didn't want to say anything. I'd become resigned to the idea of outdoor sleeping when Ma asked to borrow the phone book, paged through the white pages, then took out her phone and dialed. The other end rung for a bit, then a voice came on the line.

"Margaret-Mary?" Ma's voice was happy and nervous all at once. "Yeah, it's me. Listen, I know it's been a long time, but I need help. I'm stranded, just outside of . . ." She looked up at the mechanic.

"Gilead," he supplied.

The voice on the other end was bright, enthusiastic, from what I could hear, and Ma's face relaxed. The rest of the conversation on her end was a string of affirmative noises: "Uh-huh, yeah, sure, great. Thanks so much, I don't know what all I'd do otherwise." But when she hung up her expression was a bit grim.

"There's a vending machine if you want something to tide you over, Alex," she said as she plunked down in the chair next to me. "We might have a bit of a wait."

"What are we waiting for?" I asked.

"School friend of mine, giving us a ride to town."

"She the person you thought would be keeping us company?"

"Nope. I wasn't even planning on seeing her at all while we were here."

I looked at her expectantly, but when she noticed she just shook her head.

"I'll tell you everything once we're out of here—you can't keep a secret to save your life, kid. It shows all over your face."

When Margaret-Mary—Mrs. Rue. to me—turned up to get us I was still sulking a bit over that comment, though

I'd resigned myself to waiting for an explanation. We were both sitting in the uncomfortable plastic chairs, elbows resting on our knees, Ma skimming the paper but not really reading it—she'd been open to the stocks for fifteen minutes, her eyes fixed two inches above the top edge, unfocussed and flickering with the thoughts behind them. I sat facing her in the same position, working slowly on a bag of cheddar-cheese popcorn from the vending machine, letting each kernel stick to my tongue and melt slightly before chewing. Time had turned into lead. Then car tires crunched on asphalt and Ma looked up, and I twisted around in my seat to look, too.

A big van had pulled up, one of the ones that probably should take a special license to drive but is pretty much the biggest thing you can get before you need one. I could see the shadows of kids inside, looking at us, but they didn't hop out, sat still, waiting. Ma creaked to her feet while the driver's-side door creaked open, and as she stepped outside a tall, thin woman came around the front of the van, narrow hipped and narrow chested and wearing an ankle-length denim jumper despite the heat, her salt-and-pepper hair hanging long and braided down her back, a tiny lace bonnet pinned to the top of her head, and smiling all over her face. They collided in the parking lot, hugged and rocked and kissed on both cheeks, and I came out slow, suddenly shy, maybe of the tall strange woman but probably of all the little faces peering out the tinted windows of the van. They were talking a mile a minute, back and forth and all over each other, not bothering to finish whole sentences, and while

161

Ma had been some nervous before all the tension was out of her shoulders now, like a cut rubber band. Then Mrs. Rue saw me over Ma's shoulder.

"Glory, is that Alex?"

I nodded that it was, and she took hold of me and rattled on with all the things that people who haven't seen you in a long while do: growth and how much like one or the other of your parents you look and how long it's been since they saw you, and I just smiled and nodded like an idiot because I couldn't for the life of me place this woman—which made sense when it came out that the last time she'd seen me I'd been naked except for diapers, into everything I could get my hands on, and shaved pretty much bald because of an outbreak of lice at the nursery I went to.

Close up I could see the stitching on the little gauze cap on her head, starched stiff as plastic or like it had been soaked in glue, carefully pinned in place but not serving any real purpose, as it was too sheer to keep the sun or rain off the little patch that it covered. The girls wore them, too. I got to sit in the back in the middle with them all looking but not looking at me, so I got a good chance to study them—the little hat things covered them better since they had smaller heads. The biggest was maybe eleven, the littlest chewed blocks and stared at me head on, so I guessed three or four, and I gathered from listening that the oldest three were back home still along with the youngest, who wasn't walking yet. Ma didn't have much to say—there were probably a lot of questions she didn't want to answer—so she kept asking

Mrs. Rue questions, and Mrs. Rue was more than happy to gush like a busted fire hydrant. They'd had their ups and downs, and two of the births had nearly killed her, one with pre-eclampsia and another with post-partum hemorrhage, but all had worked out for good. The younger ones got along so well and the older ones were such a help and her oldest daughter—seventeen, she was at home making dinner—was going to get married to the son of an elder in their church soon, which meant she'd have to go back to doing all the cooking and cleaning herself; the second daughter was eleven and clumsy-handed with it, but losing the help of the eldest was worth it for the grandchildren that would be coming. Life was all she'd ever wanted it to be.

The kids kept looking at me, side eyed or full on, depending on how old they were, and the little ones argued whether I was a boy or a girl. My boyness was proven in the eyes of some because I wore jeans, but my mother also wore jeans and she was most obviously not a boy because she had bosoms, though not much of them. And my hair was long like a girl's—I hadn't gotten around to asking Ma to prune it back in a while, was weighing the pros and cons of dreadlocks—and I didn't have a beard, though that could just be, the oldest daughter proposed, because I wasn't old enough to grow one yet.

I thought it might be fun to rock their world with the concept that boys could wear dresses, girls could wear pants, and it didn't actually matter what a person had going on underneath their respective clothing, but I had a sense that sort of anarchy wouldn't be tolerated by Mrs. Rue, and since we were somewhat reliant on her goodwill I decided to keep my mouth shut as much as possible.

Ma said it would be fine if Mrs. Rue just gave us a lift into town—she couldn't guess how busy a full house must get and she didn't want to foul up the routine—but it was coming up to dinnertime and Mrs. Rue insisted we stop over. We went through the town, which was small but spread out, as they talked about it, and Ma conceded to come to dinner as long as it really wasn't a bother. I could feel my soul start crying as we passed a motel, I wanted to go to ground so badly. We came out the other end and went on and on, till we turned off at a mailbox and rattled down a long gravel driveway, and we were there.

I was done by then, over-tired, over-hungry, over-peopled and just ready for a shower and a real sleep, so I don't remember much of that visit, other than feeling the agony of the seconds ticking by as though each one was being etched into my skull. They—all the kids—had chores to do, and buzzed around doing them. Ma and Mrs. Rue sat at the kitchen table, still talking but slower now, like Mrs. Rue was finally convinced that Ma wasn't going to disappear, and drinking iced peppermint tea. The oldest daughter was cooking with the second one helping her—it was a big open kitchen—and every now and then Mrs. Rue would lean so as to get them in her line of sight and remind them how or when to do something. I didn't know what to do so I sat in a corner of the kitchen with my back against the wall and carried on a one-sided conversation with the baby of the family, who was seemingly too young for a bonnet or to really be talking. None of the kids talked all that much, or if they did it wasn't loud enough for me to hear. I imagine it was like snakes: they were more scared of me than I was of them, even though there were mobs more of them. So the kid just stood there in front of my tucked-up knees, staring at me and chewing her doll's leg and no one seemed to think it was weird, or really even notice that I was there.

The kitchen smelled odd—not bad, just like a blend of spices that I'd never smelled before—and when they gave me a drink the water tasted weird too. When Mr. Rue and the two older boys came in we sat down to eat and even the food tasted funny, cooked and seasoned in an unfamiliar way and everything just a tiny bit over- or under-done because it had all been made in these massive vats like school food had to be. The adults were talking now, about life and politics and what was going on in the world, but I didn't listen because the kids—except the oldest four—were still staring at me, so I was conscious of every breath I took and how loud it was, how the food mushed as I chewed it—it was mostly pasta, cooked the American way so as to be too soft—and how hard it was to keep the stuff on the fork and get it into my mouth neatly, so I gave up halfway through even though I was still hungry, because I just couldn't stand to eat anymore with them watching me like that, and then I became conscious of the conversation at the other end of the table, and realized that, even though it would just sound like careful politeness to most people, Ma was having a really tough time keeping a lid on herself, temper or opinion, probably both. She didn't usually bother, but she seemed to have missed Mrs. Rue and, unless we wanted to walk the miles and miles back to town and then hitchhike to the mechanic's later, we had to stay on her husband's good side. So Ma kept quiet.

There wasn't any dessert, which I was thankful for, and we only lingered in our seats for about half an hour—the kids all hopped up and cleared away the dishes, leaving me alone at their end of the table while the talking went on—before the offer was made for us to stay the night. I don't know if Ma caught the panic on my face, but she refused politely a few times, then they offered to have the oldest boy take us back to town so we could stay in the motel, and I was so relieved at this that I was downright happy to be back in the van.

When we got onto the highway I could see his face reflected in the rearview mirror every time a streetlight flashed by, not stony but set firm, like he never spoke. He did answer Ma's friendly conversation, which read more like an interrogation—she'd never been good at small talk—but he answered as briefly as humanly possible, so I was pretty sure that Ma was as relieved as I was when he pulled into the parking lot of the Lazy 8 Motel and we said goodnight.

I swiped oranges from the lobby while Ma checked us in, then made a beeline for the shower once our door was unlocked. I'd expected that Ma would want a shower, too, or would at least stay up long enough to chat, but when I came out she was dead asleep on top of the blankets on one of the beds, still fully dressed. I got into the other bed, sinking into the mattress like water, decided that not even sex could feel better at that moment, and fell asleep before I'd finished the thought.

I woke up in the middle of the night—we always say middle, but it was probably closer to two a.m.—in that sudden but complete way that I sometimes do that feels like I've never slept before in my life and never will again. Ma's bed was empty, but the front door was open a crack, one of her shoes in the gap to keep it from locking her out. I peeled my socks off to keep them clean and padded out into the cool blue moonlight to stand next to her, the cement of the balcony—it was one of those motels with all the room doors on the outside and a balcony running the whole way around—rough and pebbly under my feet.

She was leaning with her elbows on the rail, also barefoot with her hair down and wild, her undershirt and jeans hanging loose on her so that I realized she'd lost weight since we left home. The dark pooled in her eye sockets and collarbones, and she dragged slowly on her cigarette and breathed out even more slowly. The darkness washed her black-and-white, so from the back she could have been mistaken for my age, the white in her hair transmuted to starlight.

I stood next to her for a bit, not saying anything, just

enjoying the cool and relative silence—cities are never silent, nor is the country, so we had a tinny mix of both kinds of sound keeping us company, the darkness a barrier between us and whoever else might be awake, giving us a bubble of muffled privacy.

"So . . . How do you know Margaret-Mary?" I asked. And for once in my life, Ma gave me the answer that I wanted the first time that I asked for it.

CHAPTER XIV

Ma met Margaret-Mary when she was called Mags, studied biology and gave herself bad perms in the bathroom of the freshman women's dorm. She'd grown up in Nevada with very Catholic but very accepting parents, come back east to go to school, and liked girls about as much as she liked boys, but she kept that last fact under her hat pretty well until she knew that it was safe to mention it. She had short hair and dressed like Annie Hall and her favorite thing to do was kiss, though she didn't go any farther than that with anyone because it would make the angels cry. She was a wide-eyed freshman the fall my mother came back from Michigan, and she was looked after for a year by Laura and Ma and the women they hung out with. Mags wasn't a fool— she could handle herself in most rough situations—but she couldn't take care of herself in the "*Remember-to-eat-and-take-breaks-sometimes,-please,-for-the-love-of-good-sense,-Mags*" way.

Then her dad died in a car accident.

She went home for the funeral, came back and tried to get on with work, and a few months later her mom kicked it, too. She had an older sister who handled the legal part of things, so all Mags had to do was handle herself, but she couldn't quite manage that. They all tried to help her out, but there was only so much that they could do, so when she started going to church again they were relieved, because it meant that they weren't the only people looking out for her. Even though she suddenly stopped talking to her then-girlfriend—who she'd gone much farther with than the minimum distance required to make the angels cry—they hoped church was helping, hoped that with enough church and crying and time she would find her feet and find a new normal.

It was only in retrospect that they could track the downward trajectory: Mass on Sunday became Mass and confession, then Mass, confession and Wednesday prayer meeting, which was when she cut her girlfriend out of the picture. Then morning Mass every day, and Bible studies and reading on her own, and it made sense because she'd grown up Catholic, all the religion was familiar and comforting, and making it to paradise was her only chance to see her parents again. Then, suddenly, Catholicism was not enough: Mary worship was idolatry, confession a replacement for Christ's forgiveness; she had been wrong her whole life. The Catholics she knew were a bit stung by this, but they didn't say anything; they were still hoping for a happy ending. No one knew that she'd stopped doing the assigned readings, stopped going to class, stopped sitting tests, stopped writing papers, stopped thinking about anything but death and God.

Mags started going to a different church, began wearing long skirts and covering her hair, and though she wouldn't talk to them anymore they kept tabs on her as best they could, worried that she'd do something really stupid. They'd half expected her to become a nun.

Mr. Rue was touring churches, talking about the missionary work he managed—he didn't go into the field himself, but sent people out and made sure they had a place to stay, the supplies and connections they needed. She fell for him like a house under the wrecking ball, and when he went home to Texas she went with him.

After a few days of not seeing Mags leave her room her girlfriend went to the church, asked the right questions until a secretary told her that Mags had gotten engaged to a man of God and gone home with him to be married in the company of his people. They broke into her room that night, had enough of a rummage to determine that the important things—her Bible, her ID, the pictures of her parents that she stuck in the edge of her mirror frame—were missing. There was crying and wine, and talk of an intervention.

It was some months, though, before they managed, by saving a lot of their weed and movie budget and selling booze to underclassmen at a drastic markup, to get the cash together, to cram into my mother's car and take the tediously long drive down to Texas. They didn't have much time—it was spring break—and finding Margaret-Mary wasn't easy. She wouldn't talk to her girlfriend, at first wouldn't talk to any of them as she'd been warned that her old life would try and call her back, that she would need to resist the temptations and the wiles of the evil one. Margaret-Mary was already pregnant with her first child—a son who had grown up and run away by the time we showed up, and so was not mentioned when we were introduced to them—and when they asked if she was happy she said that she was dying to self in hope of eternal life. Which didn't sound like happy, but her husband didn't hit her, even if he wouldn't let her work outside the house or read anything that wasn't about God, or wear trousers, or, the women suspected, say no to him about anything, so there wasn't much they could do. It wasn't nice, but they couldn't find any definitive signs of cyanide in the Kool-Aid, so to speak, so they gave her copies of their phone numbers and home addresses, just in case, and left her where she insisted that she wanted to be left.

Ma was a letter writer, though, and she started that summer by asking for pregnancy news and trading memories about growing up Catholic, and Margaret-Mary was happy to share—even with the company of church women twice a week, they lived outside of town and she got lonely at home with no one but an infant for company. She shared a lot about her husband's church and its philosophies on marriage and childrearing, and though a lot of what she said left a bad taste in Ma's mouth she kept up the correspondence, trying to judge if Margaret-Mary was safe and happy across hundreds of miles. She hadn't worried about the kids as much— they were being raised to it, they had never known any other life—in her view it was Margaret-Mary who was stuck, who might one day want to get out. Ma didn't realize then what might happen when the kids got old enough to think for themselves, that they might decide they wanted out but wouldn't know that there was an out to want, wanted help but didn't have anyone to ask for it. Margaret-Mary knew how the world outside her community worked; she could leave if she had to. Her children did not.

When I woke up the next morning it was already closer to lunch than to sunrise, and I felt that sick, hungover way some people do when they eat too much cake too late at night. Ma was sat on the edge of her bed, wet hair straggling down her back and trying to put it up before it dried, on the phone to the mechanic's but talking quietly to keep from waking me up. Our bankroll was counted out into stacks of twenties on the night table, and I knew she'd been trying to figure out how we were going to pay for the room, the car, the rest of the distance we had to travel and whatever else she had planned. She nodded at me but stayed on the phone while I washed my face and put on my shoes, and when I mouthed "food" at her she handed me a fiver and mouthed "vending machine" back.

Going off nothing but what I could see I could have been back in Florida—same rusted balcony railing, same sad cars, same sorry part of town, but when I closed my eyes I tasted the difference in the heat and the air.

I wandered down to the lobby, nicked an orange from the bowl at reception—it didn't look like a free-breakfast type of place, but if it was I'd slept past it. I keyed in the code to get a muffin from the machine, but something went wacko and the whole column of snacks dropped, so I got a muffin and a Snickers and a honey bun, two packs of gum and a bag of Doritos. I should maybe have taken it all to the front desk, but the sign on the machine said it was an independent company, so they couldn't have put it back in anyway. So I left one of the packs of gum—cinnamon, even the smell of it made me sick—in the payout drawer, crammed my largesse into my pockets along with the change, and wandered back out.

I tried to keep casual passing the sign-in desk, but I caught sight of the little spinning carousel of postcards next to the credit-card reader. Before I realized what I was doing I had the change back out and I was asking the bored dude behind the counter if they sold stamps as well.

Daddy—

Still on the move, though coming to an end soon, I think. Stuck in Tex-ass—as you can see from the front—for a few days because of car trouble. Promise that I'll come find you just as soon as I can, no matter how long it takes. Miss you a lot and think about you all the time—Me.

PS. Promise promise promise I'll come back—if you move make sure you leave a breadcrumb trail so I can find you.

The receptionist whacked the stamp on—I hate the peel-and-stick ones, licking it was always the best part—and I dropped it in the big mailbox in the parking lot on the way back to our room. Ma was still on the phone, but when she mouthed "change?" at me I tossed her the honey bun and the pack of gum; she looked annoyed, assuming that I'd spent the money, but she ate the bun.

I waited for her to get off the phone, impatient, but when she finally did I wished that she'd stayed on for the rest of the day.

"We're going to go visit Margaret-Mary this afternoon. She's sending one of the kids over to pick us up."

"Can't I just stay here?" I asked, not daring to kick up a fuss but not quite able to keep a hint of whine out of my voice.

"That would be rude. And she wants us to stay for dinner again."

I groaned.

"It's only a few days, Alex. The car should be ready by morning after tomorrow, and then we'll be out of here. There isn't anything else to do, and I don't think she gets much adult company."

"She made her bed," I muttered and flung myself back onto my own bed.

"Life made her bed and she's laying in it the best she knows how. We'll be out of here before you know it and your bellyaching and dragging your feet isn't going to make that happen any faster, or make the interim any less painful." She stood up. "I'm going to go lay in some groceries for breakfasts and lunches—you should be thankful that we're getting hot dinners 'cause God knows when we'll be able to afford them on the regular again. Come along or stay here as you want to, but when that van drives up you *are* getting your ass into it and you *will* be in a good mood while you do it, is that clear?"

I nodded sullenly, then went and stood in the shower and let the hot water roll over me by the gallon while she shuffled around getting her shoes and keys and things. When the door slammed behind her I relaxed so much I almost fell over. I'd been feeling the grate of constant company like sand against my nerves, and the emptiness of the motel room hit me with force in that moment. And then all of the dirty thoughts that I had been ignoring since Florida out of paranoia that my mother could read my mind hit me as well.

I wanted to take my time with it and really luxuriate in the feeling, but I was so worked up I finished within a minute of beginning, and felt so disappointed that for a moment I almost apologized to myself. But the buzz came back quick, and the second time lasted longer, and by the end of the third round I'd more or less forgiven myself for my lackluster initial performance. Then came another obscenely long shower, then clean clothes and a book on the bed in the room that I had all to myself, but even after sleeping through most of the morning I only got a page or two in before the sound of the door opening woke me up, and I realized that I'd dropped the book off the bed and passed out mid-scene.

The nap hadn't really improved my outlook on life— sleeping during the day usually leaves me disoriented, if not downright murderous—but Ma wasn't putting up with anything at the moment, so I kept my mouth shut, ate the lunch she gave me, and got back to the book I'd dropped, trying to distract myself but really waiting for the van to come for us, preoccupied with my fate and unable to think beyond it. I wondered if it would be as bad as the previous evening.

The eldest daughter picked us up, and I got the idea that this was a rare treat for her, getting the privacy of an entire car for the whole drive out from the farm, and being away from work and siblings for so long. She was solid where her mother was slim, and even though she was seventeen the denim jumper she wore and her hair pulled back so cleanly and left so long made her look about twelve years old; she apologized for her mother not fetching us herself, which didn't bother me a jot. This specimen of Margaret-Mary's progeny was much more talkative than her older brother; she was still reluctant by normal standards, but compared to the other kids she was positively garrulous. I couldn't hear much, being in the back seat with the windows open, and I only half paid attention half of the time, but I caught snatches of what she said. Her name was Anna-Maria; her father didn't like that she was named after the Virgin, but her mother had been insistent. She was the one that was getting married in a few weeks.

I knew Ma was digging for information, but she was doing it carefully. She seemed to relax a bit with the description of the happy family life that Anna-Maria described, though I knew that the investigation was far from over. To keep it from seeming like an inquisition—which I pretty much knew it was, even if we were all pretending otherwise—she told a few stories about how she and Margaret-Mary knew each other, little vignettes from their college days, from which she adeptly edited out all of the lesbianism, drinking, and drug use.

This visit was better and worse than I had expected. I spent the first hour on the couch next to Ma, trying to see faces in the patterns of the paper on the opposite wall. The second hour was spent following two of the younger boys around the property to look at their goats and chickens and the pig destined to become next year's dinners, and the third hour crouched in the kitchen again, engaging the baby in deep philosophical conversation while Ma and Mrs. Rue drank herbal tea and Anna-Maria made dinner. I wasn't sure if Mr. Rue was displeased to have us gracing his table again so soon, or if he was just always grim and standoffish, but this time I could see Ma biting her tongue as he talked about politics, and joked about Mrs. Rue's housekeeping habits, and discussed plans for Anna's upcoming wedding. Mr. Rue was very proud of having brokered that. He'd been born and raised in the religious community, had never lived outside the Great State of Texas, and having married someone with such a wild past—even someone that had fully repented, been baptized and turned from worldly ways—had set him back a bit in the eyes of the church members, so the wedding was a coup for him. As for Anna, she couldn't have done better if Christ himself had come down and slipped a ring onto her finger.

I, of course, said nothing, and the kids said nothing

178

to me. When it came time for us to be taken back to the motel Mr. Rue pumped Ma's hand enthusiastically, and the silent boy from the night before took the wheel. I could tell that Anna-Maria wanted to be the one to drive us, but there were chores to be done, so her brother was selected to do the honors. Ma had given up on drawing him out of himself by then and the trip was made in a silence as complete as a body ever gets in an aging van on uneven roads.

The silence bled into the motel room; I had expected to debrief a bit before bed, at least hear an emphatic word or two from Ma on the subject of Mr. Rue, but she was quiet through teeth brushing and pajama changing.

"Has it panned out yet?" I asked her.

"Not yet," she said. "Ask me again day after tomorrow."

Again I woke at two a.m., and again I stood beside her in the pale moonlight, but this time we didn't speak. She was capital-T Thinking. I watched her turn a cigarette to ash, and then a second one, then she went back to the room. Whatever it was that was keeping her up, I'd find out when she was ready, or when she couldn't hold it in any longer. The thought that we only had one more day in that goddamned town comforted me to sleep.

Our last day in Gilead was much like the first, except with the added tension of imminent movement, the pull that migratory birds must feel in the hours before they fly. I was hanging with every nerve on the idea that tomorrow we would leave. In the moment before chance stranded us I had wanted nothing more than a shower and a bed and a little bit of a rest; now I wanted nothing more than to go, to move, to feel the ribbon of miles sliding below me as we closed the distance between ourselves and the mysterious something that my mother was so set upon and yet so casual about reaching.

It's funny how want changes that way.

Again, at a bit past two in the afternoon, the eldest daughter came to pick us up. Her smile looked plastered on, like badly done fresco that was moments away from peeling off the surface on which it was painted. She made friendly conversation to Ma on the drive, but her tone was too bright, and Ma responded by loosening, softening, trying to put her at ease. Something had changed in the dynamic between them, though she had spent too little time with us for there to be a usual dynamic. I felt like we had sat with her, made this trip with her, over and over, that the brittleness of the conversation was the exception, rather than as equal a candidate for the rule as the ride the day before. Something was going on and I didn't know what.

On this visit I utterly gave up. During the couch-sitting portion I catnapped against the deep cushions and over dinner I kept my head down, feeling something wound tight in my chest and ready to snap at any moment. Ma's tactfulness continued throughout the evening, which surprised me a little: I had half expected her, the moment that she no longer had to be perfectly polite, to tell them all exactly what she thought of their way of life and the behavior and attitude of Mrs. Rue's overbearing husband. If anything, she was even more agreeable, more polite, than she had been on the previous two nights. If I hadn't known better I would have worried that some degree of brainwashing had gone on, behind my back or right in front of me, and I was about to see my mother convert, get married and settle down, pattern her future after Margaret-Mary. Maybe they'd put something in the water they were giving us. It was a ridiculous thought, but I was still very much relieved when we were dropped off at the motel for our last night in town.

I woke up several times before morning—once during Ma's two a.m. smoke, and at least two more times in the small hours. The last time I heard birdsong, and saw a paling in the ink-dark sky, and gave up on sleep. When Ma came to I was sitting on the edge of my carefully made bed, my backpack neatly filled and zipped closed at my feet, hair damp from the shower, stomach thrilling with nerves. We were getting the hell out of here.

"Alex, the auto shop doesn't open for another two hours," she groaned, and jammed her face into the pillow.

"Breakfast first? There's a diner across the highway that does all the greasies and coffee for three dollar sixty."

"Right. Before you get in the car? In this heat?"

"They probably do fruit and pancakes and stuff, too . . ."

She had fallen back asleep.

I wanted to read but I didn't resurrect my book, hoping that at any moment she would get up and we would be off. When she finally did rise she took her time, showered and braided her hair, easing into the morning like you'd ease into a new jacket with a languor that made me want to scream.

She indulged me with breakfast, but I quickly wished that she hadn't: I wolfed mine down and then sat while she cut her banana pancakes into small squares, forked them up one at a time, chewed each one slowly with thousand-yard-stare pauses in between. When she put down her fork next to the empty plate and smiled at the waitress I tensed to go, but instead of asking for the check she got another cup of coffee, sugared and stirred it, then set it down. She dug in her pocket then and I hoped she was going for her wallet, but instead she pulled out the cellphone, snapped the back off, slid the flat oblong of battery out of it and dropped it in her shirt pocket, then snapped the back of the phone into place and put it back in her hip pocket, picked up the cup of coffee and blew gently across its surface.

"Whatcha do that for?" I asked.

"I don't want us to be trackable," she answered.

"Who would track us?" I asked.

She didn't answer, sipped at the cup of coffee, stared into space with a placidity that gave no indication that she ever intended to move from that spot again. Annoyed, I remembered all the times that she'd been the one in a hurry and I wanted to slow down, to stay put, and it galled me that she always set the tempo, that what she thought was important took precedence just because she was the parent, the adult. So I was in quite a short temper when she finally got up and paid the bill, closer to lunch than to breakfast time.

I had thought that she'd arranged a ride, that the guy with the tow truck would come fetch us or, at worst, Margaret-Mary and her caravan of kids would give us one last lift and the two of them would have the opportunity to cry on each other's necks saying goodbye outside the mechanic's. Instead we walked north to the city limits, stopped by the *Welcome!* sign, and she stuck out her thumb.

"Is this really a great idea?" I asked.

"You thought it was when you were trying to get back from 'Bama before I knew you were gone," she sniped. "Are you in some kind of hurry, chickadee?"

"I guess not really. I just don't want to be here anymore."

"If you can't be in the here and now, then where can you be?"

I didn't get to answer before a woman in a pickup pulled over and we had to hustle to get in. I was annoyed enough to sit in the truck bed, and she was annoyed enough to let me, so they got to make friendly in private until we hit the mechanic's.

I tagged along behind as she looked at the station wagon that had been fixed up for us, kicked the tires and listened to the engine, and while she hemmed and hawed

I thought for a moment that it wasn't happening, that we were stuck out there until she found a car she liked at which point the money would have run out and she'd have to take a job to get the cash to buy it—but then she had her backpack off, her plastic bag out, and was counting out a big mass of our bankroll. As relieved as I was to see the money change hands, I felt a flutter of worry at the size of the wad that she put back into her backpack.

The mechanic was kind enough to help us transfer our boxes and bags to the back of the new car, and as we stuffed them in I kept my eye open for the gun, the cigar box, anything I might want to get a closer look at, but Ma kept an eye on me, so I had no opportunity for snooping.

I put my feet up on the dash and we rolled out of there. The weight lifted from my chest, and as we rolled through town on our way out the other side I could concede that it wasn't that bad of a place, for what it was.

Then, a few miles out of town we turned off the highway, and the weight dropped back into place.

"I thought we were getting on," I said.

"We are, in a bit."

"But this is—"

"I know it. We just have one more thing to do."

I sat in stony silence, feeling my resentment build—until I saw Anna-Maria waiting for us at the end of her driveway. Ma barely slowed enough for her to get the door open and roll into the back seat, hitting the accelerator while the door was still yawning on its hinges.

"You changed your mind," Anna-Maria said in quiet disbelief.

"That I did," Ma answered.

CHAPTER XV

The first ten miles or so getting away from Gilead Anna-Maria lay across the floor in the back. I offered her water, apples, granola. She said, "I'm fine, thank you," kept her eyes on the ceiling and her breath half held, arms crossed and body stiffish like she was laying on the examination table waiting for a doctor she didn't really trust to come in and get on with things. I wasn't sure what was happening until Ma pulled over in the middle of nowhere and pulled a set of her own clothes out of her backpack. Anna-Maria wiggled into them in the tight space of the back seat, sliding the jeans on under her skirt and maneuvering the shirt on carefully. She had to turn up the ankles and the sleeves, but once she'd changed she looked like a normal kid, albeit a normal kid from a family so broke they only shopped in the dollar-a-pound Goodwill. Her hands hesitated over her hair, and you could see it in her face how much she didn't want to, but it was only a moment before she unpinned her cheesecloth cap and crushed it in her fist, like a handful of flower petals.

"Hop on up here, Annie," Ma said, gently. "It's a bench seat for a reason."

She slid into the middle and snapped the lap belt around her waist, and we glided back onto the road. In the moment she didn't seem much in the mood for talking, and Ma didn't push her, though we both noticed, and noticed each other noticing, the way that she looked at the road signs, the mile markers.

"The hard part is over now," Ma said, and I knew that even though it was just a senseless platitude meant to make the girl feel better, she was lying. The hard part was coming, would keep coming for the rest of her life.

I gleaned the whole of Anna-Maria's story—rechristened Annie by my mother—in pieces, some on the ride away from her family with the three of us sharing the front seat and the popcorn and the radio dials, some from Ma later in our journey.

Margaret-Mary home-schooled her kids, so when Annie blazed through the textbooks she was given her mother simply handed her the next one, kept an eye on her but mostly let her do her own thing. This worked just fine for all involved until Annie was fourteen, at which point she finished twelfth grade, which left her parents with the awkward problem of what to do with her, since state law said she had to have three more years of education, but there was no more education to give her short of college. Her parents had assumed that, like most of the girls in their community, she would get married as soon as she finished high school, but they had to admit that fourteen was simply too young. The easiest workaround was that she spent the day at the public library, an approved reading list in hand, and took the state-mandated tests once a year with her brothers and sisters to prove that they were keeping up with the standards of the public school.

The reading list she finished in weeks, so the reference librarian, who figured the list to be a mite scant on the sciences, taught her how to use the free dial-up, let her sit in the back room looking up chemistry simulations and calculus tutorials, but it wasn't long before she was using it to explore another world, a world where girls didn't necessarily end their education with high school, didn't necessarily have babies, didn't necessarily love men, or marry men, or have the men that they married chosen for them. Where some people never married at all. She didn't want to be done with school; she wanted to learn more for the sake of learning, the way a person generally eats cake for the sake of eating cake rather than for its nutritional value. She began planning then.

Some parts were simple: when she turned seventeen her father wrote out her transcript and gave it to her to send in to the Board of Education so that she could get her high-school diploma, and it was easy to make a photocopy for her own purposes. The SATs were more difficult—they were long and cost money, and the results had to be mailed to your house. She took the test on a weekday when she was supposed to be at the library, counted the days and picked up the mail at the post office until the results came. That didn't go entirely according to plan. Her mother saw the envelope, asked why the ETS was writing to her, but seemed satisfied with the answer that they knew she had just finished high school and were reminding her to register to take the test in time to apply to go to college in the fall—something that she had no business doing, she well knew. The applications she wrote at the library, and the librarians furnished the letters of recommendation. When the acceptance letters finally came she intercepted them in the same way she had the test scores.

Modesty and submission were the watchwords of daughter-raising, so she knew few young women with sharp tongues and sharp minds, who knew who they were and what they were doing and weren't crushed even though they bent under the weighty authority of those above them—which her mother had taught her was everyone, because the meek shall inherit the earth. Pushing back directly, telling her parents what she desired, didn't occur to her.

She had thought that she would have time to consider, to weigh, to decide whether a few more years of books were worth the effort of securing them, and how she might practically do that. But then, unexpectedly, the betrothal had come. She'd known the young man from church—by sight at least; mixing between the sexes wasn't particularly encouraged—but once the parents had decided on the pairing they were formally introduced. He was polite, kind to her, and for a while she considered giving up on the idea of going off, of resisting the future that God had so clearly arranged for her, possibly more out of inertia than desire. The world was strange and terrifying and Zacharias Habishaw, who

189

was an elder's son with a bright future as a leader in the church and manager of a local supermarket, seemed like he would make a kind husband, and she thought that she could be content with a few children and a house of her own to run the way she wanted. It wouldn't be quite the same as running her mother's kitchen and taking care of her brothers and sisters; there would probably be time for reading in the slack moments, maybe he would even get her a computer of her own, let her start a home business selling eggs or making clothes or writing workbooks for home-schooling Christian families the way many of the women they knew did.

The date for the wedding was set, and some of the parameters for their interactions were relaxed. When they were first introduced she and Zacharias had only spoken in the presence of their parents, were allowed a weekly phone call of thirty minutes with Anna-Maria's father on the line to ensure the conversation remained godly. Now they were given a little privacy at social gatherings, allowed to step away from the group so long as they remained clearly in sight and behaved themselves; her father's presence on the phone line was eliminated, frequent letters encouraged with the promise that they would not be opened or read by anyone else.

They began a regular Bible study together, conferred over the phone and, when possible, in person; this was partly at the suggestion of their parents, partly due to their own initiative, as they felt the need to get past the awkwardness of getting to know each other as quickly as possible but didn't quite seem able to—there is only so much talking about daily life one can do when one's daily life is completely repetitive, and Anna-Maria of course thought it unwise to bring up her forays to the library and how she spent her time there. She loved the Bible study—he seemed surprised at her willingness to argue with him, her knowledge of the permitted secondary texts, her ease and familiarity with the material, and if their relationship had been limited to theological debate she could have been very happy being married to him.

But Zacharias had standards. He took the opportunity provided by the Bible study and their increased communication to educate her as to the manner in which he expected his wife to behave. He was nearly twenty-three, and had had ample time to work out what that would best involve. He did not approve of inviting the outside world into his house to poison his children's minds: no television, no radio, certainly no computer. He expected her to be industrious, to keep the house clean and the children obedient, to keep a garden and preserve enough food for the off-season, to bake her own bread and sew their clothes and never contradict him, not even in private—the Bible studies were the exception to the latter rule, and he was appreciative of her fervency in that area.

All of those guidelines she could accept—it was, with the exception of the bread (they used a stand mixer; Zacharias said that hand-kneaded tasted better and allowing a machine to do her work for her was a sign of inherent slothfulness) and the sewing (they made their own jumpers, but most of the rest of their clothing they bought mail-order) quite similar to the life that her mother led, that she herself had so far essentially led, as she had moved from being her mother's little helper to the primary cook and jumper maker. She wanted to stay near her family, to remain in the church and live by its mandates—not a feasible task for a single woman unless she remained in her parents' house, which would be taken to mean that they had raised her badly, that no one would concede to marry her—so she viewed the impending wedding as a business arrangement, that would provide materially and, she hoped, intellectually for them both. She put her acceptance letters away and looked forward to being in charge of her own kitchen, to looking after her own children, and was thankful that she hadn't taken the misstep, yielded to temptation, broken her parents' hearts in the way her older brother had. She nearly burned the bundle—transcripts, SAT scores, five acceptance letters and a few scholarship offers that she hadn't expected and had rescued from the kitchen trash where they had been tossed, unopened, her father assuming that they were asking her to apply—but at the last minute she decided to keep them. They were a vanity, but she wanted to have something to remind herself that she was as smart as any boy.

Then Zacharias had dropped the figurative bomb. Or bombs, as it were. There were two, the first mentioned casually, in an offhand manner, the second developed at painful length. He thought that it was a given, clearly, or else he would have made an issue of it at the outset: he had heard that she spent an excessive amount of time in the library, presumably reading, and while that was a perfectly healthy activity for a young girl, provided the material was appropriate, now that she was an adult he expected her to put childish things aside, to paraphrase St. Paul. Only godly books would enter his house, edifying, informative books, books that spoke truth and truth alone. He would, of course, need to approve them beforehand; she was intelligent for a female but unfamiliar with the temptations of the world, and he was worried that she would pollute herself with false doctrine, or else devote time to frivolous distractions and let the keeping of the house and children fall to the wayside. She did not like the sound of that—a diet of theology alone she thought she could stomach, but what was theology without discourse, and what was discourse when only one opinion was represented?

Then he sent her some of his approved books, and her heart sank even lower: pre-digested pap. There was nothing to puzzle out or come to grips with, they just told her straight up what to think, how to behave. Even the scripture references were watered down, presented in colloquial English, with no context given, let alone translation notes. And, too, there was this issue of having the volume of her consumption limited. While it annoyed her that he assumed that she did not know how to manage her time and her work effectively, she supposed that this was because he did not yet know her. The marriage manuals her church favored recommended that husbands set their wives daily tasks as part of their role as the head of the house, which had never been very successful in her own home as her father was generally fuzzy on the daily running of the place, but she'd heard it was quite popular in other homes in the community, so she guessed that he'd come from a house of that sort. He would hopefully see how silly it was for him to write her chore lists once he learned that she could manage quite well without his direction, but she could not be sure that he would not continue to restrict how much she read even after he discovered that she was competent to manage her time and her duties. And while she considered whether this—such little problems, such selfish hesitations—were reason enough to ask to have the engagement broken, or at least reconsidered, the other bomb dropped.

They were at the beginning of one of their Bible study sessions by telephone, just through the pleasantries, and she was about to attack the reading from that day, when he interjected:

"God has told me that we should talk first, for a bit, about spousal obedience."

It had taken a moment for her brain to change tracks, but when it did, she said of course she would be obedient. It was in the vows, after all. Now, to get back to what St. John seemed to be getting at—

"Not like that, Anna-Maria, I mean *obedience*. Do you understand?"

"I can't really say that I do, if you mean for the added emphasis to indicate that you're using the word to imply other than the meaning given as its standard definition and implied in the marriage vows." The delay to their discussion, which she had been looking forward to, was beginning to irritate her.

"Oh, I very much mean obedience as defined by the marriage vows. In fact, one might say that the marriage contract exists solely to sanctify this . . . obedience."

She didn't quite understand, yet.

"Turn for me, for just a moment, to Paul's first letter to the church at Corinth, chapter seven."

That was something he did that annoyed her—gave the entire description of a book instead of using the colloquial name, "First Corinthians," as though he were in the pulpit and she in the pew. She paged through her Bible to the book.

"Verses three through five, read it just to yourself."

The husband must fulfill his duty to his wife, and likewise also the wife to her husband. The wife does not have authority over her own body, but the husband does; and likewise also the husband does not have authority over his own body, but the wife does. Stop depriving one another, except by agreement for a time, so that you may devote yourselves to prayer, and come together again so that Satan will not tempt you because of your lack of self-control.

She had read the passage before, of course, but hadn't really paid attention. She was mulling it over when he spoke again.

"Obedience makes for a peaceful house. And who would know better what will make us happy as a family than St. Paul?"

She didn't answer, but felt coldness in the pit of her stomach.

"It may be a bit improper to speak of it before we are married, but I did not want to take you by surprise. I will tolerate no arguments in this matter."

She could tell that he was uncomfortable now, but still she did not speak.

He cleared his throat. "At first, since we will be still getting to . . . Know . . . each other, I will expect your obedience daily. After some time, when we are more comfortable with each other, more familiar, that frequency may increase. Of course, I will observe all of the guidelines when you are with child and following birth."

She still did not answer.

"It is for our own well-being."

"I understand." She was surprised that her voice did not crack.

"I apologize for embarrassing you, but I felt that it was an important matter. I want you to ready yourself, for when we are married." He cleared his throat. "Now, on to John."

She had only engaged with the most superficial part of her mind for the rest of the conversation; the deeper, more essential part was preoccupied with the horror and confusion and deep discomfort that she felt in response to what he had said.

When she told Ma and me that part of the story we were sitting three abreast, drinking Coke and passing popcorn at a rest stop while torrential rain rattled down,

196

waiting for it to clear enough for Ma to be able to make out the striping on the road. I came out with some choice words for Zacharias, but Annie shook her head.

"He is a product of his environment, and even so he would have made a better husband, I think, than many men I know. Knew. We could have had a truly enjoyable relationship, if we hadn't been married to each other. He was kind."

"'Kind—' that's exactly the word I'd use to describe someone who thought it was his duty to control everything I did," I said.

"He respected me, and that's more than many of them would have. He let me have opinions."

She didn't know much about sex—she understood the biological aspect of conception, but the mechanics had not been adequately explained. Not that they needed to be for her to know how she felt about it: she was horrified at the idea of letting him do that to her, not once but repeatedly, for the rest of her life. She had no romantic feelings for Zacharias, knew that she never would, suspected that she may never have them for anyone. If she broke their betrothal she would be married to someone else sooner or later, possibly someone with stricter views, who she found less tolerable. This was what made her finally decide that she had to get out.

First, she prayed for deliverance, with the same calm persistence that she'd prayed for her mother to survive the birth of the younger sister who had come with a dose of pre-eclampsia and months of forced bed rest. Then, she considered: she could theoretically take her birth certificate and driver's license and walk away, get a job bagging groceries and start her life over, except she knew she didn't have the skills or resources to do so, and since she wasn't yet eighteen the police, if they found her, would return her to her parents. So then, what resources did she have? The acceptance letters—a place to go for a few years, a means to make up for the skills she lacked—and the brother that had run away from home five years before.

When she had time in the house alone she hunted. Her mother had secrets, kept little things from her father, and even though he had forbidden them to speak to or speak of her brother she hoped that in this case the water of the womb would prove to be thicker than the blood of the covenant. Even so, finding her brother's emails, buried in the account that her mother used for ordering textbooks and dress shirts and parts for the stand mixer, was an accident. As was finding the emails that Ma had written as well, when email started becoming as reliable as letters. At first she was confused by these, then enthralled, shamelessly read them all with the raptness with which she always approached the written word; when she recognized the veiled offerings of assistance for what they were, she realized that her finding the messages was by divine appointment. God had shown her where to go and who would get her there.

I took issue with her thinking on a whole bunch of levels, but Ma gave me the look that said "drop it," so I kept my mouth shut.

She got in touch with her brother first, explained about

her impending wedding and her need to run away. He had done well for himself, lived in a shared apartment in Utah, worked for an insurance company during the day and went to school at night, and he promised that he'd help her any way he could, she just needed to get to him.

Ma had been a little more difficult. Anna-Maria's email had come while we were in Florida. All she needed was for someone to get her out of Texas; if she were dropped by the side of the road in New Mexico she would be eternally grateful. Even with the frank descriptions of the girl's situation Ma was understandably hesitant about kidnapping—because, legally, that's what it was—her friend's daughter, had eventually agreed to meet Anna-Maria and give her a chance to be convincing in person, possibly drop in on her parents and assess the situation at home, but made no promises.

What had happened to our front wheel, Anna-Maria said, had been an act of God: three days around Mr. Rue had more than convinced Ma that there was no point in arguing him out of marrying his daughter off; seeing how it was that Anna-Maria's mother lived convinced her that she couldn't allow the girl to unwillingly share that fate. And that was how we came to have a refugee from Gilead, Texas, riding shotgun between me and Ma, glancing over her shoulder every so often but mostly keeping her eyes straight ahead, except for when she tipped her head back to drop gummy worms into her open mouth.

I made bets with myself that she'd crack, take off in

the middle of the night or just walk out on us in broad daylight and hitch her way back, but she didn't. It doesn't matter that what probably drove her to stay with us, what drove her onward, was fear of what would happen if she did go back; her courage was in facing her fear of the unknown world.

CHAPTER XVI

We could have got to Utah in two or three days of steady driving, but Ma didn't want to take any chances. She'd not written the book on how to disappear forever and never be found, but she'd read it plenty of times. Task one was simple: play the waiting game. Annie was only a few weeks shy of eighteen, and when she got there no one could force her to go home, so we dropped off the grid for a bit.

Annie wouldn't cut her hair but Ma dyed it in a rest stop bathroom in Wichita Falls at two in the morning on our first night out of Gilead, and with ripped jeans and a pair of amber-tinted aviators and a paisley-print bandana instead of her white cap covering her hair she looked like any other countrified teenage girl with questionable fashion sense. Even so we stayed away from people, didn't act cagy but avoided busy places, prime business hours, and to me it felt like the beginning again, like we were once more truly on the run. Ma didn't say anything at first, and I didn't say anything because I didn't know what to say, and Annie didn't probably because she was terrified and didn't know how to talk to normal people.

Ma had told Margaret-Mary that we were headed to Nevada when she asked, and after laying tracks north until we hit the border and Ma went in the trunk and dug out the other set of license plates, the not-really-legal ones we'd been given when we bought the car in West Virginia, the ones registered to an old woman too blind to drive. We doubled back with those plates on and struck out west—now that she was helping, Ma wasn't about to half-ass it, but she wanted to stay as much on the right side of the law as she could, and transporting a runaway minor across state lines for any purpose was right out; she knew from her parents' shady past that state lines, state cops, state sovereignty and the differences in states' laws could be used to a person's advantage.

We stocked up on field rations from an army surplus and instant coffee and drums of water and went looking for no man's land, some place to hide right in the open until we could get back to life as usual. We drove until we nearly ran out of country, stopping within a stone's throw of the Rio Grande. It was national parkland, and there was heaps of it, stretching far enough in desert and mountain that I felt like we could never be found.

And there we sat for five weeks.

There were official campsites, so we bought our permit, parked our car, and pitched our tent, and as far as anyone was concerned we were on a perfectly innocent family camping trip.

It should have been dull as hell, hanging out in the middle of nowhere, moving every few days to a new campsite within the park, just in case. At first Annie was quiet, "processing" as Ma put it, and Ma had even less to say than usual. Then the waiting started getting boring, and Annie started getting comfortable around us, and we all calmed down a bit because it's impossible to stay that keyed up for long even if you are convinced that the police have the dogs and the choppers out combing the country for you, and I realized that I should have enjoyed their silent phase while it lasted. I tried talking to Annie a bit to bring her out of herself, but every conversation turned into a debate, and you couldn't debate Annie. It didn't matter if she was right or not, or even if she thought she was right or not, she'd still win. And then I'd feel stupid and cranky, and then feel juvenile because I felt cranky and wanted to pitch a fit. I figured with all of those brothers and sisters she would have been taught the edict of "let the younger ones win sometimes."

There was only one time that Ma stepped in: like her brothers and sisters, Annie was curious as to what I was.

"I'm a human-fucking-being. I just so happen to be doing less of the fucking than I'd personally prefer." I'd thrown in the gratuitous profanity in the hope of shocking her enough to drop the question, but she was relentless.

"You have to have a biological sex—everyone does. It's part of being a 'human-effing-being' as you put it."

"Sex I may have, but what it is or isn't is nobody's business but mine." I'd been, as always, fastidious about doing my dressing, undressing, and other personal business well out of sight of everyone. "And gender I do not, and that's the long and short of it."

"Everyone has a gender," she said.

"Well, Alex doesn't," Ma cut in, her voice hard-edged. "And there is nothing wrong with that. And that is the end of this conversation."

We all retreated to our own corners after, but I had the distinct feeling that I was the only one that felt ruffled, angry and powerless.

Annie didn't turn everything into an argument when she talked with Ma, though, and it wasn't long after they got into the habit of chatting with each other that I felt something awful creeping up inside me, that made tears squeeze out of my eyes when I thought too hard about it and no one was looking. Ma loved me, but she preferred Annie. Didn't matter to me that I was her kid, that Annie wasn't long for our company, that I was fifteen and she was nearly eighteen and probably some kind of genius besides, that Ma had no other source of adult conversation and I didn't count because I still didn't dare disagree with her. Ma liked talking to Annie, and Annie liked talking to Ma, and that left me out in the cold, and feeling about five years old. I'd never been jealous of Ma's friends before, but she'd never had a friend that was so young, that I viewed as more my peer than hers.

Good thing we were out in the nowhere lands, or else I may have lost it. We could have been on a boat, with me stuck close to them every moment.

At first light I wandered out—Ma shouting after about

snakes and scorpions and flash floods, sum total of our standard morning conversation—and left them to their reading and their talking. It was and was not like the mountain I had known when we first set out. This landscape was steeper, scrubbier, the land more bone than flesh, more rock than earth. At first I thought the whole place just looked dead, kaput. But the arid land had a dusty, painted beauty of its own, and it crept into my bones as I grew familiar with the trails and overlooks and the clear bareness of it all. As much as I loved it, it did not cease to be an alien landscape, familiar only in that I'd seen it on TV, read about it in books; we could as well have been on the moon. And I missed green. I craved verdancy. I still wanted to go home.

Every morning I went walking, if only to avoid their intellectual romance, and every afternoon I meandered back. At Ma's suggestion, Annie dragged me through the schoolbooks we had—it was not as painful as I thought it would be, and she was patient, and kind about my mistakes, so that I could not help but like her teacher self. And in the evenings my mythic desire was satisfied, the one I'd had when we first left home and Ma told me a story for the first time: after dinner, as the darkness began to fall, we built up the fire, lounged around it thinking and watching the stars come out, and when she wanted to Ma would break the night sounds, not so much tell us a story but remember for us a bit of life-before-my-father. And sometimes, if I felt like it, I would recite poetry. They'd been big on us learning poetry in grade school and I had a mind like a bucket for rote memorization; I could do a lot of Frost, and heaps of the Romantics, and bunches of dirty ones that I'd found by myself, but mostly I said the ones that made something in me thrum, the ones I'd learned on my own more recently because I wanted to be able to keep them with me, if we left suddenly and abandoned the things that we'd picked up on the way. I told my mother that she was the bread and the knife, told the sky that I was myself three selves at least, and in those moments I felt that I was at least Annie's equal.

On the twenty-first of July, the day she turned eighteen, Annie was awake before both of us, standing at the edge of the campsite, watching the sky like she was about to go before a firing squad. Ma had a cake for us to have for breakfast, Lord knows where she got it, and Annie perked up some at that. Then Ma put the battery back into her cellphone—I remembered then the moment in the diner, realized that that was the moment that she'd made up her mind about kidnapping Anna-Maria—and handed it over.

"Call whoever you need to, there's a lot of credit on there."

Annie looked blank for a moment, then took the phone out of hearing and tentatively dialed a number.

"Who's she calling?" I asked.

"Her brother, I'm guessing. She didn't want him to know where she was until today, so he wouldn't have to lie if his parents asked him. Help me get this stuff in the car. As soon as she's ready we're going to roll."

When Annie came back to where our campsite had been there were still tear tracks on her face, and her nose was red, but I could tell that they were happy tears.

We stopped in the first town we came to, hit a laundromat and a truck stop to get showers—the goal up till that day had been to hide; we hadn't bothered so much with creature comforts—then we went to the big thrift store and kitted out Annie: new shirts, long pants, jacket and shoes and a bag to hold it all in. Then to a department store for things you really didn't want to buy secondhand: socks and underwear, a plastic sleeve for her documents, notebooks and pens and a Bible. She'd taken nothing with her when she'd left but the papers she had to have and the clothes that she stood up in.

You'd have thought we'd bought her the moon.

She still ducked down whenever she saw a cop, seemed a bit skittish around people, but Annie was more relaxed—she was in disguise, she had reached the age of independence, she was too far away from home for anyone to recognize her, had been gone too long for everyone to still have their eyes peeled for her.

Now that I knew our time together was coming to an end I enjoyed having her around. She smiled and cracked wise and we all sang along to the radio and ate popcorn while watching the sun set and slept in the car, and I wondered if this was what life would have been like if I'd had an older sister.

The day before we got to the brother in Utah, Ma got quiet again, and I wondered if leaving Annie meant leaving her happy mood behind. When we stopped for food for the last time Ma wrote out her cell number and made Annie memorize it until she could spit it out without thinking.

"If anything happens, if anything goes wrong, if ever you don't feel completely safe, call up and say, 'Give Alex a hug for me,' OK? I don't know if I can trust anyone with you, and I want an out for you if things go wiggy. Give me your brother's details, just in case."

We found the apartment complex late in the afternoon, outside of the city proper, where there was room for green things and breathing. It was a 1950s affair, well kept but not much prettier than the place we'd stayed in Florida. But the area looked a little safer, like the people breaking into your house would be after electronics instead of meth money, like the residents would have electronics that would make breaking in worthwhile. We sat in the car for a bit, taking in the scenery—the brother had said he'd be getting home earlier than usual, but Ma didn't seem inclined to rush. I figured she was worrying, brother or no, about sex trafficking or organ harvesting and a bunch of other sordid possibilities. Annie I couldn't read at all.

Before we got out of the car Ma pulled three twenty-dollar bills out of her wallet and made Annie put them in her bra.

"Call me and I'll come and get you as fast as humanly possible. I promise."

Then we all three went up to the door.

Annie paused in front of it, and I saw the curtain of

208

one of the front windows twitch. She was getting up her nerve to knock when the door shot open, and a young man who was twenty years or so off from being the spit and image of his father shot out, grabbed her up around the middle. Then they both started crying, and I figured Ma had been worrying in vain.

We stuck around long enough to meet the roommate—a quiet Mormon boy working towards a medical degree—see the apartment, and hear the brother's story of running away from home, which involved stowing away in a moving van and sleeping rough, and was a few hundred percent more harrowing than Annie's. Then there was hugging and hand shaking and more hugging, and then we were in the car and Annie was on the front step of the apartment with her brother's arm around her shoulders, waving us off.

It felt anticlimactic, so I was glad when Ma stopped at the first diner she saw and took a booth in a quiet corner.

"Coffee, lots of it," she said when the waitress came. Then amended: "Half caff if you can do it," when I pointed out that she'd never sleep again if she drank regular at that time of day. We sat there for a good long while, bent over two hot mugs, thinking our own thoughts, and I was sad that Annie was gone but I was happy that it was just us again, that I didn't have anyone to be constantly shown up by, that I could be unapologetically and unabashedly myself.

"Is that what it would have been like, having an older sister?" I asked, and Ma looked up sharply.

"Maybe," she said. "Why do you ask?"

"I'm glad I don't. I like it being just you and me."

"Things would have been different, if you'd grown up with one."

"Yeah, then I'd never have gotten a word in edgewise."

"She didn't talk that much."

"Not at first, but once she'd gotten warmed up . . . I thought I was in school again."

She laughed at that, then looked thoughtful.

"Speaking of, we're going to need to think about enrolling you soon. When we left Florida I thought we would have gotten to the end of the road before we got to the end of summer. School starts up in a month, and between the car and the extra slack weeks I really need to find some work—we're running out of money."

"We could go for a cheaper car," I suggested.

"No. The station wagon was expensive, but it should get us where we're going with the minimum of maintenance. I don't want another flying-wheel incident."

"Well, apparently that was all God's fault, so we're probably safe from that happening again anytime soon. How many people do you know that have joined cults that you're worried about a repeat?" I asked.

"That would depend on how you define 'know' and how you define 'cult.' A lot of people have a religious phase—some people it lasts their whole damn lives. You only need to worry, I guess, when they want to get out and they can't. Or when they force their kids into it. Kids make everything complicated."

"How do they do that, exactly?" I was just a little offended by the comment.

"They're human beings without rights, sort of potential human beings, and you get one thousand chances to screw them over before they grow up. I've known people that joined for themselves, but stayed for their kids— you can't change something that big in someone's life without giving them whiplash. You have to give Annie some credit, even if you don't like her—it takes guts to walk out."

"I never said I didn't like her."

"But you don't."

"I do too!"

"Lie to yourself all you want, Alex, but don't try it on me."

CHAPTER XVII

We sat in the diner until past dark, bathed in the steam of cup upon cup of thin, sour coffee, with dinner an intermission in the middle. Then, when we couldn't stay any longer without risking caffeine toxicity or seriously pissing off our waitress, we got back in the car. We didn't get on the highway, though, but drove just out of town, then pulled over.

"At least in this boat sleeping outside will be half comfortable," Ma said as she took the key out of the ignition and a coin out of her pocket. "Call it, front or back."

I got the front seat to myself, stretched out comfortably with my head pillowed on spare clothes, but even so I woke up periodically throughout the night and could feel that Ma was still awake, still thinking.

I couldn't get back to sleep at the point where it was too dark to see much, but too light already to go on pretending that it was still night. Ma I don't think had slept at all. When I sat up to fumble clean socks out of my backpack she was standing beside the car, smoking a cigarette and staring up at the sky.

"You worried about Annie?" I asked.

"Some, though I'm starting to think on our worries just now. Namely, how we have places to get, and reduced resources to expend getting to those places." She dug her packet from the pocket of her shirt, pulled another cigarette halfway out, then thought better of it and put them back.

"What do we have to do still?"

"We don't *have* to do anything. We could settle in right here and call it home until someone with a badge makes us move on."

I wasn't in the mood for her literalness.

"We'll be able to get moving sooner if I'm working, too," I said.

"Sorry, kid, you've got to go to school."

"But I hate school."

"Tough. You don't have too many years left of it. You can go be a bum or whatever you want to be once you've served your time. For now you're still the kid and I'm still the adult and you go to school and I work."

"That's not what you said to Annie."

"She has plans, for one. And she's older than you, two. And she's finished with high school already, three. Now quit fighting with me and get your ass in the car. We have places to be."

She sure did take her time getting us there, though. We rolled slowly back into town, ate granola bars in the front seat while loitering in public parking, then went into the diner from the night before for more fifty-cent coffee. Didn't matter if we were almost out of money, coffee was a necessity. Somewhere along the way I'd started drinking it, too, so I was pretty glad that she'd decided to cut back on cigarettes first when the purse strings started to tighten. We only had the one cup each, but we sat nursing it for nearly an hour, until it got to be a reasonable time of the morning. Then Ma pulled out her cellphone and dialed the brother's phone number.

If it had been quiet in the diner I could have heard the voice bleeding through from the other end, but because of the diner clatter all I got was Ma's end—polite but brief with the brother, then some warmer with Annie—she was nervous, I guessed, that she shouldn't have left her friend's daughter out of her sight, had done exactly the wrong thing and she would never be able to forgive herself. She nodded a lot as Annie told her about whatever there was to talk about after twelve hours of being away from us.

"We're moving on to Nevada later today. We won't be right close by, but we'll still be close enough. And if things don't work out with your brother, or with school, find me and we'll figure something out, you hear? OK. I miss having you along. Alex's right here, want me to say hi?"

I was grateful that she didn't just hand me the phone, the way my father would have done.

"OK. Keep at it—things have to look up from here. Good. OK. I'll talk to you later, baby. Keep your chin up."

That got me with a pang of jealousy. But then she mashed the off button and it was just the two of us again. She pocketed the phone and tipped back the last cold swallow of coffee, then looked at the cup for a bit.

"We can afford just one more, I think."

"Are we going to Vegas?" I asked.

"Vegas?"

"We need money, and we don't have a bunch of time."

"Kid, selling our organs would be a better bet for quick cash than Vegas. We're going to Reno, maybe, and on the way in or out the road might go through Vegas, but there will be no gambling. Real life isn't anything like the movies. You're not old enough to get in, anyway."

I put on a show of sulking, but inside I was happy: she was all mine again.

We took two and a half days to get to Reno, stopping and starting, napping on the side of the road, taking it not so seriously for a bit. And once a day Ma made the call, chitchatted some, then asked the question: "Alex's right here, want me to say hi?" She always hung up satisfied, or as satisfied as she could be in the situation, which might have been better. She would have been happier, probably, if we could have stayed with Annie, or had her come with us, but one way or another neither option was affordable for anyone concerned.

When we got to Reno we slept in the car—under the shadows of scorched mountains that were like where I had been and not like where I had been—until we found a two-room apartment that wasn't too much of a horrifying mess, with rent that we could afford. The work was thinner on the ground here, but Ma found a job mixing drinks, a nighttime job, so she would be there when I went to school and when I got back.

I woke up when she shuffled in, just around dawn, and she made me bacon before going to sleep—there was only one bed, but we traded it off back and forth. She wore low-cut shirts again, and smelled of cigarettes that other people had smoked and spilled drinks, beer and spirits and the sticky sweetness of the mixers. But this time I didn't catch the scent on her of another person—she may have been more careful, but probably she was too tired.

Three weeks after moving into the apartment I was bunged back into school, and at first it seemed like it might be better than I had remembered. I knew how to fade into the background, pretend like I belonged there, or at least had been hanging around for so long that no one could begrudge my existence. And I could concentrate more, now, felt less like I was crawling in my skin, less tortured by the presence of other people my age, by the possibilities of the flesh left unfulfilled. I no longer felt like I would kill to have sex with absolutely anyone.

I still hadn't managed to do that, had neither figured out the mechanics of the task in more than roughest theory nor met anyone that I could invite to figure them out with me, but living someplace stationary and having the comfort of my own company once again made me less despondent about that. The first night in the apartment, the moment Ma locked the door behind her, me on the inside watching the little color TV that came with the place, her on the outside in tight bartender's blacks, I got naked. Not right there; I went to the bathroom and locked the door. I'd gotten shy with myself again, felt like I had to hide it from the no one spying on me from nowhere. But I hadn't forgotten what to do. And had my body ever missed my hands. It was the reunion of the century.

My mother told stories rarely, if at all, before we left home; my dad told stories all the time. He told them slowly, did a lot of scene dressing, so you expected it to end with fireworks, or at least sparklers, but they never had real endings. Which is true to life, I guess, since it's so rare that reality rustles up a satisfying narrative shape, the edges rounded off and the ends tied up. It's rare that you get finality to things, the way we like our books and movies to end. Life so often goes flabby and peters out at the finish point instead of clicking satisfyingly, like the sound of a box being shut. That's why we read, and watch, and listen, because we want that click and life never hands it over. You can go the regulation eighty-odd years without getting one neat chapter break, forget about a "The End." It just goes on and on, like snail slime.

But back to Dad.

One of the stories that he liked to tell was of the first time he saw a car that had a television. He was in school like every other kid on a day like every other day, when he got called to the office. His grandfather and older brother—two years ahead, in the fifth grade—were waiting for him there, and his grandfather was signing them out to take them to the dentist with a wink at my dad, because no dentist's appointment had been made and they all three knew it. Instead, there were hamburgers and milkshakes and a drive into D.C., which was a rare treat.

It was crowded—they stopped on a side street, doors locked and windows up, watching the press of people, shouting and waving, marching, chanting—and then a gold Oldsmobile glided past, and my father caught the flicker of the tiny television built into the gap between the two front seats so that the people in the back seat could watch it. And that was my father's clearest memory of the 1968 D.C. Race Riots, of King's assassination, of the issues of import that shaped the world of his childhood.

I was annoyed when I first heard it that the story had no end, and seemingly no point, and I demanded of him a better story to make up for it.

With benefit of hindsight, I realize that the point was that his perspective was the wrong one. I was looking at the wrong end of things, not realizing that what he was trying to tell me was that we aren't always the heroes of our own stories.

Reno was like Florida without the water: same routine, same sense of waiting for the other goddamned shoe to drop. I tried to fly under the radar, but now that we were

older—it was my first year in high school, and it immediately made me miss the relative innocence, the
insulation, of middle school—there were questions. Not
from the teachers—my memory blots them out cleanly,
they were so unimportant—but from the other students.
We were at the age of transformation; everyone else
seemed to be in the process of morphing neatly, if spot-
tily, from *child* into either *man* or *woman*, and so my own
refusal to pledge allegiance became suddenly noticeable,
something that everyone around me seemed to think
they deserved to have an opinion about.

And so came the questions.

"What are you?"

"My mom was born in Sicily, but we don't know
where my dad—"

"Not like that, I mean *what* are you?"

"My grandparents used to take me with them to an
Episcopal church—"

"I mean sex."

"I imagine I'd like it if I ever get the chance—"

"Quit fucking with me. Are you a guy or a girl?"

If the questioner had gotten that far they were either
looking about as uncomfortable as I felt, or getting pissed
off, depending on the person, so I usually closed with,
"In case you're confusing 'sex' with 'gender'—I don't
have one."

It was unnerving at first, to be confronted like that;
then I started to enjoy winding them up. They were
assholes for thinking that it was any of their business
in the first place, and why did it matter whether I was

evolving into man, woman, or an entirely different species? Knowing someone's sex doesn't tell you anything. About that person, anyway. I suppose the need to know, how knowing changes the way you behave towards them, the assumptions you make about who they are and how they live, tells an awful lot about you.

It's bothered me for as long as I can remember, the way the human compulsion to classify stands at odds with my feeling of falling outside the available categories. When I was a child at home it mattered less: my father was Man, my mother was Woman, I was myself. But when I went out into the world, or even to my grand-parents' house, everyone seemed determined to put me into a box that I had no business being in, expected me to think and act and want in ways that were consistent with a label with which I could not identify.

When I was seven my mother had to come get me from school because I had run away from my teacher rather than line up like I'd been told. On our drive home I explained it was because the teacher had told us to divide up, boys in one line and girls in the other, and I just couldn't make myself get in the wrong line one more time, that there wasn't a right line for me to get into.

She looked at me in the rearview mirror, swinging my legs in my booster seat and waiting for her to start yelling at me, and I remember feeling as though she could see inside my brain, as if she were seeing me properly for the first time.

"If that's how you feel, then that's how you feel," she said. "Let me know if you change your mind."

I suppose she'd spent too much of her life being pushed into being what she wasn't, and doing what she didn't want to do, to have it in her to do the same to me, but she still asked whenever the topic came up if I'd changed my mind yet. It wasn't until I was almost a teenager that she took me at my word. And in the end, the joke's on that teacher: I still haven't joined either of the lines that she tried to put me in.

Of course, there was one area where sex was an issue. In Florida I had gotten out of gym and so avoided locker rooms, made sure to only ask for the bathroom pass in the middle of the class period so that no one would see that I alternated between the boys' and girls' rooms. But now that we were all expected to be settling into our adult bodies—and since the school wouldn't let Ma opt me out of gym—that wasn't so easy to do.

I'd gotten permission to use the single-stall handicapped bathroom off the teachers' lounge for getting changed; most of the teachers knew me on sight from my passing through and were pleasant. And there was only so much harassing other students could do between classes. So all was good in my queer little world until a group decided that, if they couldn't get me to cop to what variety of crotch giblets I was keeping in my pants, the next best thing would be to catch me naked. At first I wasn't sure if that was really what they were after, or if they were all locking on to what they saw as a good target for extracurricular pummeling, but either way I didn't like it.

I was half expecting the first fight when it came. I just wasn't expecting it to be started by a girl. Maybe I should have started it myself, chose the biggest, ugliest motherfucker there and knocked his face in, established myself as top of the heap as early as possible, like we were in prison. I wanted to be a badass, but I knew that I wasn't.

First fight: walking down the hall, squeeze past a group of girls, feel hands on my head and shoulder, then the hands bounce my face off the metal of a locker door and I feel my nose crunch. Turn around. She's my height, her hands coming up for my face, but I'm quicker: knee drives up into her kidneys, sweep her feet out from under her and I fall on top of her. Her head makes a dull sound as it hits. Then a teacher is pulling us up, and I don't continue it even though I want to and I know she's hurting, even though she's not showing it. My face is bleeding everywhere.

"I'm sorry, I'm sorry, we tripped, I'm so sorry, are you all right?"

She takes my lead, and we both play it beautifully, get ourselves out of suspension, detention, whatever they do to kids that try to beat the suit out of each other in the hallway. I miss the next class because I'm sitting in the nurse's office even after the nose stops, because I can't calm down: I don't feel things, I don't cry, I didn't know that I was angry. But I was. I hadn't been afraid when I felt my nose crack, I'd been enraged.

And now I wanted a reason to keep swinging, because getting that girl on the ground had felt better than anything I could imagine. Every face for the rest of the day was an invitation, begging me to hit it, to knock it clean off, to show it just what I thought of the world.

When I got home that afternoon Ma took one look at me and pointed to the door.

"Out. You've got a chip on your shoulder about something and you're getting out there and running it off. I don't care what he said she said, I want your ass pounding the pavement for an hour. When you've calmed down you can come back and tell me about it."

I didn't want to—I wanted a fight—but she still had her mother voice, so I went. When I told her about the nose and the locker she didn't have much to say at first.

"Don't kill anyone, OK, kid? I didn't want you to have to deal with this, but it would be pretty silly to think that 'want' would stop it from happening. Next time, you might want to try taking a fall; give the principal and everyone reason to get involved, and they'll have to defend your ass. Or, if it happens, make sure it's the last time. Might get suspended, but everyone will know not to mess with you. I can't advise either way. I always took the 'end it' approach, but we didn't get in much trouble for fighting back then."

The second fight was a guy, and he was just a bit bigger than me, and it was outside of school, just after, on the walk home. It was a clean invitation: he started with insults and then socked me in the gut. He was big, but he wasn't very good at bullying: there are off-the-shelf slurs for every group on the planet, but he didn't know what to shout at me, so most of it missed the mark, and just made me confused. He should have won, but he expected me to be scared; he didn't know about the anger. It was hot, it made my head fizz, got me so high that I didn't feel pain, just the crushing desire to make him cry. Which he did, when I got him on the ground and rubbed his face against the sidewalk like I was grating cheese for spaghetti. I let him go and he tried again, and I got him down again. I wasn't sure I could trust him to let me be when I let him up the second time, so I reached back and whaled away at his ass like he was a disobedient kid. The humiliation might have been a bad idea, but he let me walk away afterwards, high on the victory even if I was the worse for it. When the bruises colored up Ma wanted to call the school, but I wouldn't let her; it had happened outside of school hours, off school property, and I hoped that it was the end of things. I had faked being a hardass twice, it should be enough to get them to leave me alone.

It was maybe a week after the second fight that I was late getting moving for gym. It was mostly because we'd be playing volleyball; I have the hand-eye coordination of a squashed slug, and I hoped that if I slipped in late, with my excuse that I'd had to go farther than everyone else to get changed, I'd be allowed to sit out at least the first game. I'd lingered in the class before finishing up my notes, taken my time getting my athletic clothes out of my locker, and when I got to the teachers' lounge it was already empty. It struck me as odd, when I opened the door, that the bathroom light was off, but I figured someone had been trying to save energy. When I reached to switch it on and a hand grabbed my arm I nearly jumped out of my skin.

It took all three of them to get me into the bathroom, their hands on my wrists and in my hair and clawing at my clothes, the four of us fighting silently except for angry, bitten-off whispers that "You jumped too fucking early, Chad; we'd have got it inside easy if you'd just fucking waited!" I don't know why I didn't scream, why I saved my mouth for biting. The scare of being grabbed from the dark had gotten my adrenaline going, and I wasn't thinking. But they were, and they got me off balance and into the little room; then they closed the door and locked it.

The bathroom floor was cold on my face and through my shirt; the hands were still in my hair and on my wrists and there was weight on my back, and I wanted to kill them. I wanted to rip them apart with my teeth. When they flipped me over I saw that I'd already made a start: one of them was holding his arm, but it wasn't until later that I realized that he'd been muttering, "It fucking bit me!" and meant me. Another one of them straddled my stomach, reared back and punched me in the face.

I'd never been punched in the face before: at first I didn't realize what had happened, didn't feel pain but dizziness, my ears ringing. The guy on top of me knew what he was doing; I noticed, just before he punched me again, that he'd wrapped his hands the way boxers do. It felt like I was stuck to the floor, like I'd never be able to overcome gravity enough to sit up again. The one on top of me shifted his weight down, and I felt cold air on my stomach as someone yanked up my shirt.

"No tits," he said.

"That doesn't prove anything—half the sluts here are carpenters' dreams."

"Yeah, but how many of them don't wear no bra?"

"I dunno. Just all the dykes and skanks, maybe? Move your ass—we came here to get proof."

The weight shifted up to my chest, and for a moment I couldn't breathe. My vision was weird, but as I blinked I saw that one of them was sitting back on his heels, camera phone out and at the ready. The third guy was straddling my shins, and as I tried to make sense of "proof" he began fiddling with my belt, yanking down my jeans.

Suddenly I got it.

My thrashing only slowed them down a little as they tried to keep me pinned and get my clothes off at the same time. But my anger at being jumped had morphed into terror, hot and choking, underlaid like a baseline with the memory of hitchhiking in Alabama, of having my head forced down. I started screaming then, and the guy sitting on my chest flailed, trying to cover my mouth, let go of my arm so he could do it and I clawed him across the face, gouging at his eyes.

Then the bathroom door opened, swung inward and cracked against my shoulder hard enough that I was glad it wasn't my head, and a booming voice asked, "What the hell is going on here?"

CHAPTER XVIII

I spent the rest of the day in the nurse's office, wrapped in blankets and shaking. People asked me questions, and I wondered if the guys had gotten the pictures they were after, if the people asking questions had seen the pictures, and I wanted to die. Then I heard my mother, her voice thundering down the hall as she reamed the principal or whoever was with her at the top of her lungs, and I wasn't surprised that he wasn't answering back very loudly. She came in, paused in the doorway to look me over, pushed past the flailing nurse and hugged me.

"Oh. My. Fucking. God. You've had my kid sitting naked on an exam table for over two hours, right through lunch I may add, and you only now call me?"

"There was blood on my clothes, so they took them as evidence," I muttered, and looked down at the floor. She kept her language under control after that, at least, but not her volume, and not her tone. You could have felled trees with her voice as she spoke to the principal, the nurse, the police, and anyone else in hearing range, and though I knew that I wasn't the one in Dutch even

I quailed a little. She made them hand over my gym clothes since they didn't want to give back the ones I'd been wearing, made them leave me alone so I could dress, then she tried to take me home. The principal insisted I couldn't go yet, that I had been involved in a fight, had bloodied at least one face and almost gouged someone's eye out, and was looking at suspension. She looked like she just might strangle him with his own tie in that moment, then swept me off the table in a bridal hold and went to carry me out of the school. I insisted on being put down before she got to the door, walked out under my own steam, looked straight ahead as I passed students in the hall: I'd had enough humiliation for one day.

We drove home in silence. When we got in she made me food, watched me eat—she'd already found someone to cover her shift, was staying with me that night. It reminded me of the night that I got back from my ill-conceived trip to Alabama, and as I forked up tortellini I considered for a second telling her about the man in the car. The time seemed right for it, if there really can be a "right time" for that sort of thing, but when I opened my mouth the words died in my throat: there were still words I just couldn't say.

"How do you feel?" she asked after the food.

"Pissed off as fuck that I didn't hit 'em more," I said. She laughed, but it sounded weird, like she was doing it to keep from crying.

We watched movies on the couch for the rest of the night, me snuggled into her like I was six again. But something was off—when I poked around in my head, there was a blank. The day hadn't happened. I'd boxed up the feelings and put them away. And under the blankness I felt scared, not that someone would jump me again, but that what I wasn't feeling would all come out when I didn't expect it, when I couldn't handle it, that someone else would do or say something to trigger the avalanche and I wouldn't get to choose how or when it happened. I put that away, though, enjoyed the feel of Ma's arm around me, the feel of being a kid, and tried not to think directly about the blankness in my head, tried not to let it know that I knew that it was there.

Ma had to go back to work the next night, but I didn't have to go to school. Which was a massive relief. I didn't want to be anyone's special case, anyone's exception to the rule, but more than that I didn't want to worry about getting jumped, worry about people trying to see things, to have to wonder if someone had managed to get pictures after all. To wonder if the person sitting next to me had seen them.

I stayed home for three days solid while Ma made calls and arranged things, shouted at officials and social workers. When she wasn't slinging drinks or passed out in bed she was yelling at people about me or giving me her funny concerned look, the one that told me that she was worried and she had no idea how to fix any of the things that she was worried about. I kept a low profile, or as low a profile as I could manage in such a small space with a mother on the warpath. Then, on day four, Social Services sent over a tutor, and things quieted down some.

The in-home tutor was usually reserved for kids so bad they weren't allowed back in school, and at first they didn't want to dish him out to me—it didn't look good for them to seem to be punishing the victim of what was being called a hate crime, but Ma wasn't sending me back. So the tutor came two days a week to go over everything, check my homework, and mete out assignments, and we generally muddled along OK. Ma looked over his shoulder the first few visits, but gave over when she'd satisfied herself that he was a decent guy who was giving me a decent education; the lessons were in the middle of her sleep time.

Besides what now passed for school there were few draws on my time. Once you took away all the trappings school didn't take that long to get through, and was pretty mobile when I wanted it to be. When I found my courage again—a considerable amount of it had been left on the floor of the handicapped bathroom—I went forth into the wide, wide world just to prove to myself that I could. And though high school is, in ways, a microcosm of the rest of society, I didn't get any more attention on the streets of Reno than the women—not the prostitutes, but the women in general—did for their heels and modest skirts, and far less than the cross-dressers and drag queens.

It wasn't long before I got bored. I knew that what had happened at school had frightened my mom, knew that she'd always been afraid that she'd use her fear as an excuse to keep me from doing things; when I'd wanted to learn to rock climb at age nine she'd taken me to try it, and when I hit the top of a wall for the first time I'd looked down to wave to her and saw that she had her hands over her eyes, found out on the ride home that she'd spent the entire afternoon not watching me in terror that I'd fall, even though I was harnessed and helmeted to hell and back. So I leveraged that knowledge when I asked if I could get an after-school job. She'd been on the fence until I pointed out that, if she said yes, then I'd naturally keep her posted as to my whereabouts, where if she said no then I'd probably do it anyway and not tell her. So she gave grudging consent, so long as I kept her up to speed on where I was and what I was doing, which left only the problem of finding work.

With all the time on my hands I'd been thinking too much, and not necessarily of happy things. So when the time came to assess my skills, parlay them into work, the memory of the man in Alabama returned, and an insidious voice whispered, "*Sex work is all you're good for—even a stranger saw that much.*" And for a moment I believed it, considered listening to it and wasn't sure if that was because I knew the voice was right or because I wanted to punish myself by making what happened in that car happen again. But I knew Ma would kill me if she found out, knew that if I went down that road I probably wouldn't ever see my dad again.

I'd been thinking about him a lot in my free time as

well, wondering what he was doing, if he expected me to come back someday or if he'd moved on. I missed him still, but it wasn't a sharp missing, the way you feel about someone close who's just died, but rather the dull familiarity of a well-established absence. When we first left home I hadn't known that I should feel the sting of loss, had taken it for granted that, no matter what Ma said, I'd be seeing Dad again soon, had felt about his absence the way I had when I was small and he left for work in the morning; part of me had assumed that he'd be home in time for dinner, had assumed that since he hadn't come home then dinnertime had yet to arrive. I hadn't known to miss him until I'd already become accustomed to his absence.

Dad didn't like to drive; the car was decidedly Ma's territory. So the times that he did drive stuck out in memory.

Whenever I got in trouble—sassing teachers, starting fights, sledding through the neighbors' azaleas or I don't know what—court was convened at the kitchen table. Ma got louder and louder asking why I'd done whatever it was that I'd supposedly done and then answering her own questions, working out an entire psychology for whatever crime had been committed while I stood with the fear-shame-anger axis of awful in my belly, until she burned herself out. It happened every few months, and each time I told myself that it was the last time; I hadn't seen this screw-up coming but by God I'd see the next one.

Then Dad handed her a beer, took the keys in one hand and my shoulder in the other, and steered me through the door to the front seat of Ma's car. We usually drove around for maybe thirty minutes first, not saying anything, keeping to the back roads so we could go slow, so I could calm down. Then Dad would ask one question, like I'd told him an interesting story and he'd missed an important part, and he'd let me spew, out of order and angry, what I remembered of the incident *du jour*. It didn't matter if my memory didn't jive with whoever had already got their version in; he kept his eyes on the road, and if I paused for too long he gave me a little nudge to get me going again. I talked with my eyes straight ahead like in confession, and afterwards we stopped for a chocolate milkshake to break up the hard lump of unshed tears in the back of my throat, throwing away the empty waxed paper cups on the way home because Ma wouldn't have understood why I deserved a treat right then. When we got in she'd be sitting at the kitchen table, the empty beer bottle in front of her, and I'd apologize as best I could, and we'd sit down to figure out what came next.

I hopped from odd job to odd job, bussing tables, selling popcorn, washing floors, spinning a roulette wheel until someone realized that I was far too young to be in a casino, working for cash paid under the table, carefully squirreling away my own bankroll. I made friends with the dancing girls and bouncers and drag queens, coaxed war stories out of anyone who would tolerate my presence, tried to make the most of the time I had in a place I didn't really want to be.

More than ever before I was feeling the restlessness, the longing for motion, that I imagined my mother felt, but now I also wanted not just to be moving but to be the one deciding in which direction the movement would take me. I was beginning to think about going back to Virginia, considering what I would have to do in order to get there.

There didn't seem to be any good solution. I could wait until I was old enough to tend bar and follow in my mother's footsteps, but that was too far off. I could save up enough for a train, which would just leave me broke on the far end. I could hitch and walk my way across the country and run the risk of winding up dead in a ditch. There were options, but none of them were practical, workable options. So I hoarded my cash, made and discarded plans, and became one with the city in a way I hadn't in Florida—it wasn't my home but I knew the streets, knew the weather, knew the overhanging mountains, could cup it in my hands and suck its marrow, so to speak.

And so the months passed, a fall and a winter and a spring that were missing some of the seasonal earmarks, bisected by a Christmas and New Year's when neither Ma nor I touched down in the apartment for more than six hours at a time, working all of the shifts and jobs that no one else wanted because they had people to spend the time with, traditions to keep, ascribed some importance to the time of year. When the holiday cacophony settled down Ma took me for Chinese food as a sort of conciliatory celebration, and I kept the calendar that they gave us at the restaurant, hung it in our kitchen so that I could periodically cross days off, feel the way time slipped by, measure the distances with my fingers: so many knuckles from today to next week, so many hand spans from this month to next month, so little distance between the present and the future. Just a matter of waiting, of working, of crosses on cheap paper, and we would be on the road again.

OK, I was going to leave this bit out. But I like to think that I've gotten too old for shame, too wise to want to apologize for who I am or what I've done. And I can always comfort myself with the knowledge that there's no telling how much of it is true, how much an intentional fiction—or how much the distortion of time and wishful thinking.

Just before Christmas I settled into regular work at Cojones, a little club where the main draw was drag shows and female impersonators doing stand-up, and where I collected empties and cleaned up at the end of the night. One of the waiters at a restaurant where I'd washed dishes for two weeks had sold me a fake ID that said I was old enough, and they paid under the table, so no one scrutinized it too closely. Ma, when I told her what I was up to, had shrugged and said, "Sounds like a fun place. If anyone offers you drugs, don't take them," and left it at that.

The performers fascinated me: a hairy, coarse, earthy

man became, through the application of makeup and packing tape and magic, the essence of feminine beauty, his voice and movement and bearing completely changed and yet something essential preserved. Most of them took to me, or at least tolerated me, and I loved being able to watch snatches of the shows in between running my ass off.

I met Simon my first night there, but it wasn't until a week or so later that I actually noticed him—or he noticed me, rather. Simon was an eighteen-year-old Adonis, muscled, bronzed, and camera ready in his street clothes; as Ina Propriate he made the room roar with laughter and question their sexuality. In or out of drag he was a flirt; I brought drinks back to the performers ahead of the show and he introduced himself by saying I was so adorable he wanted to eat me.

We slid into being friends probably because we were the youngest two there, though I'd like to think that Simon found me as alluring as I found him, that attraction was one of the reasons that I wound up at his apartment drinking cheap rum, shooting the shit, watching bad movies, and every now and again having a field day in his closet. He presented himself as a manly man, a bit of a musclehead, but in private he was an utter whore for clothes. The first time he dragged me home was because he couldn't live another moment until he'd gotten to dress me up, and since he seemed to want to play with my genderlessness, rather than overwrite it with what he thought I should be, I let him.

I wouldn't let him see me naked, so he picked out the

costumes and let me don them in the bathroom, then attacked with a basket of pins and a roll of garment tape, let me try on the skin of a roaring twenties dandy in plus-fours, a Gibson girl complete with Ina's fake bosom, a flapper with my own flat chest under the drop-waist dress, and a passable imitation of the Thin White Duke—at least from the neck down. It was strange and not unpleasant, walking out into his living space—which was about as big as his closet space—and turning in front of the full-length mirror propped next to the television, swapping back and forth between man and woman, man and woman, and I could see where Simon's glee came from: a touch of powder, a bit of padding in chest or shoulders, and I could be anything. And it was thrilling, too, trying on the identities that I could take up, the trappings of gender that made me look alternately like my mother or my father, as though I were dressing myself up as one or the other of them and so summoning their essence in my own frame. But no matter what clothes he put me into, how much makeup he slapped on or scraped off, there remained something off, something other about the character I saw in the mirror, and our play only confirmed what I'd long felt: being either and neither and both at once fit me more closely than the other options on offer.

After I'd let him dress me like a doll and heard him rattle on about his childhood and family, ex-boyfriends and girlfriends and one-night stands, while he pinned his clothes to fit the narrowness of my body—the alcohol or the energy drinks he'd been mixing it with had given him hummingbird-like energy—I couldn't feel awkward around him, didn't feel nervous drinking alone with him while watching *Alice in Murderland* and gossiping about people from work. So I guess what happened was only natural.

Even with the distraction of paying work I was still thinking about what happened in Alabama, had sudden, unwanted memories, sometimes images but more often a smell, a taste, a full-body sensation that I hated, that I wanted to be rid of. I couldn't talk about it, but I wondered if there was another way of dealing with it. If I couldn't erase the memory, maybe I could overwrite it.

We were sharing his couch late one night after work, were both feeling loose and fuzzy with how much we'd drunk, were nearly to the end of a black-and-white film whose plot I hadn't been able to follow because all my attention was on him, on what I was going to try and do.

"Hey, Simon?"

"Hm?"

"Would you do me a favor?"

"Depends what it is," he said. "I'm good at romantic advice but bad at all the other kinds."

"Would you let me suck your dick?"

He blinked, and I immediately regretted asking.

"Alex—" his voice was slow—"I think you've got it backwards. The suck-er is the one that's doing the favor—the suck-ee is the one that usually has to ask for the favor."

"So that means no, right?" My whole body was on fire from shame.

"Well, I mean, why do you want to?"

"To see what it's like," I mumbled. "And, I mean, it's only my mouth. No other bits get involved so it doesn't matter. You can pretend it's someone else doing it—"

He pulled me over against him—I felt the muscles in his arms bunch, felt myself burning hotter—and stopped me mid-sentence with his mouth on mine, with a kiss that made me want to cry.

"Now," he said in Ina's voice, syrupy and Southern, "don't go around treating yourself like some crusty sock, because you're so much better than that." Then in his own voice, he said, "Never given head before?" He watched my face, saw how I debated the merits of lying to him. "Or never done any of it before?"

I hid my face in the sofa cushion. "I did it once, a while ago, but it was awful and I want to replace it with a better memory. Of someone, y'know, I like."

I hoped that he would latch onto the "like" part, but he didn't, went for the word that I'd hoped he'd ignore.

"What made it awful?" he asked.

He was leaning back into a corner of the sofa, had pulled me so that I was half laying on him, could feel the heat of his body and the play of his muscles, smell the sweetness of cola and rum on his breath and the bitterness of his sweat, feel the way his words rumbled in his chest. His hands were resting on my hips, felt like they were burning my skin through my shirt. And I felt safe and scared, painfully aroused but still so scarred. So, with my face in his shirt so I wouldn't have to see his reaction, I told him about the first time.

He wouldn't let me do it, not after I told him why I wanted to, and for a bit I regretted having said anything, having not gone straight for his crotch without a word. But he didn't seem disgusted with me, and he didn't throw me out; when I woke up the next morning we were still sprawled like that across the couch, me with my face pillowed on his right pectoral and drooling on his T-shirt, him with his head fallen back on the armrest and snoring, open-mouthed.

I expected him to distance himself after that night. When he woke up he made us breakfast, and when I saw him at Cojones the next day he smiled and waved and flirted with me like nothing had changed. Later I asked if he would let me blow him just because I wanted to. He said no, and he kept saying no for the rest of the time we lived in Reno. But even though he wouldn't let me, I guess now that it wasn't because he didn't want to. He got in the habit of leaning against me, putting his arm around me, kissing my neck in the long slow way that I'd longed for when I watched the teenagers on the beach in Florida, touching me in the warm, tingling ways that people reserve for lovers.

CHAPTER XIX

This was the second Virginian spring that I had to imagine without being there, a full two years since we'd left—which meant that my birthday was drawing close once again. I didn't mind as much as most people would have that, since leaving home, we'd already let two of them pass without remark: birthdays to me had always meant phone calls to relatives that weren't sure how old I was (my father's parents), pretending to like presents from people I had to pretend to like (my father's brother and sister-in-law) and admitting to myself and my parents that though I had sort-of-friends that I spoke to at school, I didn't have any friends worth inviting to share the cake that was usually a disappointment in some way. So the lack of notice I quite enjoyed, especially the absence of uncomfortable phone calls. The thing that got to me was that I was another year removed from my father, that much farther from a point that I was increasingly uncertain I would be able to get back to.

It was sometime in March, when I had grown sick of waiting but hadn't gotten close enough to a time when we might actually be leaving to begin looking forward to packing up and getting out, that I thought again of trying to get in touch with him. I had written a postcard or two to let him know I was all right—without giving the details of what had happened at school and how I was keeping myself busy now that I didn't have to go— but it didn't occur to me until then that everything would probably be fine if I just tried phoning him; Ma had never outright told me not to, had even said before we left Florida that she was keeping him informed of our location, so I didn't have to worry about letting it slip the way I had when we first left home.

For the sake of discretion I went a few blocks over before looking around for a pay phone, just in case it did backfire on me. I dropped in a handful of change and dialed the number, then hung up and dialed again because I'd forgotten that I'd need the area code since I was out of state. There was a bubble of excitement that could have been fear pressing up on my diaphragm, but then came three harsh, ascending tones, and *"We're sorry, you have reached a number that has been disconnected or is no longer in service. If you feel you have reached this recording in error, please check the number and try your call again."*

I tapped the cradle button until I got a dial tone, fed more coins in, tried the number again. Same tone, same message. The bubble in my belly had turned to worry. Maybe he had changed his cellphone since we'd been gone; I'd thought it would be the best way to get hold of him, figuring that he'd be at work at that time of day, that day of the week. I hadn't considered what might happen if he answered while he was at work, that it might be hard for him to hear from me, unexpectedly and after so long. Maybe it was a good thing his number wasn't working; leaving a message at home would be better.

I counted out my change, fed it in, punched 1-434, and paused: I couldn't remember our home phone number past the area code. I was stuck, and for a moment I panicked. Then I pressed coin return, held down the cradle button so the call wouldn't go through, and tapped numbers until my hand remembered the pattern. The relief of remembering was almost as strong as my fear, my excitement, and I promised myself that I would not forget again. As I put in the coins and dialed for real the sensation bubbled under my ribs, and I wondered if he'd changed the answering-machine message, or if it would be the same one we'd always had. I waited for the ring, but instead came the three tones again, and then: *The number you have reached has been changed to a non-published number.* The voice repeated itself while I stood there trying to figure out what the hell the words meant, why it wasn't ringing, and then the obnoxious "beepbeepbeepbeep" came and I slammed the receiver down.

I wasn't sure what it meant, other than that I should have thought of calling sooner, should have tried calling sooner, even if I had been too nervous of making my mother angry, of touching off some new conflict between them, of letting slip something or just telling my father where we were and having him come after us. Maybe

I had put off calling for so long because I was worried that this would happen. I walked home dejectedly.

When I was younger Ma vanished sometimes for a day or three but rarely more. She never told us beforehand that she was going—I would wake up and her car would be gone, and when the sun rose it saved the dew in the oblong where her blue Honda Civic should have been, and ate that last.

I always thought that, in the moments before I was truly awake, I could sense her absence the way I could sense her eyes on me before I turned around. Now I know it must've been that I couldn't smell her smoke from the porch under my bedroom window, where she stood to have her first cigarette of the day while I slowly woke above her. On the mornings that she ran away I would lay there for a few moments, feeling the portentousness of my mother-tracking sixth sense (breathing in the absence of cigarette smoke), then surrender to the need to actually get up, because a world without mother was a world in which all of the rules were suspended, at least until she came home.

I would come into the kitchen drunk on the intensity of light unsullied, undimmed by the monotony of life, and find my father flipping banana pancakes, boiling a saucepan of coffee, peacefulness cool and heavy over the whole kitchen. We ate in silence as the sunlight flowed through the backyard, over the grass and budding things—we never talked until he'd finished his coffee— and then life began with a snap like an engine starting:

sandwiches and water in a knapsack, thick socks under our walking shoes, and out the door before the syrupy rays of sunrise had dripped and diffused into the more mundane pale light of day.

Often we walked into our own wood, that was not our wood but protected national parkland, down to the bottom of our backyard and into the trees, past the graveyard—which my parents could not explain no matter how many times I asked why people were buried behind our house—to the river, to follow its sanded banks, jump from boulder to boulder up the center, feel the rush of water in our blood. Other days we got the bus—a little way, but at that age every moment was so great a fraction of my life that the ride felt eternal. We stopped at the entrances to other stretches of parkland, walked bravely into mountains not our own and followed paths that we had not cut, losing and finding ourselves in a memory of wilderness. And when, exhausted, I fell asleep on his lap on the ride back or in the sun on the stubble of our infrequently cut lawn Dad carried me in, took me through the motions of bath and dinner and sleep, so that I learned how to half suspend the rules, to go out with eyes open and know the long way back.

Where my mother went on those days, I never knew. Her absences could have been planned, to give her breathing space or to give my father and me some time together, but I doubt it. They were like each other and not like each other, wanderers in different ways, speakers of different languages, and though they both felt the desire to share their hidden places, they could not share them with each other.

Maybe they could have worked it out, maybe it was better that they didn't keep trying, that Ma left when she did. I don't know if it would have been better if she hadn't taken me with her: what so irritated her about me were all of my similarities, all of the ways I was my father wrought small. I was her also, but those parts were less glaring: one doesn't recognize oneself staring out of another's face.

It was the end of May, a few weeks before schools let out but close enough to summer that they were more or less out of things to teach, when I came home to Ma sorting and tossing and packing us up again. She'd given her two weeks' notice, was ready to get the hell out of there. The tutor told me that he felt bad making me work because the public school was giving half-days and showing movies, so it wasn't difficult to get him to sign off on my having completed the year to satisfaction. Ma spent the days before we left lightening our load, bagged up things for me to take to the Salvation Army while she was asleep during the day. The apartment smelled like anticipation.

I went home with Simon after work the night before we left, snugged up to him on his sprung couch and fell asleep watching a movie with my head on his chest like it was any other Saturday night and we'd be seeing each other later in the week. I woke up before him to morning light coming in the windows and wished I didn't have to go, wished that he and I had gone farther, done more, and at the same time glad that he hadn't let me. He woke up as I was putting on my shoes, insisted on making me breakfast before I left, kissed me before he'd let me walk out the door.

When I got back to the apartment just after sunrise I felt peaceful in the head but tense as a bowstring in my entire body, ready to travel; started pulling out the back-packs and milk crates and odd duffel to corral what things we were taking with us. The key rattled in the lock just as I finished—Ma coming in from her very last night of tending bar in Reno—and I stopped to scramble together a breakfast for her before getting after the packing. She slept—I knew that it was death to wake her—while I boxed and bagged our mutual and my personal things, carried them quietly down to the car, then spread out on the couch, holding a book but not really reading it, too wound up to concentrate.

She emerged at a bit past three in the afternoon dressed in her traveling clothes more because she didn't go in for bathrobes than because she was ready to go. She ran a hand through her hair and observed, "You're wearing my clothes."

"They're our clothes," I answered.

"Are they now?"

"That's what you used to say when you stole Dad's shirts." The shirt of his that I'd been wearing when we left home still got traded back and forth between us; most of the clothing that we owned was technically men's and fit neither of us especially well. But women's clothing was less durable and had too much allowance for curves that neither of us had.

"Do I get nothing to call my own?" She meandered to the kitchenette, began to make coffee.

"I haven't touched your hairbrush."

"If only you would," she sighed.

"Or your gun."

"And I'm hoping you keep it that way."

She ate the breakfast I'd left for her, went and packed her own small collection of things. It shouldn't have taken twenty minutes, but she stretched and yawned until one in the afternoon, when she asked me to pop her backpack in the car while she went down to turn in the apartment key. I was waiting with my feet up on the dash and road atlas across my knees when she came back, firmed up some now but still a little sleep blurred around the edges, and as she slid into her seat and popped the ignition she asked, "You ready to learn to drive yet?"

"I'm pretty sure that isn't legal without a permit," I answered.

"Pity. We'd get there so much quicker if we were trading back and forth."

"Get where?"

"California, for now—it depends on how current my information is where exactly we go once we get there. Don't know how long we're staying either, so no point asking me."

My late night and early rise caught up with me as we left Reno. I closed my eyes, just to rest them, as we started west, and didn't open them again until we hit the city limits of Davis, California. The landscape had changed while I slept, become more familiar not because we were in a place I knew myself, but because we were in a place almost every American knew, the setting of half the movies and television shows I'd ever seen. I'd always suspected that it wasn't a real place, that people didn't actually live there, go to school and hold down jobs and get on with their daily lives, but that everything that happened in California happened for the benefit of the gawking nation, that it was a state called TV World and everyone lived on a sound stage.

It was disappointingly normal.

We wound up downtown, in the cute part where it was easier to walk than drive and half the shops sold overpriced food that looked too healthy. It felt much later than it was, still a ways to dinnertime, my body clock thoroughly annoyed with me. We left the car in a parking garage and wandered the convoluted streets, going quick down the straightaways, then stopping to study signs, building numbers. We meandered in that manner for perhaps twenty minutes, skittering fast, then drawing up to look around like quail in a cornfield. I was following, head down and groggy, and nearly walked up Ma's heels when she suddenly stopped outside of a recessed black door, the stair up to the apartment over the shop on the ground floor, which belonged to a real-estate agent. She stayed still for a moment, reading the listings in the window or the name next to the doorbell, then took my hand and pulled me across the road to the café on the corner. There were tables on the sidewalk, but she pulled me inside, put me into a two-top against the front window, stepped into the end of the line leading up to the counter and the bright copper-topped espresso machine. I had to admit, Californians looked . . . not prettier, really, but healthier, like they'd been fed good food and beat up less by life than the people I'd grown up around, like they exercised on purpose instead of working themselves into the ground.

Ma sat down on the other side of the table, placed a wide-mouthed mug and a jar of sugar in front of me.

"We'll get dinner in a bit," she said. "For now it looks like you could really use this."

She watched the realtor's window across the street, sipped her four shots of espresso stretched with water, laughed when I sheepishly pulled an apple, a hard-boiled egg, and a granola bar out of the pockets of my cargo pants.

"I had a friend in school that used to hoard food," she said, waving away the offered half of the granola bar. "Her mom was a lifetime dieter, all bony by then, but she'd been chubby as a teenager, and didn't want her daughter to have the same fate. Fat-free everything, no snacking allowed. Except she had a brother, and the mom kept junk food around for him because guys need more calories or something. So she knew there was crap food in the house, and she knew that it was being eaten, but she wasn't allowed any of it. By the time she got to be seventeen or eighteen she was paranoid of having no food, so she always had carrots and apples and things under her bed, in her closet, in her backpack, but she couldn't make herself eat them if anyone was watching. Poor girl felt so damn guilty about it, and she was always starving." She pulled out a cigarette, then slipped it back into the pack, tapped her lighter against the table. "It was almost like she wanted to disappear completely." She'd been telling her story to the air in front of her face, like she usually did, but then her eyes focussed on me and I felt uncomfortably exposed, my upper lip painted with foamed milk. "I always thought it was weird—you try your hardest to not mess up your kids and that's how you screw them over for life."

We sat there for a while, in the sunshine, drinking slowly and not talking, but in a good way, and I'd just gotten used to the idea that this was going to be our afternoon, sitting and sipping, when Ma's eyes locked on something and she sprang up, tense again.

"Come on, time to get hustling," she said, pulling coins out of her pocket to leave as a tip with one hand while scooping up the cigarette pack and lighter with the other, moving fast without seeming hurried. She pulled out a cigarette one-handed on the way to the door while I tangled in my chair and sucked down the last inch of my coffee; she paused just outside to light it and give me a chance to stumble after her, then started off down the street with me in her wake, puffing streamers of white like a steamship, leaning slightly forward and taking long steps, shoulders square and hands jammed in her jacket pockets, not looking back to check if I was coming after because I *always* came after, clumsy and stumbling and two jumps behind.

We turned corners, found a square crammed with white canvas booths stuffed with things for sale. I kept losing her in the people—she'd finished her cigarette and not lit the next one; this wasn't the type of place you smoked tobacco in public, so there were no white plumes to follow. There was homemade cheese and barrels of brined olives, mounds of the usual vegetables plus the weird-looking varieties, hand-dyed wool, vegetarian food and Lebanese food and all the things you'd expect or hope for, but every time I started to get a good look at something I had to break off, run after to catch up to the dark hair and breadth of corduroy-covered shoulders that was leaving me behind. I hoped that this would turn out to be the source of the dinner that had been foretold, but it was not: we passed quickly, if meanderingly, through without even a sprig of cilantro to show for our time. We settled down in another coffee shop, this time opposite a hair cuttery, and when Ma brought my cup—and an egg sandwich—to the two-top by the window that she'd pushed me into this time, I asked, "Are we following someone?"

"Why do you ask that?"

"It's either that or you're gearing yourself up to commit a murder. Or maybe you've had a psychotic break and we're going to erratically walk the city like the wandering Jew until caffeine poisoning sets in."

"You were so nice to be around before you became a teenager."

"It comes with the territory. Now please tell me what's going on."

"OK. We are following someone."

"Are we going to kill them?"

"No."

253

"Are we going to make them think that we're going to kill them?"

"Yeesh, where do you get your ideas?"

"I dunno, maybe somewhere between Florida and Reno? You remember that time when you pulled out a gun and made it look pretty damn certain that you were going to, don't you? Because I'm pretty sure that I didn't just imagine it."

"My mother always told me that one day God would punish me by giving me a kid exactly like myself."

"I'm pretty sure that at the very least I drug less than you did, and we both know that I run away less. Now, who are we following?"

"Eat your sandwich."

I took a massive bite, then asked again, muffled by bread and mouth as wide open as possible without losing the bite, "Who are we following?"

"No talking with your mouth full, that's disgusting."

I chewed and swallowed, and repeated my question.

"Someone."

"That narrows it right the hell down."

"I can always lock you in the car until I'm done."

"This is California, there'll be a massive uproar. Might even make the newspapers."

"You're not a dog, no one would care."

I sullenly chewed the sandwich and watched her watching the doors across the street, not wanting to push her too far—she wouldn't bother with dragging me all the way back to the car, but she might leave me alone in the café for a few hours, which was not something I really wanted. I devoured the sandwich but nursed the coffee. I was feeling buzzy already and if I finished it she might get me another one, to legitimize our claim to the table. I stole one of the inner pages from the drifts of random newspapers on a bench by the door, found a pen and the crossword, and tried to think like a smart person. Which was entertaining for maybe five minutes. I wound up holding the pen over a nine-letter word for "*ennui*" while staring out the window, taking note of who went in and out of the hair cuttery and of the apartment doors to either side, but mostly thinking about people I've hated and what I wished I could say to them.

I noticed the couple because of the way that Ma tensed up, how her breathing changed, not like a Predator with Rambo in sight but like she'd seen something she didn't want to see but couldn't look away from, like she'd burned herself.

It was a young guy and a girl, maybe ten years older than me—but I've always been bad at guessing ages—and I recognized the girl, or felt like I should. Maybe we'd been chasing her across the entire country. She was neatly dressed, the kind of person who wore outfits rather than clothes, and I just knew that her bookshelves weren't only alphabetized, but stayed that way.

"Is that Laura?" I asked. They were holding hands on the sidewalk for a moment, finishing a conversation before they got going.

"That's what I called her, but that's not her name anymore."

"Is she an old girlfriend?"

Ma was out of her chair, sliding her jacket off the back and drinking down the last of her espresso with her free hand.

"What? Christ, no, what kind of cradle robber do you make me out to be?"

"You don't look that much older than her."

"I was seventeen when she was born, you can do the math for me."

"OK, that's a bit of an age gap, but—"

She shushed me as we stood in the doorway to the café, as she shrugged on her jacket and took my hand and we began walking. We followed them, on the opposite side of the road and a ways behind, as they went to a park and listened to the reggae band playing for free, then onto a university campus. We should have been caught in the last place; it was a Sunday evening and not many students were around, but locals were playing fetch with their dogs, enjoying the space. We hung back as the girl let the two of them into the Thurman Laboratory with a keycard, settled under a tree to wait.

"What if they're spending the rest of the evening in there?"

"They aren't—she's either checking an experiment, feeding the birds, or picking up some work to take home with her."

"How do you know?"

"She's working to become a large-animal vet. She pretty much lives here."

"How do you know this?"

"I'm good at finding things out."

CHAPTER XX

She didn't explain until later that evening, after we'd called it quits for the day. We'd trailed not-Laura and her boyfriend the rest of Sunday, across the university campus to the library, through town and back to the apartment, sat on a bench on the opposite side of the street until it seemed pretty clear that they were in for the night. On the walk back to the car I dropped hints until Ma consented to stopping for an actual dinner, though she wouldn't go so far as to spring for a decent place to sleep. Instead we moved the car out of the garage to the parking lot behind a church, put the blankets in the windows to block out some of the light, and settled in. I was half asleep when Ma began telling the story.

It was just after her stay with the artist, when she was living with her parents for the last time and working her way slowly through eleventh grade. This final stab at a normal home life ended when it was discovered that, somewhere between the end of summer and the beginning of winter break, she'd gotten pregnant. The circumstances under which this had come about, who the father was, she refused to say.

She'd spent the first four months or so in complete denial, unable to accept what was happening inside her body, to her body. Though she told no one, the father didn't have the same qualms, and when her brother brought the rumor home that she was pregnant her parents investigated. This was followed by a month of indecision, of her mother crying and her father angry and her brother hiding from her as she crept through her life, as if by not drawing attention to herself she could slide back into normalcy when it was all over. A quick wedding was difficult without a groom. Abortion was, religiously and culturally, out of the question; single motherhood was likewise gaining acceptability in wider society but still a badge of shame in the world her parents inhabited.

She couldn't remember if it was more the case that her parents had thrown her out, or that Social Services had taken her away. It may have come down to an agreement between the two that she was sent to a group home, given a place to hide until her condition passed, allowed to finish out eleventh grade at a public high school because the parochial school she and her brother had gone to had expelled her when she started to show.

It was pretty much accepted from the word "go" that she'd be surrendering the kid when it came; no one even asked her how she felt about that. No one told her much about the situation, either. Not her social worker, or the councilors at the home, or any of her teachers; they all seemed to assume that, since she'd managed to get a baby in there, she should already know what to expect when it came to getting it out once it was cooked. The baby will be born; a nice married Christian couple with a house and money will adopt it and give it everything it could ever want; you'll forget all about it and your life will go back to normal. That was what they told her, over and over, when she met with her social worker and with the woman from the Catholic agency who was handling the adoption. All she had to do was sign the papers when the time came, and it would be as if this part of her life had never happened.

Her water broke in the middle of the night, and she'd had no idea what was going on, thought that she'd spilled something on herself, that one of the other residents had pranked her. They'd taken her to the hospital, left her alone for hours as her insides worked and kneaded and she wished that she could die, or at least pass out. And when it was over a nurse laid a blanket-wrapped bundle on her shoulder, said, "Congratulations—it's a girl," and she'd been too shocked to do anything, somehow hadn't equated the previous hours of agony with the inevitable appearance of something wiggling and alive.

"They handed her to me, and she squished her face against my neck, started batting her hand against my mouth—probably looking for food—and something happened. For months I couldn't wait for it all to be over, wished that she'd just go poof! and stop existing, but the moment I smelled her I didn't want to put her down."

Seconds later there was a flurry of whispering and another nurse swept in.

"Whoopsie! That wasn't supposed to happen," she'd said in a sing-song, and snatched the baby away. Weak and confused and out of her mind on drugs, my mother let her go.

Over the course of the three days that my mother stayed in the hospital they allowed her to hold her baby a handful of times, and always reluctantly; it wasn't until she was getting ready to leave that she realized it was because she wasn't meant to have caught sight of the child, that they were supposed to have been separated as quickly as possible after the birth. The baby was sent to foster, Ma back to the home she'd been in immediately before. She was in pain and being driven crazy by post-natal hormones, wanted to hold the baby that she hadn't been able to accept she was going to have, unsure of what would happen to herself next and frankly uninterested, and that was when the caseworker appeared to have her sign the surrender form.

She'd refused to do it at first, argued for an hour, but the woman wore her down: what she was feeling, her need to keep the baby, was nothing more than hormones, and the moment that she recovered she would realize that giving her up was the only right thing to do. She had no husband, no job, nothing to offer a child; she'd been stupid and selfish in getting herself pregnant but she could turn the situation to good by letting the baby go, giving a childless couple the chance to raise her as their own. The agency had paid her hospital bill with the understanding that she would surrender the baby; was she prepared to pay them back all that money, now that she was refusing to give her up? Was she even able, or would her kid sit in foster care for years while she tried to earn enough to pay the fees, earn enough to support the two of them?

The woman wore her down, then sweetened her with promises: the adoption would be open, she'd know where her baby was living, know about the parents, get yearly updates on how she was doing. It would almost be like she was off visiting relatives, like Ma hadn't given her up at all.

Those promises were what got her to sign in the end; she didn't know that you couldn't trust words unless they were in writing. The people who took her daughter didn't want to meet her, see her, acknowledge that she even existed. There would be no news, no updates, no information whatsoever. It would be as if she never had a baby.

When she realized what had happened she bussed her way across two counties, back to her parents' house, broke in while they were both out, took everything she'd left behind, and walked out for the last time. For a few weeks she slept in her car, until the idea of killing herself became far too appealing, and she realized that she needed help. So she phoned her social worker, the one that would push her to go to college, and checked herself back into the system.

Her requests for information about her daughter were blocked until the girl turned seventeen, when the parents said that she'd run away from home. Then they'd initiated contact with the birth mother, trying to get some answers.

They had never told her that she was adopted, but they suspected that the drugs they assumed that Ma had done while pregnant had screwed up her brain chemistry, her behavior, permanently. There had to be a reason for how rebellious she was, how much she pushed back against their efforts to do what was best for her. They hadn't believed Ma when she insisted that there hadn't been any drugs, was no reason that she knew of for their daughter to be acting out apart from the environment in which she had been raised, the person who she naturally was. They had ceased responding to her then, but Ma didn't care: she had something to go on, finally. It had taken her some time, using the tiny amount of information that had been revealed by the adoptive parents' short communications, but she had tracked their daughter down—and that was why we were in California, following a young woman who looked uncannily like both of us, who didn't know that she was adopted and who probably wouldn't know what to do if a woman who claimed to be her birth mother appeared out of the blue.

"I thought that it would be enough to look at her, know that she was alive and healthy, see if she looked happy," Ma said. "If I can't talk to her by tomorrow night, we give up and move on."

We were at the coffee shop again when she came out her front door the next morning. Ma tensed to stand up

262

when she emerged, but to our surprise she crossed the street and came in the café. She joined the line up to the counter, and I recognized in her my mother's wild hair, her narrow shoulders, the economy of movement when she reached for her wallet. The woman greeted the barista by name, got a latte and took it to the condiment counter to be doctored. I kicked Ma under the table: do it now. She stared at me, not looking at me but rather actively not looking at her other child. I kicked her again, and she rose up in her seat a little, then settled back down. Her daughter—the cashier had called her Carla— snapped a lid on her cup and walked out. When the door closed behind her my mother moved, leaving me to flounder two steps behind as we left the café, nervous-excited and wondering why she hadn't spoken in that unexpected moment of proximity.

We followed her to the university, up to the doors of a lecture hall, turned back and settled on a bench in the sun a few hundred yards away. Sometime after the first hour I fell asleep, leaning against Ma while she read a paper that someone else had left behind. The recent spate of car-sleeping hadn't been treating me very well.

I was elbowed awake what felt like mere moments later as Carla left the building. I tensed to get up, but needn't have bothered: she crossed the green space where we sat, head down and steps purposeful, and keyed herself into a building on the opposite side. It was an improvement on the lecture theater in that, with a judicious change of bench, we could watch her through the broad windows as she dumped her gear into a locker, moved her ID card and lanyard from trailing out of her jacket pocket to around her neck, then plunged farther into the building, out of sight. I was acutely aware both of how creepy our behavior was and of how extremely boring stalking was. Ma still had the newspaper that she'd picked up, but she was only holding it in front of her now, looking instead to the horizon, the sky, the movement of students back and forth and around us. I made her give me a middle section of the paper, both to hide behind and as a prophylactic to boredom. I felt bad for her, for what had happened and for the naked longing on her face, and because I felt that the whole thing couldn't end well, that whatever she wanted to result from this exercise wouldn't go to script.

When Carla emerged and strolled away we waited a few breaths and then followed: to the café on campus to buy a sandwich, to the quad to eat it, to the library for an hour and then to another lecture theater, where we waited outside, Ma's eyes on the door and my attention fixed on the watch on her wrist, on the change in texture from noon sun to the thicker syrup of pre-dusk light.

"We're running out of day," I said. Her eyes remained fixed on the door of the lecture theater; I wasn't sure she'd heard me. "Time's almost up. You need to do it soon."

Still no answer.

"You don't have to do it this way—maybe you should try writing her a letter first. Or try a phone call. Something a little less difficult." *And weird*, I wanted to add, but didn't. She was reminding me of the girls I'd gone to school with, who obsessed over certain boys, kept their pictures up in their lockers, followed them in the hallways and watched them across classrooms but never introduced themselves. To see her like this made me deeply uncomfortable, and had I been less reticent, less self-conscious, I might have charged the girl when next she emerged, tackled her into the grass, forced the interaction.

The theater door opened to disgorge a mass of students, and Ma was alert once again, if she had relaxed her vigilance in the first place. We followed her through the dusk—she was leaving campus, going home probably.

"If we follow her home again she's going to call the cops," I pointed out. I didn't think Ma had heard me, was going to elaborate on my point when she put on the speed, and I had to trot after her.

"Excuse me, excuse me! Miss!" The girl turned, and Ma stopped dead.

"Yes?" she asked.

No answer, not a sound.

"Can I help you? Are you lost or something?"

Ma didn't respond. She was frozen on the spot, mouth half-open. Seeing the two of them feet apart, gazing at each other, made me want to smack them both, to ask my mother if she was crazy and my sister if she was blind, if she didn't see herself in our mother's face, if she didn't have the eerie feeling of doubleness.

"Did you drop this?" Ma held out her own wallet, and the girl looked at it for a second before shaking her head.

"No, it isn't mine. Security can find the owner, though, if you found it on campus."

"Sorry to bother you."

I wanted to kick her.

The girl turned away. Ma was still standing, offering up the wallet, and I wanted to kick her even more. Only when the girl had disappeared into the distance did Ma move: she put her billfold back in her pocket. Her shoulders dropped. She turned to go, and I followed just a bit behind, not wanting to break into her personal space, wanting to give her some privacy with thoughts and feelings I couldn't understand, but as we went she reached behind her back and took my hand, pulled me up under her arm like we might have walked in a life where I was that kind of kid and she was that kind of mother. That didn't work—I was too tall for her to get her arm around my shoulders anymore—so she let it settle on my waist, and I was the one who draped my arm across her shoulders, held her close to me as we walked back to the car.

She didn't say anything as she got in the driver's seat, buckled her belt, and reached for her cigarettes. She dropped the pack, balled her fist and punched the dashboard, once, with a swallow that was more a sob. Maybe it would have been healthier if she'd talked about it—if we'd been the kind of people that talked. But she shook her hand, picked up the cigarettes and shook out one, then looked at me as if she couldn't remember whether I was at an age to be smoking or not.

"I'm not *that* old yet," I said.

She waited until we were on the road to light up, blowing out the first plume of white as we turned towards the highway. Heading north again.

"We're almost there, aren't we?" I asked.

"In the grand scheme of things, yes. We don't have very much farther to travel. End of the line is just ahead. I think."

"I saw your map," I said. She didn't seem surprised. "There isn't anywhere planned out after what comes next. We're staying when we get there, right?"

"I don't know."

"How do you not know?"

"Some people, when you show up on their doorstep for the first time in ten years, they're happy to see you— some people call the cops. Most people would only expect you to hang around for a day or three."

"So she isn't expecting us?"

"Not really, no."

"What do you mean, not really?"

"Well, I made promises a long time ago, and I don't think that she believed me."

"What kind of promises?"

"First one was, if we got to forty and were both still single we'd move in together. Second was, if her husband ever left I'd take his place. Half joking but not really, you know how I mean."

"What if she doesn't let us stay?"

"Then we figure something out on our own."

267

"I'm getting pretty damn tired of sleeping in the car."

"And I'm pretty damn tired of living in motels, but we'll figure something out."

"Which Laura is it?"

"Say what?"

"Which Laura are we going to see?"

"I've told you all those stories and you can't guess?"

"Not really, no."

She gave me a look, wiggled her eyebrows at me, but didn't answer.

I waited a few minutes before asking, "And no plans after that?"

"None whatsoever."

"Does . . . my dad still know where we are?"

"He knows that we're safe."

I hadn't known what to call him, didn't know if mentioning him would upset her.

"Can I talk to him sometime, or something?"

She looked at me for a moment, then said, "Haven't you noticed yet that there's pretty much zilch I can keep you from doing once you've decided that you want to do it?"

"Does that mean I can quit school?" I asked.

"You're getting pretty close to the age where you could, if you want to. I think when you turn sixteen you're allowed to try for your GED rather than serving the rest of your time."

I waited a few minutes before asking, "Does that mean I can go back east?"

She waited a few minutes before answering.

"Just be careful. And maybe let me know ahead of time, OK?"

For once the sun did not chase us into darkness, but sank off to the left, beyond the cities and people, as we went north now on the last leg—or what I hoped was the last leg—of our journey.

CHAPTER XXI

I woke up to the thought that we were on our way home. Virginia home: the mountains were low and small, the scrub sandy, and the ocean nowhere in sight.

"Are we . . ." I began, then glanced at the clock and the sun and figured that we were traveling pretty much dead north. "Are we there yet?"

"It's about a thousand miles altogether, kid, give it a day or two."

"Are we stopping for breakfast soon?" According to the clock I'd only slept a few hours. What looked like an evening sun was in fact a barely risen sun.

"Soon. I'm going to get a few hours' sleep when we do, no sense wrecking when we've come this far already."

The strange sleep cycle, or rather the lack of one, had put me in an odd mood, and I didn't try to winkle any more stories out of her as we rolled north, but sat and stewed in my own thoughts. I'd spent a decent amount of the previous few years of my life holding absolutely still while at the same time moving relentlessly, unstoppably forward. Time was a hard thing to get a handle on. Every day had the capability of being the carbon copy of the days that preceded it, so it was hard to remember that the days added up, that I wasn't living the same day, day after day, into forever, but that each day was a measured segment of something set and finite. That I too would die. Could die, in an instant and in any instant, and that would be it. That no law of the universe guaranteed that I would make it back to see my dad, that he would be there to see if I did make it back. It terrified me, that we all live relentlessly, that we all die eventually, that we have no real knowledge of what happens after, that we can't say, "Stop the ride, I want to get off."

Humans—most of us, at least—have the incapability of pondering the really terrifying things for any serious length of time. It's probably what keeps us from throwing ourselves off cliffs in mass fits of existential crisis. I watched the mountains and the tractor trailers bearing down on us and wondered about death, until my stomach started to growl. Then I began wondering about food, and was saved from myself. We think we're evolved, but we aren't, at least not as far as we like to think that we are. The feral part requires appeasement before it will allow *sapiens sapiens* to pursue its intangibles.

We stopped at a rest stop that modeled itself on the sort of place that wagon trains would have paused to water the oxen and stock up on ammo in the days when both oxen and ammo were given possessions for someone on the road. Now it offered hot food and free refills of coffee, coin-operated showers with towels for rent and a three-washer laundromat; there were some family cars and little trucks but big rigs, circling the diesel pumps or clustered together like a herd of mammoths, dominated the asphalt. Ma parked somewhere that wasn't really a space, leaned back in the driver's seat and sighed before switching off the car.

"Shower?" she asked.

"I dunno. They got curtains or something, or is it open-plan like we're animals?"

"Going to have to see, aren't we? If it's too uncouth you can always do without until we find someplace to your liking, but I can't promise that that will be on this side of the border. It isn't too busy this time of day, at least."

The showers turned out to be unisex, little lockable closets with one showerhead apiece and a door that went floor to ceiling, and the water was hot and came out strong. We had our own soap and towels, and when I locked myself in and breathed out, in private once again, I almost curled up on the floor and fell asleep, it felt so good to be alone. I whacked on the water and let the thoughts roll through my head without having to worry about what my face was giving away, leaned on the wall and let the stream roll hot down my back, feeling the aches and the tight places, and I knew that on the other side of the wall Ma was doing the same thing. She used to take me in the shower with her when I was a toddler, because she couldn't trust me on my own with the run of the house. I'd play with bath toys sitting on the bottom of the far end of the tub and she'd lean against the tiled wall, letting the water wash over her like she was under a waterfall, enjoying holding still, being warm, not having to think or do anything.

I got out first and waited for her, damp with my cleanest clothes sticking to me, drying my head under a hand dryer because I hated having wet hair dripping on my shirt. She staggered out when I was nearly done, the wet clumps of my hair hanging down and the dry sproinging in my face so I looked like Shirley Temple on a six-day bender and couldn't see anything to the front or sides, only down.

We ate burgers in the diner but didn't have coffee for once, and as she began to fall asleep over her plate I asked, "Want me to take a spell, driving?"

She snapped awake. "I had a friend in high school that read palms. She told me that I'd die in a violent manner, but at an advanced age. I'm not letting you turn her into a liar—I'll sleep in the car for a few hours, and then we'll carry on. We're almost there."

I followed her to the car, took the back seat as she took the front, stretched out and listened to her breathing, listened for it to change. She usually shifted around as she fell asleep: one, two, three; lower back, shoulders, then neck, getting the stiffer places comfortable. This time she just went out, like her falling asleep was an actual fall, sudden and into unimaginable depths. I tried to follow her, but the seat was hard underneath me, my neck at the wrong angle, and even though my body was tired my mind was wide awake. Eventually I gave up, wormed my way out the door making as little noise as possible, stepped into my half-laced boots and crunched towards the truck stop.

I'd thought I'd just have a little walk, knock the keen edge off my wakefulness, but when I got halfway around the truck stop I realized that there was another side to the place, literally—the buildings were pushed back to back, one side with the showers and diesel and chewing tobacco, the other side oriented to families, with a tacky souvenir barn, picnic tables . . . and a dark blue U.S. Post box.

As I poked through the junk on the shelves I realized that, were the air of a different quality, I could have been back on the east coast. People went on and on about how unique their little part of the country was, and while the landscape had changed as we went it had still been Wal-Marts and McDonald's from sea to shining sea. It was one size fit all, the family places bought out by companies that shipped and sold in value size. Maybe if we'd strayed farther from the highways as we'd gone along we could have found the little places that remembered the differences between GA and CA. But who has time for that? And who wants to stray too far from what they know? One day—maybe even yesterday—we'll find that we no longer have the option of leaving the familiar behind.

Between the novelty outhouse magnets and the off-color bumper stickers I found the cards and stationary, stopped and read a few off the bottom rack—the kind you need to stick a finger through for the joke to work, that I was too embarrassed to pick up and read if someone else was standing with me—then shuffled through the postcards and Post-it notes, looking for something cheap. Behind the pack of "to do" pads and unicorns and flowers was a pack of notepaper, marked down because half the envelopes were missing from the set. I considered walking out with it, reconsidered and picked out a gel pen, paid with bills from Reno that had been washed in the zipper pocket of my cargo pants and were softer than their fabric, opened it all on one of the picnic tables and immediately had to chase down half the paper because there was more of a breeze than I'd realized. At least the table wasn't wet.

Dad—Still don't know Mom's plan, but we're almost out of country. Should make our last stop in a day or two, then I guess I'll be coming back. You can tell from the postmark that we're on the west coast—we've come farther than I thought we would. Also, it's taken longer than I thought it would. No surprise there. I thought I'd be back long before now, else I would have written more. But you were the one who told me that life never follows the plan. Ma keeps her cards close to her vest, so I guess I can't really know that we're almost done. But I can promise that I'll be headed towards home by the end of the year.
    Me

I had no way to know if I would be headed home, by the end of the year or otherwise; I had no idea what the date was, whether we were really stopping soon or if we'd continue through the Arctic Circle and on into Russia. But I felt like I had to give him something. If I made a promise, I'd have to keep it.

Ma woke before I did, started the car and reversed out while I was still sprawled across the back seat.

"Hang on, I get sick sitting back here."

"Still? Your pediatrician told me that you'd grow out of that."

"Doctors are idiots."

"You can be so negative sometimes, Alex."

"Did the doctor tell you that I'd grow out of that, too?"

"We're in rare form today."

"I didn't sleep long enough. Or I slept too long, take your pick."

"A little bit cranky?"

"Just feeling weird." And I did. She snapped on the radio and I leaned back in the passenger seat and put my feet on the dash, wanting to grouse and snipe but unable to interrupt the music.

I thought we'd have longer. That I could be grumpy and she could cheer me up and we could have the miles going on and on, just us. Then came the signs: BORDER CONTROL—HAVE YOUR TRAVEL DOCUMENTS READY FOR INSPECTION PLEASE, and I realized that things had greened up, cooled off, that the road had run out while I was still taking it for granted. FERRY AHEAD—ALL FORMS OF PAYMENT ACCEPTED.

"We're—uh—they're not going to arrest us for having the gun, are they?"

"Hm? Oh, that. I sold it while we were in Reno."

". . . Anything else they could, you know, arrest us for?"

"We should be golden, kid. Quit worrying."

We sat in a cloud of exhaust, inching towards the ferry, waiting for everyone in front of us to have their little books stamped. At our turn, Ma handed over the passports nonchalantly.

"More than ten thousand USD in cash or goods? Plants? Animals? Soil? Food? How long is your stay and what is your destination?"

"Just prepared food. We're visiting a college buddy on Vancouver Island, should be a couple-week stay at the longest." She dug through her billfold and handed him an envelope with our address in Reno on the front and one from British Columbia as the return. He looked us over, looked in the back of the car—we'd packed it neatly, all the edges square, but it still looked like we'd been road tripping—flicked through our passports, then bang-bang, bang-bang, stamped them both. Ma shouted, "Thank you!" as she rolled up her window and we rolled slowly down into the belly of the ferry and into the parking space an orange-jacketed young man waved us towards. She cut the ignition, grabbed her backpack from the back seat and rolled out of the car, and as she opened the door I was hit in the brain with the smell of exhaust and fuel oil and decay. We hadn't started moving yet, and already I felt sick.

Once I got out of the auto-fume fog and into the fresh air on the deck I felt not sick, which isn't quite the same thing as not feeling sick, but damn it if the ferry itself didn't make me supremely nervous. I'd never been on a ferry before, and as we pulled out into the water I wished immediately that I had been allowed to continue in my ignorance. We were trapped in a sardine tin with miles of water beneath us, rocking slowly along with no way of getting off.

Ma had a book with her, some oranges, a blanket—she could have stretched out on the bench where we'd huddled against a bulkhead to get away from the kids screaming in excitement as they watched the land recede, but instead she sat next to me, hunched forward with her forearms braced on her thighs, her shoulders tight and her eyes fixed in a thousand-yard stare. Every now and again she would open the backpack, shuffle through the contents, take a gulp from the water bottle, then settle back, alert but watching nothing. If I didn't know better I would have thought that she was nervous. Doctor's-office nervous. First-date nervous. A nervous that I should be nervous about.

When we hit land once again she continued to sit, braced for impact, until the ferry had mostly emptied out, then went slowly down to the auto deck and drove us out into the cloudy light of Canada—which looked suspiciously like the cloudy light of America that we had presumably just left.

"Is something wrong?" I asked.

"Not as such," she answered.

"That's not an answer."

"Depends on who you ask."

"Do you know where we're going?"

"Does anyone?"

We rolled slowly through streets lined with shops to a more residential part of town, the houses wide spaced, or appearing so because of how small they were, how precisely the gardens were laid out. She squinted at the house numbers, got to the end of the road and doubled back, stopped in front of one of the smallest. The paint was peeling slightly, the house itself looked vacant. The garden was why we'd passed—a hedge of overleaning cypress trees, so that the house had a tucked-in, leave-me-alone look to it, as if we weren't supposed to be looking at it, as if the residents didn't want to be seen. We sat on the shoulder of the road, Ma not looking at the house but rather at her hands on the wheel. She pulled the keys out of the ignition and rolled out of her seat. I didn't want to go with her, but I followed.

The path to the door was overgrown; there was one of those cutesy ceramic plates next to the bell that said, *Cypress Cottage, 42*, that we couldn't see from the road. Ma stood for a few minutes, studying the door, the dark window, then pressed the bell.

The held-breath waiting went on too long, then we heard footsteps inside, slow-stuttery footsteps. Ma had tensed to walk away. She looked old to me, tired and frayed at the edges, and at the same time so young, so hopeful, so scared. A key rattled in the lock, and the door opened on a chain, showed a slice of a hollow-chested woman, her skin yellowed and papery.

"Hey, don't let me bother you—" Ma croaked.

The door slammed shut, metal rattled on the other side. She flinched like she'd been hit.

Then the door slammed open, the woman shot out like an arrow into my mother, knocking her back not very far because she was so thin, the two of them hugging and crying, and I knew that our journey was over.

CHAPTER XXII

Her husband's affair had been going on for seven years when she was diagnosed with cancer, so he'd had somewhere else to go. She'd come home one day and everything he owned was gone, along with most of the furniture: there were gaps against walls, spaces where things should have been, dark oblongs in the paint and wallpaper haloed with sun bleaching. Laura's voice was merry as she told us about it—she had a habit of running her hand over the short grey hair that frosted her scalp that made me feel that it was OK to look at her directly. I was silent as they talked, hoping to be forgotten. Ma hadn't known about the cancer when we left Virginia, or we would have probably come straight here, as quickly as possible.

The letter she'd gotten with the almost casual aside halfway through of *and Phil left me for his mistress* had been the thing that actually made her leave, had made her decide, right in the middle of one of her endless fights with my father, that she wasn't going to spend another moment of her life shouting back and forth in that kitchen with him.

"It doesn't do any good to just run away from something, you've got to be running *to* something," she said when I asked why she'd waited so long. She'd been planning on leaving, in the right way, at the right time—the backpack that she'd taken with her, which had sat with the shoes all through my childhood, had held her green card, my birth certificate, our passports, all of the papers that she would need to start her life over—but life kept getting in the way. First she'd had me, and at every stage of my growth there had been another reason for her to postpone leaving, until one day she just did. As we'd traveled she'd continued getting letters from Laura, but it wasn't until Reno that the second bomb was dropped.

"So I have no ovaries and no eyebrows now, but I'm in remission and not entirely bankrupt. I should be celebrating, I guess, but it feels a bit like a massive anticlimax. I mean, I had cancer, and now I don't. What do you do after that?"

Ma hadn't waited around long enough to respond properly to the letter, just dropped a postcard in the mail that said she was on her way and gave her notice at the bar where she worked. We'd been meaning to go, sooner or later; she'd thought we'd hang on until I was out of school for the summer, but the news made her re-evaluate: "remission" didn't mean the exact same thing as "cured."

"Why didn't you tell me at the beginning? I would have come sooner, I could have helped."

Laura was quiet for a long time. A bottle of wine had been opened, and we were perched on high stools

282

around the end of the kitchen counter, them drinking and me with a soda, over crackers and cheese and containers of leftover olives and marinated vegetables from Laura's fridge scattered across the granite, half a fancy hors d'oeuvres party and half the random mess of teenage girls just home from school with every possible snack laid out as they chatter all the stopped-up words of the day. The kitchen was nearly empty of furniture, but that made it feel light; in that house the few objects that remained had a special weight to them. Her husband had taken the heirlooms that had come from his grandparents' houses, left only the things that were truly hers.

Ma plucked at a cigarette, looked at Laura.

"You don't anymore—do you?" she asked.

"Well, I shouldn't, but—" Laura looked at me. "If you're not going anywhere, I could skin up . . ."

"I thought—"

"Got back in the habit recently. It helped with the nausea."

The smoke flowed in heavy ribbons from their mouths, and in that moment she was all of them: the white-haired old artist that had taken my mother in, the street-smart young girl whose kiss she couldn't forget, the one that got away and the one that she'd run away with, and still the little girl who stole dimes from her mother's purse and shared cigs behind the hedge with the damp ground slowly soaking the seat of her pleated wool skirt. They were old and young at once, outside of humanity, the way that lovers always are.

And there we stayed, I don't know for how long exactly. There was a gentle quality to the days, as if time weren't passing, as if there was nowhere that I needed to go. As if I'd come home. Then I started to feel a tingle in my bones. An itch. And I tried to ignore it, but then the question started sounding in my head: whose child are you?

It was Laura who set me free.

She and I were sitting one evening in the sunroom at the back of the house—we had already made a habit of sitting there together, her of telling me stories about her own life and about my mother's life. Ma was cooking dinner, banging pans around and far enough away so as not to hear, and Laura said:

"If you go, we'll be here when you get back."

"I never said I wanted to go."

"You haven't said that you want to stay, either. If you're itching to leave, go. And then come back."

"Why do you think I want to leave?"

"By this point I know the signs. Birds before they migrate become disturbed. They cannot settle. If you were to confine them they would beat themselves to death on the walls of their cage, trying to follow the pull. When the travel urge comes, they have to leave. They know it—any sensible person watching knows it. They grow more and more agitated, and then the moment comes, and they fly."

She dug in her pocket, handed me a key on a braided leather band.

"That's in case you want to go out for, I don't know,

ice cream in the middle of the night and we're not awake when you get back. But you get to choose how you use it."

I waited three days, until the fizzing I felt, the odd, anxious itch in the back of my head and down my spine, could no longer be ignored. Neither of them said anything, but I could tell by the way they looked at me that they knew, that my mother saw in me herself at my age, and the fact that she didn't say anything, that she didn't try and stop me, I took to be her blessing. That, and when she brought me a pile of clean laundry a few days later my passport and birth certificate and a little pile of money were stacked neatly on top of them.

I packed mostly dry, light food, thick socks and spare underwear, put the money I had hoarded and my passport and the key in a zippered pocket close to my skin, and disappeared. I should have left a note, perhaps at the spot at the kitchen counter where my mother sat when we ate dinner. Left a drawing of a bird in flight, at Laura's spot. I didn't, didn't think to do it until I was already on the ferry, watching the line of coast recede, a different line of coast approach. I trusted that they would understand.

Thirty years on and what I remember is more likely to be not what I said, but what I wish I had said, putting words more polished into my past mouth. We don't have memories as we like to think of them: perfectly preserved snippets, here's-what-happeneds, certainty and clarity.

All we can really have are mythologies, fragments pieced together and made to cohere, to have pattern, to explain life so that, even if we can't feel good about it, we can believe we understand it.

I get to tell this story because I'm the last one standing. Even in her final months, when all she wanted to do was sit and remember, Ma would not remember for me the details of our journey. Whatever I told her had happened, she seemed content to accept as truth. Laura was the one who told me that it was my story now, that I got to decide how it all happened, that I was the only one who could tell it.

It is strange to think that all that's left of her on earth are the stories that she told me, and even then, they aren't the stories that she told me, but her stories as I remember them. For years I blanked over that part of my life, glossed it, pretended that I'd forgotten the time when we were on the move. If I'd never had to put her in the ground, I may never have come back to it, never thought again about that time except in moments when some smell, some sound, called up an unwilling memory, dropped me for a breath back into that awkward, anxious adolescent body.

Now that she is gone I want to send my teenage self back to her, settle the person who I was happily into Laura's house with her, make myself content with stillness. But who I am now does not negate who I was then: I have to admit that, at the time, I wanted more than anything to be back on the road, to find the way back to my father, to fly, and there is no shame in that.

EPILOGUE

Sitting on the ferry surrounded by people with shopping and kids and luggage and screaming babies I was more alone than I'd ever been before in my life and fairly thrumming with the possibility of it, the freedom to do what I wanted, to go where I chose, and the responsibility of living with the consequences of those actions, whatever they might be. Surrounded by the consequences of my fellow passengers' decisions in stereo and Technicolor I had the time to reflect on just how far it was, one side of the country to the other. I had turned sixteen while we were in Canada—there had been a cake, which surprised me a little bit, and a night out at a cult movie house, which surprised me even more—a few years older than my mother had been when she ran away from home and hiked the Appalachian Trail, not so much younger than when she'd gotten pregnant with my sister. It was a long way, but I figured that I could make it. I'd done it before, after all, albeit not on my own, and it had taken a damn long time. I reckoned I could do it the second time quicker.

The ferry hadn't even cost twenty bucks, and when I put my feet back down on solid land I found that the bus left from mere yards away, so I gave in to impulse and bought a ticket for Seattle, managed to keep my insides on my insides for the three-hour ride, got directions to the Greyhound station from the driver and dropped the money I'd expected to spend on the ferry on a ticket to California, to go and do what my mother couldn't do, before my nerves failed me.

There was plenty of time for nerve failure in the four hours I had to wait to be able to use the ticket, though. I went looking for cheap painkillers but found first a packet of motion-sickness pills that the pharmacist wouldn't sell me because I was too young, then an adult willing to buy the pills for me because there was no way I was getting on a bus again without them, then a discount bundle of grocery-store sandwiches, then three thrift-store paper-backs, because if I was going to have the option of reading while in transit opened up to me by the magic of the pills then I was going to damn well take advantage of it.

It was an overnight ride, made somewhat longer by the fact that the guy who sat next to me between Tacoma and Portland decided that I of course had a burning interest in the saga of his love life, and that my raised book was mere politeness that should not prevent him from telling me in detail about all of the bitches and whores that had done him wrong and turned his kids against him. The pills worked, but knocked me out, which was a small price to pay for not being sick. After the talker left I dozed, waking each time we stopped, and people shuffled past me getting off and then getting on, dropping back off as the gearbox ground and we got on the road again.

At half past six the next morning I staggered off the bus in Sacramento with an hour to burn before the next bus, bought a cheap breakfast that I ate slowly because my stomach felt touchy even with the pills, and considered my situation. It felt odd still, being on my own; I couldn't shake the feeling that Ma should be coming back any moment, that she had just gone to the women's room, just gone to pay the bill, was about to turn up next to me with the news that it was time to get back on the road. It didn't make me as anxious as I'd thought it would, though: she wasn't there to make sure I was all right, she couldn't fix my mistakes anymore, but she also wasn't there to see them when I made them, wouldn't be disappointed in me when I inevitably proved how foolish and young I still was.

After the food I poked around the bus station, read the timetables, bought some discounted sandwiches for later, then picked out a postcard.

Ma—

Banking on the possibility that we breed true. I'll let you know how I'm getting on, and when I come to roost for a while I'll send you the address. Let me know if you all do any relocating; I'll be back sooner or later. Hug Laura for me. I love you.

—Me

*

I found Carla as she was leaving the avian lab that afternoon and followed her for a bit, trying to decide on an appropriate place to talk, the best way to approach her. Ultimately I didn't have to: she turned down a side street that wound up being a blind alley, was waiting behind the corner when I turned down it after her, got me face down on the ground with her knee in my back and both wrists held before I could figure out what the hell was happening.

"Why the fuck are you following me again?"

"I'm sorry! I'm sorry! I just need to talk to you a minute!"

"The hell you do. I'm calling the cops."

"Just five minutes. I've got to tell you something important."

"Tell it to the judge, you pervert."

"You were adopted."

"Fuck you." She was rummaging in her bag, for either pepper spray or a phone.

"Your mom—the lady I was with before, the one with the wallet—she was seventeen when she had you. She gave you up because she didn't have any other options. She wanted to tell you herself but she was too scared, and if you'll let me go I'll give you her name, address and phone number and leave you alone, I swear."

She paused in her rummaging.

"What the hell. Seriously. What the hell?"

"I know, it's weird. She only found out who you were and in what city you lived in the last year or so."

"Is this some sort of prank or something?"

"I promise it's not." She hadn't let me up yet, but she'd let go of one of my wrists to grope in her bag, and I took the opportunity to pull out the piece of paper that I'd written Laura's address and phone number on, handed it up to her. She hesitated a moment before taking it from me.

"How do I know this isn't some kind of weird scam? I figured out I was adopted a few years ago—I've been trying to find out who my birth mom was. How do I know that you didn't find that out somehow and now you're trying to scam me?"

"You figured it out?"

"Blood types."

"Ah. I guess you can't know, really. If you'll let me up I promise I'll walk away and never bother you again. You can call that number or not, chase it up or ignore it, it's up to you."

She was quiet for a minute, then took her knee out of the center of my back, let me roll over and get slowly to my feet.

"I guess that makes us half-siblings or something. I'm sorry I had to tell you this way, but I thought you deserved to know."

"How do I know you're not lying?" she asked. "That you're not a pair of psychos that want to make my bones into wind chimes?"

"Who knows? Hell, half the time I don't know if I'm telling the truth or not. You're the smart one. I bet you can figure out a way to check out my story, meet up with her somewhere safe, and find out whether or not she's your mother. You don't lose anything but time checking it out."

I left her in the alley; I looked back once and saw her holding the paper and looking after me. I wanted to keep talking, convince her to call our mother or just get to know her because I wanted to be a person with a sister, even a sister I never saw. But I kept my head down and kept on walking.

She was the one who got to decide whether she wanted to be part of my story.

North America is wide. It's easy to forget that, when you look at a map or sit in a car or get in a plane and watch it all whip past. I walked and thumbed, and this time I knew what to do to people that tried to take advantage, knew what the more subtle forms of trying to take advantage looked like. I was careful now about where I slept and whom I rode with through the Midwest to the other coast. I wanted to stop and kiss Simon one more time and ask again if he would let me go farther, to see how Anna-Maria was getting on, see if the Michigan nightclub was still in business, go down to Florida and dip my face in the sea and catch a wave with the people I had known there, but I couldn't: they were not my mission, and I was afraid that if I paused, if I deviated, I would never get where I was going, that the part of my makeup I'd gotten from my dad would take over and I'd find myself wedged in, unable to leave. There would always be the opportunity to go looking for them after I found my father.

I crossed into Virginia without knowing that I had, only realized it when I got into the mountains and things started looking familiar. I began to pass through places I'd been before, places I'd once known, that, callous to the time I'd been away, had refused to change. I had been gone so long, gone so far; everything should have been different. The truest marker that I had been gone, that I hadn't dreamed it all, was that the trees were just beginning to change their color, there was a snap of fall in the air.

There were little things, new stoplights, some shops closed and different ones open, but for the most part the place had been caught in amber, frozen since I'd left. I walked down streets and along the shoulders of highways, cut through woods and backyards and schoolyards and places where I probably shouldn't have been, found the long winding backwoods road with my home past the point along it where you expected to still find homes, looking just the same as when we'd left in the middle of a chilly spring night.

Except someone else lived there.

I walked up the gravel drive slowly, turned over the hide-a-key under the porch steps: it was empty. Maybe Ma had taken the key when we left, maybe Dad had moved it. So I knocked on the door, rang the bell, and felt shock explode fizzily in my chest as a woman I'd never met before, a young woman with a toddler on her hip, answered the door. She was polite, but she didn't

293

know where my dad had moved to, clearly wanted me to go away, so I apologized and walked quickly back down the driveway towards the main road, listened for her to close the front door over the sound of my feet crunching the gravel.

I went a little ways back along the main road, then cut off into the woods, circled round and found the fort that Dad and I had built just across the property line on national parkland, that the new people didn't appear to have found yet, and slept off my disappointment.

Our old neighbors still lived in their house, still remembered me and remembered liking me, but couldn't tell me where Dad had moved to, just that he had left perhaps a year, a year and a half, before. They fed me dinner, and lent me a phone book, let me copy down the three possible addresses, and I was thankful that I'd always had a less common last name. They offered to let me use their phone, but I didn't take them up on it—I had developed a bit of my mother's aversion to phones over the course of my trip.

Instead I went myself to the addresses I had found, knocked on doors because that seemed like the right way to do it. Two, of course, were strikes. The third was an apartment block where he had lived but didn't anymore, and this time the superintendent knew where the occasional piece of mail was being forwarded, and I was thankful for the dinner I had been given as I walked across town to yet another apartment block. I was tired, in the body and in the head; I'd been keyed up for too long for a reunion, I couldn't maintain the excitement anymore. Which was why, when no one answered his door, I settled down with my back against it and fell asleep.

I was woken up by a shoe gently nudging my ribs, a voice I recognized saying, "Hey, kid, you OK? You can't sleep here."

When I looked up I got to watch the shift in his expression as he recognized me, the realization like a glass falling from a countertop, shattering on the floor. Then he held me so tightly I couldn't breathe, like he would never let me go.

He had gotten my letters and postcards and wanted to write back but hadn't known where to send the reply; had been kept up to date on my health and well-being by semi-regular phone calls and occasional emails from my mother and had always meant to talk to me, to ask her to let him talk to me, but never had. For a while he'd managed to hang onto the house, but had to let it go when he lost his job.

For the first week whenever he wasn't at work, morning and night, I filled him in, told him the stories of where we'd gone, what we'd done. There were parts I left out, parts I couldn't tell him about, but not many of them, and he was good at listening, good at letting me spin it all out the way I wanted to.

I was sleeping on the sofa in his apartment, borrowing his clothes the way I'd borrowed my mother's, spending the days while he was at work reacquainting myself with the town I had left. We talked about me quitting school to get a GED, finding a job, possibly getting a bigger apartment so that I could have a bedroom, and for a few days I looked forward to settling back into a life like the one I had known, to habits and rhythms and weekends that were distinguishable from weekdays. But then I came to the end of my stories, and as the words began to run out a tingle grew in my spine, an itching at the back of my brain.

I interrogated it while I lay awake in the dark, listening to his breathing on the other side of the apartment. I'd sent a postcard to Ma and Laura to let them know I had gotten back in one piece, had received one in return to let me know that they were still where I had left them, and at first I thought that it was the missing of my mother that made me itch on the inside.

It wasn't until I spent a day in the mountains, wandering for the sake of forward motion alone, that I realized that what I felt was a sort of anti-homesickness, a sick-of-home homesickness, that home for me was a place I was going to, rather than a place I could occupy. Nature or nurture, something I had been born with or something that had grown with every step and mile, it didn't matter which. I had my mother's restlessness.

For a month or so I studied for the exam that would get me out of school forever, tried to sleep at night and went out to the mountains with my dad every spare moment we had, trying to kill the growing urge that felt like it would make me lose my mind. He was amused that, after so much traveling, I still wanted to spend my weekends on my feet, and I couldn't tell him why, didn't want to tell him why, tried instead to settle to the life I had come back to. But he had lived with my mother for fifteen years before she left him, and he knew the signs that Laura had described: the way I could not settle, the way I couldn't stand the confine of walls, of roads, of anything smaller than earth and sky.

He walked with me to the center where the exam would be given, and I expected that once it was over I would feel light, freed from the requirement of public education for the first time in my life, and that the ability to go forth and find work and live as an adult would calm me, that being formally allowed to do what I wanted would lead to my not wanting so much. It turned out that the reverse was true: with nothing making demands on my time besides searching for work, which took up considerably less time than studying had, my unease only increased.

He watched me pace and rock and scratch absently at my arms until the skin was raw, growing more agitated as the days went by, but he said nothing. Maybe I wanted him to tell me that he wanted me to stay, wanted him to try to fix me there, to remind me of the parts of myself that I got from him, the ability to be happy wherever I was, the passiveness that had gotten me through the journey from east to west in the first place. But he never tried to stop my mother when she left, whether it was for hours or days, and when the time came that I could no longer hold still, didn't think I'd last another day, he did not try to stop me. I could see it in the way he moved that he knew that I would be leaving, that he didn't want me to leave, but he wouldn't give voice to it, wouldn't try and lay claim to me. I don't know if I hated or loved him for that.

I lasted a week of sleeplessness and pacing. It was four in the morning when I broke, began rolling my clothes into the backpack I had brought with me from California, picking out my thickest socks. Dad came out of his room and watched me stuff things into pockets, didn't speak until I zipped them closed and set the bag upright, then said, "Wait a minute," went into the kitchen and made a half-dozen bologna sandwiches, pulled me into a hug when he handed them to me.

We stood for long moments, him on the inside, me on the outside, neither of us willing to close the front door. He left it, stepped back and then turned and went into his room, so that I had to close the door after myself, pull it to make sure that the lock caught. It hurt to walk down the stairs of the apartment block, and I wondered if I was screwing up, if I should go back inside and get ready for a normal day. But when my feet hit the pavement the tingle up my spine, the itch inside my head, stopped.

As I walked away I probed for the uncertainty I had felt when I was first alone, on the ferry from Canada, but all I felt was peace. I was on my own, could go and find my mother, or see if Simon would have me, or winter in Florida before I made up my mind. I didn't know where I was going, and I didn't have to know. The road was beckoning; all I had to do, all that I could do, was follow where it led.